OF SPELLBOOKS AND THIEVES

OF SPELLBOOKS AND THIEVES

THE LEGENDS OF ANTICUUS
BOOK ONE

ROBIN WINCKLER

PROLOGUE

12/2/T/xx-80

Someone once told me people are not to be judged by what they look like on the outside, for it is the heart that truly matters in the end.

He should have known this better than anyone as this lesson was a nightmare he lived. With scars that covered every inch of his body, and eyes that mirrored the look of a starving beast, he could be called a monster. Even so, I trusted him—as foolish as it may seem.

Pausing in his writing to look out the window, Tobias released a deep sigh. The last golden rays of sunlight streamed through the open curtains, painting the pages he wrote on a warm yellow. Black ink had smeared across his hand, and his fingers were starting to cramp. His chair at the desk had been comfortable when he first sat down, but now he couldn't stop shifting in it.

He had promised them a record of the events, but introductions were so frustratingly difficult. Once he got past the hard part, he knew the story would flow easily. It still sat at the forefront of his mind, even after all the years that had gone by.

He shook himself and tilted his head downward to face the scribbled words once more.

"Don't judge a book by its cover" is something we are often told, but the ones that tell us are usually the ones that ignore their own advice.

Maybe it is fear that drives us to make these choices. Maybe it is a cruelty we all deny we have. We think ourselves to be above things that are different and therefore look down upon those things. Is it, perhaps, our need to conquer? As humans, do we feel insignificant and require something to suppress this?

He stopped to stare at the words. Muttering to himself, he resisted the urge to tear the page into a million pieces and start all over again. The record had to be written, lest the whole ordeal happen again.

Whatever it may be, he wrote, *I was challenged to see past it. I found allies within my enemies and enemies within my allies. That is the twisted way of life, is it not?*

Ah, but my story does not have an exciting beginning like some do. It began just as any other day would: with clear, autumn skies—the season called Xenah in Calistie. My story started with a book I could not understand, a tree, and a woman I'd go so far as to call annoying.

PART ONE
THE THIEF'S GAME

"A thief who thinks like a dragonborn is a thief to be feared,
no matter the object she steals."

I

STOLEN

7/3/D/xx-68

THE OLD DOOR creaked on its hinges as Tobias pulled it shut. He lingered outside of it for a moment, staring down at the key tightly clenched in his fingers. A sigh slipped through his lips.

Another day under the tree, huh? He twisted the key, satisfied as the locks clicked in place. *Dad and Talia should hurry back before my eyes turn into an old man's.* The trail of thought withered as quickly as it had come. He stayed behind of his own choice, but he never imagined how lonely it could get at home while they were away.

The carvings in the mahogany door greeted him as his gaze traveled away from the lock. In the early morning light, the red highlights buried deep within the wood seemed brighter, as if the door were bathed in flames. It was warm and comforting, like the hearth when he could sit around it with his family during the cold season of Sefah.

When the house was empty—as it had been for the last several weeks—it was suffocating to sit there alone. Though outside, surrounded by the winds of the changing seasons and the distant cries of the dragonborn people, the tree provided a moment of peace for Tobias that the empty house would only snuff out.

Standing up straighter, he dropped the cord that bound the key over his head and tucked the cold metal into his shirt. Once he was certain that the small key had been safely hidden away, he gripped the strap of his satchel and spun on his heel. The grass rustled beneath his boots as he walked away, trekking down the slight slope from the house to the old oak in the distance.

The monotonous walk drowned away beneath the buzz of Tobias's thoughts. It was the same thing every morning: wake up, pack, head out to the tree. After repeating the routine for the umpteenth time, the excitement and curiosity had dulled, swaying more into frustration. The only reason he began his morning in such a way was to avoid the work he knew would be waiting for him at his desk when he returned.

If I have to choose between staring at words I can't read, and staring at words I wish I couldn't read, I'd choose the first any day. There were only so many unedited manuscripts he could skim in a day before he began to long for the mystery that occupied his mornings.

Dropping his bag beside the roots of the oak tree, Tobias sifted through the contents until he dug up the source of it all: the curiosity, the excitement, the frustration, and the scolding from Talia had come from this. His fingers brushed against its spine, feeling the ridges along the middle from where the book had been bent a little too far back.

A blank, white cover met him as he turned it over. The empty, fingerprint-stained face mocked him.

Another day under the tree, attempting to uncover the mysteries of the stubbornly confusing script between the stained covers.

Tobias frowned at the white leather-bound book in his hands. The weathered pages, turning yellow at the edges, taunted him. The neatly-formed letters were beautiful to stare at—crafted with a steady yet graceful flow—but the words they created were gibberish to him.

He knew one thing for certain: he *hated* the white leather-bound book. Its gold embellishments shone too brightly in the early morning sunlight that filtered through the auburn leaves above him. Flipping the page only revealed another set of words and symbols that meant nothing to him.

He had been staring at the same stupid book on and off for six years whenever he got the chance, yet not one person he had consulted had been able to tell him what it was or what the words meant. Not even his older sister, despite all her wisdom and knowledge. The confusion etched into her face when he showed it to her for the first time was something he could never forget.

"If there's anyone who can figure this out," she had said, *"it's you."*

The only thing he had figured out thus far was that he hated that book more than he hated his own lack of knowledge about it. No amount of note-taking or attempted deciphering could uncover the mystery behind its delicate, handwritten script.

He sighed and leaned his head back against the tree behind him. Clouds rolled over the deep blue sky, briefly blocking the bright sunlight. The wind picked up and breezed through the book, turning over several more pages before he finally slammed his hand down to stop the motion.

He glared at the book, like it was the one at fault for the cold winds. One of these days, he would bury it in the ground and forget all about its secrets. He had no use for something he couldn't understand, and all it ever seemed to do was frustrate him.

And yet... He never did toss the book. The mere thought of doing so pulled sharply at his gut. After all, what if it turned out to be important somehow? The world he knew had changed significantly in the six years since he found it abandoned in a forest near the mountains.

With restless hybrids beyond the border, a new High Summoner to rule us, and a new batch of Dragon Riders for my sister to teach, the world isn't what it once was anymore. It's bound to need this... book. Whatever it is.

Or at least, that was how he justified his holding onto it.

When the wind died down again, he smoothed his hair back and turned his gaze toward the Hybrid Territory. Beyond the forests to the east of his home lay the border to the land of the Draconic people—the pure dragonborn and their half-breed offspring, the hybrids. A roar resounded from somewhere beyond the border, sending a shiver down Tobias's spine. Despite how often he had heard the rough sound, it never ceased to make him wonder what—or who—had become the next victim of the monsters' insatiable hunger.

The sound died down, gradually replaced by the morning calls of birds. His shoulders relaxed, and he leaned back to look up at the red-brown leaves of the old oak tree. It had been his favorite place to read for years; now, he wondered if it would stay safe.

Although, with Deiah's warm season coming to a swift end, many of the dragons would soon begin their hibernation. The leaves had darkened, and the cold had settled in much earlier this year. Tobias could only hope the abnormality would put an end to the noise of the hybrids, too.

"What are you reading?"

Tobias shot to his feet and scrambled away, looking left and right for the source of the voice.

A woman laughed before stepping out from behind the thick trunk of the tree, her hands clasped behind her back. She looked to be about a year older than him, having just entered her twenties; in spite of this, her voice was high-pitched and curious, like that of a little girl. Dark brown hair spilled down her back in loose waves; it was paired nicely with her tanned skin—earned by many hours spent in the sun. When she smiled, her eyes narrowed slightly.

Tobias huffed and straightened the front of his tunic, tucking the white book under one arm. "Why does it matter to you?" He hadn't heard her approach at all. How long had she been there watching him? Had she been there all morning? Had he been so lost in his thoughts that he hadn't noticed?

As soon as the question left his lips, however, he winced. He could have told her the name of any novel; she might have accepted it and left, but he just had to be curt and rude right off the bat. *Way to go, Tobias. Now she'll want to pester you even more.*

"Pardon me," she said, tipping her head to the side. "I was just curious. I've been to this spot many times before and have never seen you here." She fixed him with a sharp stare, a mischievous gleam in her sapphire blue eyes.

Tobias came to the tree to read—or *stare* at the white book— every day. He was the one who had never seen her. A red flag went up in his mind. Gritting his teeth, he scooped up his satchel from where he had dropped it in the grass and slung it over his shoulder, holding tight to the white book.

"Leaving so soon?" she asked. "Before you go, might I ask you a question?"

"You just did. Twice, actually."

He caught a glimpse of her rolling her eyes as she stepped toward him. "A different one."

Frowning, he narrowed his eyes and met her stare with one of his own. She blinked, smiling innocently. One question couldn't hurt. With a sigh, he waved his hand for her to continue.

"Where did you find such a book? I must say, the cover is

beautiful." She tilted her head to get a better view of the book in his arms, her chestnut brown hair spilling over her shoulders. Leaning forward, she reached to touch the book.

Tobias jerked back, putting another couple of steps between them. *Beautiful* was not the word he would use to describe the plain white cover: it was stained with dirt, grass, and fingerprints from years of use. Even the gold embellishments Tobias hated were being worn away from touch.

He shrugged off her question. Despite the warnings in his mind, he couldn't help the curiosity that stirred beneath his wariness. Did she know something about the book that he didn't? "What do you want?"

She huffed and folded her arms over her chest, increasing her childish air. When she narrowed her blue eyes at him, he caught a certain spark of gold in them, glowing in the bright sunlight. It flickered with a life of its own, clearly not just a reflection of the light in her eyes.

"Aren't you just *so* polite!" She pouted, and the spark of gold vanished.

Annoyance overtook his wariness and deepened his frown. "Polite? Well, excuse me!" He snorted at her look of indignation. "You're one to talk. You seem convinced you know something about me—convinced enough to strike up a conversation."

There was a slight chance that she might have been sent by his sister—Talia would send her friends with messages on occasion when she couldn't come herself. But no sooner had the thought occurred to him than he tossed it aside. Even Talia's friends thought to introduce themselves before beginning a conversation.

The woman raised a thin brow and rested a hand under her chin. "You really don't know anything, do you?" She sighed and tsked, using her fingers to comb her long hair back over her shoulder. "He did say you might as well be living under a rock."

He? Tobias shoved the book into his bag, biting the inside of his mouth. A tug at the back of his mind urged him to leave, but another question kept his feet rooted to the ground. The wind toyed with his hair and clothes again, like it too was urging him to give up on his rising curiosity and go.

All the while, the woman's gaze never left him.

With a shiver, he noticed it was more like she was looking *through* him. Her eyes were glazed over and the only thing that shone with life was the sparkle of gold he'd seen before. It danced and swirled, much like the look of the magic wielded by Mages.

She shook her head, and the moment vanished, just as the wind fell silent once more. "Well?"

"How am I supposed to know anything if no one tells me?" he asked. His hands itched to take hold of his sword, but when he lifted his fingers to grab it, they closed on empty air. Eyes flicking to the spot at his waist where it should have been, he found that there was nothing there.

Of course, he thought bitterly as he bit the inside of his cheek. *I forgot it again.* Subconsciously, his hand reached for the key around his neck. The cool metal pressed against his chest. He exhaled slowly in relief. At least he still had that.

The woman didn't bother to answer this time. Rather, she leapt forward and thrust her hands into the bag at his side before he had a chance to pull back. With a triumphant smile, she yanked the book free and danced away. Holding it up, she gazed at it with a strange sort of fondness. Tobias leapt back on instinct, eyes wide and mouth ajar. At the sight of his surprise—or just the feel of the book in her gloved hands—laughter spilled from her lips.

"If you want to know anything, you should start by paying attention to what's going on around you," she said with a hum, waving the book in his face.

Warmth flooded his cheeks; he shot her his best glare. This only made her laugh again, hands on her knees with the book under one arm. He curled his fingers into a tight fist, clenching his jaw.

"Return that to me," he snapped. "It doesn't belong to you."

The woman looked up, wiping tears of mirth from her eyes as she finally caught her breath. She cleared her throat and pulled the front of her red blouse straight again, adjusting her collar and smoothing her skirts down. Her lips twitched with a suppressed smile. She held the book out for him to take.

Eyeing her, he reached to take it back.

With a gasp, she pulled it back and cracked it open, holding up a finger when he opened his mouth to protest. "Let me just take a look at something!"

Rage swept away the previous warnings in Tobias's mind, wrapping him in a burning desire to strike her. But he refrained, curling his fingers into tight fists at his sides. If there was one thing his sister Talia had drilled into his head, it was that he couldn't hit a girl.

He wondered if that included annoying, thieving girls too.

"Can you even read this?" she asked, pointing at the very same page he had been staring at earlier. The neatly written words and carefully drawn images still looked like gibberish to him, though beautiful enough to stare at for hours.

"No." He curled his lip. "Why should that matter to you?"

She frowned, her nose scrunching up as she stared down at the book. "I'd bet anything it's a spellbook. Did you know Mages write in a secret code to keep nosy people from learning their spells and twisting them to their will? As though people who have magic powers aren't trained to read the code, but whatever." With a shrug, she snapped the book shut.

Tobias studied her, mulling over her words. Could it really be a spellbook? His eyes narrowed as he wondered what else she might know about it. Anything he could glean from her would be a step forward, but a thread of impatience and mistrust wound tightly around his thoughts.

He only knew one thing for certain, and that was that she couldn't keep the book. His gut twisted at the very thought of it staying in her hands.

Shifting his feet, he lunged forward. The woman met his eye and smirked. She twisted and swiped his feet out from under him, placing a hand on his shoulder and sending him crashing to the ground. He gasped as pain flared in his back. Before he could right himself again, the cold blade of a knife landed at his throat.

The woman planted her knee on his chest, leaning down so that she was face to face with him. Her knife pressed against his throat, making him clamp his mouth shut as he stared up at her.

"I think I'm going to keep this book. I know someone who needs it more than you do, but I'm sure he'll thank you for holding it for him until now." She chuckled, and a wicked smile twisted her face. "The Mage it used to belong to was rather protective of her spells."

She pulled back and stepped away, sheathing the knife at her waist, where an array of others lay in wait—previously hidden beneath a swath of red cloth. "The name's Eira, by the way. I suggest you not be so careless next time we meet! I may not be feeling as merciful then—oh! And your sword is in the tree if you want it back." With another wink, she pressed her lips to her hand and blew a kiss before taking off with the book.

Tobias rolled to the side and pushed himself to his feet with a grunt. He looked at her, then up at the tree. Sure enough, his sword had been wedged into the branches just above his head.

He cursed and scrambled up the tree to get it. Wrapping his fingers around the sheath, he pulled until it came free. He leapt down and turned to face the way she had gone.

Eira was still within his sights. Tying the sheath of his sword to his waist, he gritted his teeth and rushed after her.

Just like that, the book he despised so much had been taken.

The thing that caused so much frustration for years was finally gone.

But it didn't matter. "Eira!" he yelled after her, his feet pounding against the worn dirt roads that led away from his home and his tree.

He was going to get that book back.

2

KASE

TOBIAS'S SIDE ACHED AND his legs screamed in protest. He was too slow—Eira had vanished in the direction of Floridus, the next town over, already. Tobias cursed, using words he knew his sister would hate. How could he have been so stupid? He let the book go from right under his nose; and if that weren't ridiculous enough, he had been oblivious to his missing sword for who knows how long. If she hadn't pointed it out, he may never have noticed.

He slowed to a stop in the middle of the road, resting his hands on his knees as he gasped for breath. With a frustrated groan, he raked his fingers through his hair, pushing it out of his face. *Talia will never let me hear the end of this.*

Lifting his head, he only saw the empty road. No thief, just the town in the distance and a red dragon circling over it in the clear blue sky. The sun rested in the middle of the open expanse, marking the time as just past noon. A whole morning, wasted. He thought back to the documents waiting for him at home and their deadline looming over him. A grimace pulled sharply at the corners of his mouth. There were other things to get done.

But he *had* to get that book back. If it really was a spellbook, like Eira had said, then who knew what would happen if it landed in the wrong hands. And she was bringing it to *someone*. Each time he recalled the swirling gold in her eyes, a shudder passed through him. Something about it all wasn't right.

He gripped his sword hilt. What if she wanted to turn the spellbook over to the Draconic people? Their Golden Head Dragonborn, the strongest disciple of their most prominent goddess, was said to hunger for magic. Blood stained his hands and painted the runes of his spells. If the spellbook landed with him…

Tobias shook his head vigorously. She's a thief. She probably just wants to make money off of it." *And Floridus has many places for her to sell it.*

With another deep breath, he sped off down the road toward Floridus, shoving his other nagging questions and worries aside. He locked his gaze on the red dragon above. It beat its wings and circled again, gliding effortlessly through the air. Dragons were something he knew. The sight of it brought him back to normalcy, pulling him out of the confusion of spellbooks and thieves. It seemed strange to be so attached to dragons when the dragonborn and hybrids lingered in his worst memories.

"Dragons are much the same as the Draconic people," his sister would say. *"They deserve the same caution, Tobias. Don't let your fascination and curiosity blind you, alright?"*

He frowned at the memory.

The dragon was too far to see properly, but he could tell from the way it angled its head down that it was searching for something—or perhaps waiting. He swallowed thickly, momentarily wondering if his real concern should be the dragon and not the thief.

A shrill whistle pierced the air, echoing in the silence. The dragon snorted in response and flew downward, landing in a field outside the town. Tobias released the breath he had been holding. If it answered to a whistle, the dragon must belong to someone.

If it belonged to someone, perhaps there was a Dragon Rider in town. That thought straightened his back and renewed his motivation. He couldn't screw up while his sister had an ear to the ground.

The gravel road faded into cobblestone streets as he passed through the entrance to the town. Bustling as always, Floridus's marketplace presented itself with a myriad of people and sounds. He made a point of steering himself away from the print shop, where he knew he would be hounded for the editing he had yet to do. Instead, he followed the scent of freshly baked bread, foreign spices, and herbs to the opposite side of town's market.

Women crowded the streets, stalls, and shops. Many of them had the same dark brown hair as Eira, or her tanned skin and angled features. Some of the women even wore the same green skirt or red blouse as the thief. They went about their own business, milling from one shop to another, calling out to each other in loud voices, or simply chatting the afternoon away.

Tobias gripped his sword and shoved his way through the crowd. "Eira!" he called. He tried to ignore the looks cast his way despite the fact that they burned the back of his neck with the same intensity as the sun. "Eira!"

He called and called, wandering and shoving his way through the marketplace, tapping the shoulder of too many similar women to count. By the time he had made his way to the outskirts of the town, the sun had sunk to late afternoon and his throat burned from all his shouting. Frustration itched at the back of his mind; when he finally came to a stop, his foot tapped irritably against the ground.

Gritting his teeth, he stared into the street he had come from. She *had* to be there somewhere. He must have just missed her. She couldn't have gone off somewhere else. If she had, how was he supposed to find her? *Which would be the point of her going far.*

"Eira!" he called out again, inwardly cursing himself as more people turned to stare. "I know you're here! Return what you stole from me, Eira!"

A hand landed on his shoulder. Tobias jumped, spinning around and drawing his sword. A pair of dark eyes stared back at him, blinking as they shifted from his face to the tip of his blade. A man stood there; hands raised innocently as he took a cautious step back. He was at least a few inches taller than Tobias, dressed in a black tunic with a red coat, a white hood pulled over his disheveled black hair. A small, red gem kept the hood of his cloak pinned around his shoulders.

Disappointment clouded Tobias's surprise. The man was, quite obviously, not Eira. With a growl, Tobias sheathed his sword—though he kept his hand against the hilt. He wouldn't take any more chances with strangers until his luck cleared up. The gods themselves had clearly decided it was a day to mock him.

"Sorry," the man said, his eyes darting around and his voice low. "Didn't mean to scare you."

Tobias narrowed his eyes. "Yes, well, I'm in the middle of something."

The man chuckled, brushing his hood back and letting it rest on his shoulders. Combing his fingers through his hair, he said, "I know, I could hear you from miles away. You're looking for a thief, right? Eira?" He reached into a pocket in his coat and fished out a silver pin with a red gem in the center. Etched into the flat, round surface was the image of a dragon. On the other, a human. The symbol of a Dragon Rider.

Recognition overcame annoyance, and the tension in Tobias's shoulders relaxed. The red dragon he saw earlier must have belonged to this man; the pin marked him as a dragon-bonded who had been certified by his sister. The silver it was crafted from labeled him as a dragon's partner, the red gem identified the class of his dragon.

"You're... a—"

"Dragon keeper," the man said with a smile, revealing pearly white teeth. His tanned face was smeared with soot and dotted with freckles. He pocketed the pin again. "Come with me."

The man turned, motioning for Tobias to follow, and made his way out to the field behind the town, sliding down the soft, grassy incline with ease. Tobias stared after him, bewildered by his sudden appearance. Although the pin couldn't be stolen from the person it was given to—it would always reappear back in the hands of the original owner—he was no longer sure he wanted to wander after strangers. As much as he trusted his sister to pick good Riders, and dragons to bond with good people, the incident with the thief still sat fresh in his mind.

Tobias's chest tightened. How easily she had snuck up on him and disarmed him without his noticing. How quickly she had manipulated his curiosity. He had been too wrapped up in his own thoughts to stop her from stealing the book from his very hands.

Still... He glanced back at the crowded marketplace where he had made no progress in his search for several hours now. *Do I have any better ideas?*

Somewhere, tucked away on one of those crowded streets, he would find a very angry supervisor with an earful of complaints about his unfinished work. Although that was an easy problem to solve, his heart sank at the thought of letting the book go and resigning himself to work. It may have been a nuisance, but the book was still valuable to him. It was a treasure trove of secrets untold—secrets he desperately wished to uncover if only to turn Talia's head. It was in his care, and he was the one that screwed up.

No, he admitted. *I don't have a better idea.*

With a sigh, Tobias fixed the strap of his satchel and

followed the man. The dew of the grass clung to his boots as he stepped away from the gravel and stone of town. When he caught up with the man, they walked side-by-side toward the center of the field. Scorch marks stained the ground, and massive footprints marked the mud. They were the right size and shape for a red dragon.

Awkward silence stretched between them. The wind whistled through the knee-length grass of the field, carrying the sharp scent of ash. Tobias tilted his head back, gazing upward in search of the red dragon.

"My dragon and I didn't agree to complete Head Dragon Rider Talia's training," the man said. "I ended up becoming a Mage Guardian instead. But, um… my Mage isn't around at the moment, and my dragon is growing old and lazy—though he still acts as high and mighty as ever…" He trailed off as he rubbed the back of his neck.

It wasn't unusual to find a Mage Guardian on their own. Mages had been disappearing all over the country only to be found dead later, their bodies blackened and sucked dry of life. It was a popular story that had spread to both news and fiction, and Tobias had read more than his fair share of it from those who knew nothing of the suffering it brought. Even on their own, the Guardians were always tight-lipped about their Mages.

The eagerness written on the man's face—his openness to discuss whatever seemed to cross his mind—brought hesitancy creeping into the back of Tobias's mind.

"What does that have to do with me?" he asked with a pointed stare. While he was always happy to have something explained to him—as it kept his curiosity at bay—he couldn't help but wonder why this man had come to him. Unless he was somehow working with Eira and was there to distract him.

Tobias gritted his teeth and resisted the urge to take hold of his sword again. One look at the man was enough to tell him he stood no chance against him if they ended up in a fight. Not to mention the man had a dragon on his side, flying somewhere above their heads.

When they reached the center of the scorched part of the field, the man looked over his shoulder. Something unreadable sparked in his dark eyes, lingering in his expression as his brow knit together.

"I know Eira. I have a score to settle with her." Without waiting for any questions, he lifted his fingers to his lips and whistled. The shrill noise echoed in the still air, and a few seconds passed before a roar answered.

A blur of red and orange flashed across the pale blue sky and a dragon descended from the clouds. Its wingbeats were powerful enough to send Tobias stumbling back, shielding his eyes from the wind. Gentle despite its size, the dragon landed in the grass a few yards away from its master. Once grounded, it folded in its wings and lifted its massive head.

Tobias blinked, rubbing his eyes as he stared at the dragon. Two twisted horns rose from its head; its jaw was decorated with a series of spikes. Its scales were a mix of ruby red and amber, and it breathed a cloud of smoke through its nose when it exhaled. Long talons jutted out from its paws, and its head rose even with the roof tiling of the buildings of Floridus.

Despite this, it looked down on him with soft amber eyes, lined by age and swirling with magic.

A Celestial Class dragon. It perfectly matched the description his sister had read to him as a kid. She spoke of higher class dragons with a gleam in her eye, and he had always shared her fascination from afar. Now, standing at the foot of one, he was choked with awe.

"Woah," he breathed, taking an involuntary step back.

"This is Smoke," the man said, stepping forward to pat the dragon's side. Even when he stood next to it, his head barely reached the base of the dragon's shoulder. "He's the one who told me to go get you. You're going to need help if you want to catch Eira. She has a knack for getting under your skin and, unfortunately for you, she's good at what she does."

Tobias looked from the man to the dragon, wondering if it was possible he could still be dreaming. Maybe he never even got out of bed that morning, and this was all an elaborate story created by his subconscious to entertain him.

The cold edge of Eira's knife against his neck rose to mind, and he swallowed hard. He quickly shoved the idea of a dream away.

"Why are you really helping me?" he asked.

The man frowned, his eyes going distant and hazy for a moment. His gaze flicked away. "Like I said, I have a score to settle with Eira."

Tobias scrutinized the man, weighing his choices. Suspicion chewed at the fragile trust he wanted to place in this man. On the other hand, Tobias found himself in awe of the man's ability to tame and bond with a Celestial Class dragon. There weren't many Celestial Class dragons out there, and they were said to avoid bonding with humans. Talia had always said it was her dream to meet and bond with a Celestial dragon. Tobias wondered if she was disappointed when she met a Rider who had already bonded to one and then had denied the training she offered.

He picked at the hilt of his sword absently. "Can you tell me your name?"

"Didn't I already?" The man furrowed his brow in concentration. "I must not have, sorry. The name's Kase." He held out his gloved hand to Tobias. "At your service, uh…" He trailed off, expectant.

Tobias took Kase's hand and shook it. "Tobias. And I'd be happy to have your assistance—yours and Smoke's."

If his sister had trusted Kase enough to give him the pin, Tobias would trust him too. Two were better than one; perhaps he could make use of Kase's knowledge of Eira.

3

THE DRAGON KEEPER PIN

"So, she took your book and ran off?" Kase asked after Tobias told him all that happened in the last few hours. The dragon keeper took a drink from his flask, his face scrunched up as he thought. When he was done, he screwed the cap back on and shoved it into his saddlebag. "Yeah, that sounds like Eira all right."

Tobias plucked at the grass, twisting it in his fingers as he stared up at the sky. The sun had just begun to set, painting over the fair blue of daylight with a deep purple. The last of the brilliant rays of light streaked the sky with pink and orange. The two of them had sat in the scorched field, watching the sky grow steadily darker while Tobias dumped the entire story of the thievery onto Kase—who listened intently to every detail. He wasn't sure what sitting around and talking was going to do to help catch up to Eira, but each time he had mentioned that, Kase told him they needed a plan first.

Tobias grumbled to himself. He *knew* they needed a plan, but all he wanted was to have the book in his hands. He wanted to skip all the middle steps and just get to the end.

But of course, those middle steps wouldn't allow themselves to be skipped.

Sighing, Tobias leaned back on his hands and forced himself to stop picking at the grass. "You said you had a score to settle with her, right? What kind of score? What did she do?"

Out of the corner of his eye, he saw Kase shrug. The man reached into his pocket, pulled out the pin from before, and began to fiddle with it. "Just something that happened a long time ago. I don't like to talk about it."

Right. Should've known. Since that thread of conversation wasn't going anywhere, Tobias shifted to a new one. "Do you know my sister, Talia? When you spoke about her earlier, you seemed pretty familiar with her." Tobias always noted how people spoke his sister's title—usually with awe or sometimes even fear. But Kase had said it with a friendly gleam in his eyes. There was something about his face—or perhaps his name— that seemed vaguely familiar to Tobias. Like a stubborn memory that sat at the very back of his mind, just out of reach.

His curiosity leapt at memories like those, eager to sift through them for anything he could learn. This one in partic- ular presented a struggle, but it could be easily solved depending on Kase's answers.

Luckily, Kase nodded eagerly in response to the new ques- tion. He looked down at the pin, a fond smile curling the corners of his mouth upward slightly. "She was good friends with my Mage and was eager to teach me more about my bond with Smoke." He smoothed his finger across the surface of the pin, staring at it for several more seconds before he pocketed it again. "She talked about you sometimes, but I doubt she mentioned me. I think she was disappointed I didn't drop Avi— my... Mage to become a full-fledged Dragon Rider."

He leaned forward and put his head in his hands, combing his fingers through his raven black hair. "But she's a good person," he added as an afterthought. "I admire her."

Tobias thought for a moment, mulling over Kase's words, wondering if Talia had ever mentioned Kase to him. She was often quiet about her students, but Tobias was certain she wouldn't be able to resist telling him about Smoke had she met the dragon.

His gaze strayed to the red dragon, who was curled up behind Kase with the tip of his tail draped protectively across his master's lap. His amber eyes were watchful, and thin wisps of smoke trailed out of his nostrils each time he exhaled. Any time Kase fell silent and stared blankly at his hands in his lap, Tobias wondered if the two were conversing through their bond. A twinge of envy twisted his gut as that thought solidified.

Kase cleared his throat, rubbing the back of his neck. "How is she, by the way? Talia, I mean."

"She's fine," Tobias bit back. He bristled at the question, though Kase's tone was harmless. "She's busy. She had to step away from the school because she's..." He trailed off and fiddled with the blade of grass in his hands. With a sigh, he finished, "She's getting married soon."

It wasn't news to Tobias yet admitting it out loud always seemed to twist his gut. He ducked his head to avoid Kase's gaze. *But here I am: always a burden, always making her worry.* The blade of grass split between his fingers, tearing evenly in two.

"Ah," Kase murmured. He heaved a sigh and rested his chin in his hands. "She deserves to be happy."

Tobias nodded, but his tongue tasted bitter. She deserved to be happy, but he knew she never would be as long as she was worried about him.

"Well, anyway. What I don't understand is why Eira would want a book." He narrowed his eyes at the grass as if searching for the answer somewhere beneath it. The only answer he got was from the crickets, chirping louder as the sun sank lower.

Tobias shrugged, leaning forward again when his palms

began to ache from the press of the earth against them. A soft, steady flow of heat from Smoke's scales warmed him as the air grew colder. The first few stars began to appear alongside the waning crescent moon. It snatched his breath from his lungs as his gaze lingered on the sky, awe sinking into his thoughts. Tobias couldn't recall the last time he had been out at night. He always returned to an empty house as soon as the sun sank behind the distant mountains. By closing the curtains and lighting candles, he rushed to shut out the world outside. It was strangely comforting to be in the company of someone else: beneath the stars, smothered in a dragon's warmth.

The distant roars that carried across the border of Hybrid Territory painted his memories in blood red, locking him up inside his own house until the sun rose again. Even if he spent every day and night alone, he took comfort in his safety.

Only now did he notice that he had been painfully lonely.

He shuddered and shifted closer to Smoke subconsciously, pressing his palm against the soft fabric of his tunic where the key dangled beneath. The dragon greeted him with a snort, and the warm air around his scales increased. Tobias nodded his thanks, meeting Smoke's amber eyes and searching their depths for some kind of hint to the bond he shared with Kase. When he could find nothing but that old look of wisdom, his throat constricted painfully.

But then it was gone. The choked up feeling vanished as quickly as it had come. He swiped at his eyes, just in case, before facing Kase again.

"I don't know why she would want the book," Tobias admitted in a soft voice. "It's just something I found about six years ago, with words I can't read. It intrigues me, so I kept it around, but… I don't know why she would want it." He had always felt drawn to it, and now that it was gone, an emptiness had settled over him. Did Eira feel the same pull?

Kase froze, sitting up straighter. His hands shot out and

grabbed Tobias by the shoulders as he twisted around to face him, his eyes wide and sparkling with excitement. "Six years ago, you said? What does the cover look like exactly? Describe it to me!"

Tobias's brow furrowed and he peeled Kase's hands off his arms, scooting back a little more. Kase muttered an apology, but the spark in his eyes didn't fade. He trembled, shoulders tight, body leaned toward Tobias. His gaze kept flicking back and forth between Tobias and Smoke; the dragon was probably speaking to him. Tobias had seen similar moments when Talia and her dragon would talk privately with each other.

"Yes, six years ago, give or take a bit." He folded his arms over his chest and gave Kase a firm stare. "Dirty, embellished with gold, and made of a white leather. Probably dyed. It had all these tiny fingerprints, and the pages were folded down at the corners."

"Oh my—gods above!" Kase shot to his feet, beaming as he raked his fingers through his unruly black hair again. He let out a laugh as he turned to the dragon. "Aviva! It must be Aviva! That's why Eira wants the book!"

"Aviva?" Tobias asked. Kase rushed to tighten the straps of Smoke's massive saddle. "Who's Aviva?"

"Never mind that, I have a plan." Kase grunted as he pulled on the leather straps of the saddle, buckling them several notches down. Smoke rolled over with a groan, pressing the saddle straps to the ground. Kase gritted his teeth. "Get up, you old fart! You already had a nap today—no, by my count, this must be your fourth!"

With a heavy sigh, Smoke slowly rose to his feet and shook himself like a dog, before unfurling his wings and stretching out each of his legs. He lashed his long tail and almost swept Kase off his feet, but Kase leapt out of the way at just the right moment. Tobias smiled to himself, watching Kase scold the dragon the way he would a child.

With a final glare at his dragon, Kase spun around to face Tobias again. "Have you ever heard of the Beast Master of Ruber?"

Pausing for a moment, Tobias nodded slowly. He had heard rumors of a wild girl who lived in the forest outside of the small town of Ruber. She was whispered to be under the influence of *beastic no norai*, the Beast Curse, which was placed on shapeshifters who used too much of their magic. Some had said she was no better than the Draconic hybrids—monsters born from the goddess's "perfect" dragonborn which devoured the flesh of humans. Others simply said she was more interested in sulking than killing. Either way, Tobias wasn't entirely sure why he would want to meet her.

"She can track Eira and tell us where she's heading," Kase said. "On top of that, I need to pay a visit to my cousin, who keeps her in check—Oliver is his name. Plus, I bet he'd be thrilled to hear your story!"

My embarrassing story of how I couldn't keep a thief from stealing my book? Tobias frowned, reluctantly rising to his feet. "So this Oliver will take us to see the Beast Master, who will take us to Eira?"

"Yeah, basically."

"You're not taking me on this trip just because you have family matters to settle with your *cousin*, right?"

Kase shook his head. "Of course not. I'm not here to waste your time, I promise."

Tobias sighed, shaking his head as he pressed a fist to his temples. More steps in the middle was the opposite of what he wanted. He bit his lip as Kase checked over the saddle again, once more scolding Smoke for something he had said through their bond—which made the dragon laugh in the strange, chortling way that dragons did.

If Tobias turned this plan down, he would be chasing Eira blindly. He had done that once—stumbling after her as she giggled and ran away with his book. His neck burned with shame.

He nodded. "Alright. You know better than I do, I'm sure. Lead the way."

Kase grinned and gestured for Tobias to climb into the saddle on Smoke's back. "It's only a few hours away if we fly there. We should arrive by morning, and you can sleep on the way if you want." He bent down and offered Tobias his hands as a stepping stool.

Tobias put his boot in Kase's hands, and Kase hoisted him up. He scrabbled against the warm, smooth scales but eventually gripped the saddle and pulled himself onto Smoke's back. His arms ached from the effort, and he frowned at how effortlessly Kase managed to climb up.

To be fair, his mind whispered, *he probably does this several times a day. You don't.* The only dragon he had ridden on was Talia's, and Sikii was much smaller than Smoke. If he put the two dragons side by side, Sikii's head probably barely reached the base of Smoke's neck.

Tobias shoved the thought away and gripped the sides of the saddle as Smoke unfurled his wings again.

"Be gentle," Kase advised, patting the dragon's neck.

Smoke pushed off the ground with a grunt, catching the winds effortlessly. The leap into the air forced Tobias to tighten his grip, squeezing his eyes shut as the wind rushed past him. Taking off was always the worst part.

As simple as that, they were flying, heading one step closer toward the thief and Tobias's book.

And yet, he couldn't help but look back down at the ground far below. His gaze drifted to the oak tree and his house nestled in the distance. It was barely a speck, overshadowed by the heavy darkness of the night. High in the sky, it seemed so small and insignificant. His chest ached.

I'll come back soon, he promised himself as he faced the front again, tightly gripping the thick leather of the saddle. *First, I have to get my book back. Then I can go home—if that loneliness is still even considered home.*

The thought turned sour, and he reached for the key dangling from his neck once more. *No,* he rectified it. *It is home. I'll come back to it.* With that promise to spur him on, fresh confidence flooded through him. He had a dragon keeper by his side, after all. Getting the book back now couldn't be *that* hard.

After all, what thief would defy a dragon?

4

HUNTER IN RUBER

SMOKE FOLDED IN HIS WINGS and began his descent, jolting Tobias awake. He couldn't remember falling asleep, but the change in the sky told him it had been at least a few hours since they took off. Night had begun fading out as the sun rose, and a thick layer of dark clouds had gathered over the pale blue sky. The frigid air hung thickly around him, biting through his tunic. But he was too busy gripping the sides of the saddle and squeezing his eyes shut to bother much with the cold.

Below, talons scraped across dirt; Smoke's body straightened as he landed, flapping his wings a few times to settle himself before folding them in at his side. Tobias pried his eyes open as Kase swung his legs over the side and leapt down. He tripped and landed on his side in a spatter of mud with a yelp. Smoke chortled, flipping his tail in amusement.

Kase shot him a glare. "Oh shut up, you… three-legged chair!"

Three-legged chair… Tobias rolled his eyes. The insult made no sense, as Smoke had all four of his legs intact. He slipped down from Smoke's back, landing evenly on his feet. His legs did feel stiff, but he felt a flicker of pride at the fact that he

31

didn't fall over—unlike Kase, who was an experienced rider. He made a mental note to brag to Talia next time he saw her.

Kase mumbled something to himself as he rose from the ground, brushing dirt and grass from his pants. A smear of mud covered the back of his cloak, and Tobias barely bit back his laugh as Kase twisted and strained to get a better look at it. Smoke stretched his neck forward and stuck his tongue out. With a yelp, Kase jumped back.

"Do *not* lick me! That never washes out, and I'll smell like your mouth for weeks." Kase froze, his frown deepening. "Yes, that would be worse than the mud!"

A small smile stretched across Tobias's lips, and he rubbed the remains of sleep from his eyes. Though Kase was loud, always wrapped up in some kind of conversation with his dragon, Tobias was glad he wasn't traveling alone. If he were, he probably would be overloaded with anger and frustration, with no clue where to go and no idea how to even begin. He might have even still been wandering the streets of Floridus, searching for a thief who wasn't even there.

"Anyways," Kase said with a final, pointed look at Smoke. "Ruber is just over there. Smoke, you can go find yourself something to eat. Rest up but try to stay close by so I can call on you more easily this time. Don't leave me stranded again."

Smoke stretched and arched his back, shaking out his body like a wet dog before spreading his wings and taking off again. The gust of wind sent Tobias stumbling backward, nearly landing in the same mud as Kase had.

"Come on," Kase said once Tobias had righted himself. "Oliver will take us straight to the Beast Master, and then we'll get that thief."

Tobias nodded and followed Kase down the road to the little town in the distance. Unlike Floridus—a popular town for trade since it was so close to the southern ocean—Ruber didn't have a paved, cobblestone street that led into the town. Instead, it was constructed of hard, packed dirt. It was uneven in places, and Tobias nearly tripped over a small rock in the path.

As the buildings grew closer, Kase's steps quickened. His pace was fast enough that Tobias kept falling behind and had to take larger steps to keep up.

Kase muttered to himself and fiddled with the silver pin, combing his fingers through his hair as he walked. However, he didn't seem nervous; Tobias couldn't spot the trembling in his hands that most people gained when frightened. Rather, he looked almost excited. Each time Tobias got a brief glance of his face, his dark brown eyes were alight and there was a barely contained smile on his lips.

Puzzled, Tobias fidgeted with the strap of his satchel. Kase had mentioned having other reasons for needing to see Oliver. Knots of anxiety formed in Tobias's stomach. He had no idea what Kase was truly after. He could only hope this detour wouldn't end poorly for himself.

The town of Ruber opened before them, much smaller than Floridus. The buildings that lined the streets weren't stalls and markets, but houses, each one marked with a red roof: the feature that earned the small trading town its name. Kase looked back and motioned for Tobias to follow before speeding ahead.

"Hey—wait!" Tobias called. When Kase didn't stop, he gritted his teeth and raced after him.

The earthy scent of the charcoal fires slammed into him as he stepped through the town's entrance; unlike Floridus's, it was unguarded. Not only that, but the streets were entirely empty. It was still early in the morning; the sun had barely risen past the horizon to cast its weak rays across the town and its neighboring forest. Tobias faltered at the emptiness, his breath catching in his throat.

He caught a glimpse of red and white as Kase hurried around a corner and disappeared down another road. Shaking away the tendrils of unease, he chased after him again. "Kase, you're killing me!"

When Tobias finally caught up to Kase, he stood in front of a small house with a dark red roof. A single window faced them on the left side of the door, but a set of tattered curtains obscured their view of the inside. The walls were stone; the door in front of them was stained wood, worn by deep scratch marks across its front. Kase's hand hovered over the curved handle, his brows drawn together and his lips pressed into a thin line. His other hand remained clenched at his side, his shoulders tense.

Tobias sighed. He pulled Kase aside and knocked on the dark wooden door. The knock echoed hollowly on the other side of the door. Tobias winced as he withdrew his hand.

No answer came.

Kase gave a nervous laugh. "Classic Oliver. He never answers the door." He put his hand on the handle again. This time, he twisted it and pushed the door open. Sunlight flooded into the room through the open doorway, and a dog's bark greeted them as they stepped inside.

They entered a small kitchen and a breakfast room, though it seemed to be swept clean of activity. No dishes sat on the counters, nor any pots or other cooking utensils. Tobias frowned thoughtfully before turning his attention elsewhere. A hallway opened up to the left, leading away into the rest of the house. On the right, a staircase rose, with a door beneath it that appeared to be a closet. A table stood at the far end of the room they were in. On it rested a full quiver of arrows, and beside it sat a chair.

The barking grew louder, paired with the clack of nails against wooden floorboards. A black and white dog burst around the corner, head tossed back as it howled. As Tobias closed the door, it rushed toward them. The dog jumped and scratched at Kase, nearly knocking him over, barking all the while. Tobias went stiff in the face of the dog's attack, but Kase laughed. He scratched at its ears, grinning as the dog flopped on the ground and offered its furry white belly for scratching.

"Such a good boy you are, yes you are. So much better than Smoke." Kase bent down, petting the dog all over and combing his fingers through its fur. "You've grown since I last saw you, yes you have. You used to be just a little guy!"

The dog's tongue lolled out the side of its mouth and the barking quieted. Its tail thumped on the wooden floors.

"Axel!" a voice called, down a hall to the left. "Get back in here! Hudson, I hope that's you. My bow needs fixing again, and I—" A boy rounded the corner and stopped short at the sight of Kase. Unkempt, coal-black hair hung in his tanned, soft face. Beneath the black locks, his eyes widened. The armful of books and papers he was carrying slipped from his grasp, clattering to the ground. He didn't look down at the mess at his feet, but kept his gaze locked on Kase. The surprise vanished as quickly as it had come, and his face twisted with anger.

"Kase," he greeted with a slight growl.

The dog, Axel, rolled over onto its feet and raced back toward the boy, wagging its tail and barking some more. With the snap of his fingers, the boy sent Axel down the hall from which he had originally come. Once Axel disappeared from the room, silence fell over them. With a pointed glare at Kase, the boy bent down to pick up the books and papers he had dropped.

Kase squared his shoulders. Any excitement Tobias had seen previously had completely vanished, leaving him stiff and unreadable.

"Oliver, I—"

"Well, this is disappointing," Oliver interrupted, crossing to the table at the far side of the room. He dropped the books onto it with a thud that made Kase wince. "And here I thought my morning was going well so far. What can I help you with? Did you come to ask more favors of me? Or make some more promises you don't intend to keep? Please, Kase, enlighten me as to why you've barged into my house with another one of your problems for me to solve."

Tobias reached for his sword, biting down on his tongue. Oliver's sharp tone grated against his nerves, making the hair at the back of his neck stand on end. Despite the small spark of frustration that lit in his chest, he couldn't help the way his gaze drifted back to Kase. Uncertainty quickly smothered the spark. Was Kase truly that fickle? *No.* Tobias jerked his focus back to Oliver. *Don't rush to conclusions. If you do, you'll lose your shot at getting the spellbook back.*

With that in mind, he studied Oliver more closely. Aside from his tone and his foul attitude toward Kase, there were deep, dark circles under his eyes. His clothes hung loosely on his thin frame; his tunic tucked hastily into the belt around his waist. He looked small and frail. Perhaps his tongue was his best method of defense.

Oliver pulled the chair away from the table and dropped himself into it with a heavy sigh. His hands brushed against the hilt of a small knife at his waist, pausing for a moment before he drew it slowly from its sheath. Eyes fixed on the blade, Oliver turned his head away from them. Strands of unevenly cut black hair fell in his face, obscuring it from view.

Kase took a deep breath before speaking. The playful excitement sparked by his brief encounter with Axel had slipped away, replaced by a dark, disappointed glaze in his eyes.

"I guess… you're still upset about that?" Kase asked in a low voice.

Oliver drove the knife into the tabletop, his head shooting up to meet their gazes. His amber eyes flashed; Tobias took a step back instinctively.

"Upset? That's putting it lightly!" he snapped. "I don't owe you any favors, so stop coming to ask for them! I told you I was done with you and your… *nonsense!*"

"It isn't 'nonsense'!" Kase protested, his hands curling into tight fists at his sides. "It's—" He cast a sideways glance at Tobias and clamped his mouth shut, turning his head away. A heavy sigh left his lips.

Silence smothered the room like a thick, heavy blanket. Tobias poured his attention into keeping a blank expression for fear that too much interest would only stir the tension in the room. It was suffocating enough as it was; he didn't need to push it. *I shouldn't be here at all.*

Finally, Oliver took a deep breath and dragged a hand across his face, pushing his coal-black hair out of his eyes. "What do you want, Kase?"

Another beat of silence passed before Kase lifted his head again. "Well." He cleared his throat and gestured to Tobias at his side with the sweep of his arm. "I'm on a mission with my friend here, and we need your help with something."

Oliver's gaze flicked back to Tobias, who stiffened under his sharp glare. He lifted a questioning brow. "Get to the point. What is it you want?"

"We want to see the Beast Master."

Oliver froze, his eyes widening. Shakily, he wrapped his arms around himself. When he lifted his head to look back at Kase, his amber eyes had taken a different appearance. Gone was the glare, the look of hatred, and in its place was cold fear, a pathetic, helpless look that sent a shiver crawling down Tobias's spine. His trembling became even more evident when he grabbed a fistful of his loose, forest-green tunic at his shoulder, bunching the fabric in his hands.

"The... the Beast Master?"

Tobias shot Kase a look from the corner of his eye, fear worming its way into his chest. Oliver was supposed to be her keeper.

And he was downright terrified of the very mention of her name.

Tobias shook his head, biting down on the inside of his cheek and steeling his nerves. He stepped forward a bit. Oliver flinched, his eyes lingering on the sword at Tobias's waist. Calmly, Tobias lifted his hands.

"Can you take us to see her?" he asked softly. "Kase tells me no one can visit her without your permission, and I really need her help with something."

"What could possibly be so important?" Oliver stood up and dropped his hand back to his side. It trembled slightly, and the wrinkles from his tight grip on the fabric of his tunic lingered. "I... You don't want to see her, trust me. Nothing is that important."

"We need her tracking abilities," Kase added with a quick glance at Tobias. He stuck his hand into the pocket where his pin was, facing Oliver with soft eyes. "Please, Oliver."

"Then I can lend Axel to you! He's an excellent tracker!" Oliver argued, gripping the table with one hand and leaning against it. His eyes narrowed; a tight frown had formed on his face.

Kase sighed deeply. "If I had wanted a good tracker, I would have just asked Smoke! I *need* Arayna's magic if I'm going to help Tobias catch this thief."

Oliver flinched at the word *thief*. In the blink of an eye, he pulled the knife from the table and whirled around to face Kase, blade pointed at him. "What thief?" he spat, his eyes narrowed and sharp.

Kase stared evenly back at Oliver. Any emotion Tobias had seen before was masked—even his dark eyes had gone blank. Dull. Lifelessly tired.

Tobias bit the inside of his cheek until the coppery taste of blood leaked into his mouth. Though the knife wasn't pointed at his face, he could practically feel its cold blade against his skin. Maybe it was Oliver's burning glare, or maybe Kase's sudden mask, or maybe just the way the knife's silver blade glittered in the light. It was stifling; the air was so thick with tension that he could no longer draw in a breath without worrying that he would shatter the brief moment of quiet and send the two spiraling.

Nothing is that important. Tobias grabbed the hilt of his sword, squeezing until his fingers ached. As much as he wanted the book back, was it even worth the struggle?

A sinking feeling gripped him. Perhaps his obsession had pushed him too far.

5

THE BEAST MASTER

"What thief, Kase?" Oliver snapped, his hand trembling at his side. He inhaled sharply through his nose and narrowed his eyes further. "What do you really need Arayna for?"

Tobias stepped forward, pushing himself between Kase and the knife. Although his heart raced with the blade inches from his nose, he faced Oliver with a solid glare. "There's no need for this. Kase and I can find another way to catch the thief. She stole a book of mine, that's all. If you aren't comfortable with assisting us, we'll leave." He held Oliver's gaze for another second. When Oliver's expression didn't waver, Tobias sighed. True to his word, he turned and grabbed Kase's arm, steering him toward the door.

It was just a book, he told himself firmly. *She was lying when she said it was something important. She was teasing. You don't need it, especially not if it's going to cause this much of a problem.*

He didn't need it, but his head throbbed at the thought of letting Eira get away with the theft and that emptiness within him deepened. As it always did when his head clouded with anxiety, his mind drifted back to Talia. What would she do?

Would she go after the book regardless of the drama it created? Would she have let it go? Would she never have let it get stolen in the first place?

Before Tobias could settle on an answer, Kase planted his foot. He yanked his arm free and spun to face Oliver, who hadn't moved. Oliver tilted his head slightly, eyeing them with suspicion. The knife was still pointed at Kase, glinting in the light.

"Eira," Kase said, barely above a whisper. "The thief is Eira."

Spouting curses, Oliver raked his fingers through his hair. "I told you I wanted nothing to do with her!" he snapped, his voice pitched high and choked with desperation. Again, he drove the knife into the table and leaned against it, pressing his hand to his shoulder. "I will not take anyone to see the Beast Master —*especially* not so I can get dragged back into Eira's schemes!"

"But, Oliver—"

Oliver visibly tensed when Kase spoke. "But nothing. There are no buts to discuss here." He fixed Tobias with his hardened amber stare. "I don't know what he told you to rope you into this, but maybe you should ask him a bit more about what happened the last time the Beast Master and I had a little *disagreement.* She's become a monster, and I don't want to be responsible for what she does to you if she learns of why you've come."

Tobias reached up to grip his shoulder, in the same place Oliver kept touching his own. Realization hit him like a slap to the face: the Beast Master must have wounded him. That was why he was so afraid. Slowly, the edge that sharpened Tobias's tongue began to diminish, and he swallowed the last of his unspoken retorts.

"Then... we just won't tell her," he murmured, ignoring Kase's curious glance. "There are other thieves in the world. Surely she could believe it was any of them—Eira might not even come to her mind."

Oliver sank back into his chair, his forehead pressed into his hands. He said nothing for some time. The silence pressed heavily against Tobias's shoulders, like someone had piled a bunch of books on them and expected him to still stand upright under the weight.

Fidgeting with his gloves, Kase spoke up. "Arayna deserves to know it's Eira," he said softly, keeping his head bowed. "She deserves to know what's going on, especially if… if the book is what I think it might be."

Oliver fixed Kase with a firm stare, leaning forward to rest his elbows on his knees. The shadows cast on his face by the flickering candle made him seem so much older than he was, like he had lived a longer life than sixteen or seventeen years. He sighed wearily, and his shoulders drooped. "Even if she does, I don't want anyone else to get hurt. I don't want there to be any more blood on her hands. And if you're so certain the thing Eira stole is what you think you need, maybe ask yourself why you've dragged your new friend along. This isn't about him, is it? It's about you. It always is."

Kase looked at Tobias; his face fell, and his hands clenched at his sides. He pursed his lips and turned his head the other way, reaching up to grip the red pin that kept his cloak around his shoulders.

Tobias frowned. *Selfish* was not the first word that came to mind when he met Kase, and it certainly hadn't surfaced since. Until Oliver planted the seed. It was true that he didn't know anything about Kase—what he wanted, why he came, or where he intended to go next—but he hadn't thought it was necessary. An inkling of doubt diluted his thoughts, wearing down on his resolve until it was barely even a thin wall between him and the goal. And yet, the emptiness left behind by the book ached. His fingers itched to flip through the pages.

I should never have picked it up in the first place. It was never his to begin with, just something he found and obsessed over. It had brought him nothing but trouble, frustration, and misery. *Why do I even want it back? It's not that important, right?*

"You exhaust everyone around you, Kase," Oliver muttered, snapping Tobias out of his reverie. "Let go of your fantasy already. Aviva is gone; Eira had her killed. Arayna and I don't want a part in your outlandish dreams anymore."

Tobias gritted his teeth and stepped toward Oliver, putting his hand on the hilt of his sword. This time, Oliver didn't flinch away, but Tobias didn't care. It was more for his own comfort than for a threat.

"I don't know what happened in the past, but Kase didn't drag me along." Determination welled inside him, overflowing with each word that fell from his lips. "I came of my own choice, and I'm chasing Eira for my own reasons. If you can't or won't help us, we'll go. But you're not going to fix the past by running from it."

Before either of them could argue, Tobias spun on his heel, his face warm with frustration. For the second time, he grabbed Kase by the arm and hauled him toward the door. Selfish or not, Kase was his key to reclaiming the book. He wasn't foolish enough to think he could do it on his own.

This time, Kase didn't stop him. The door swung open and the two stepped outside into the sunlight. Without so much as a goodbye, Tobias slammed it shut behind the two of them.

Tobias sagged against the door. Storming out might not have been the best idea, and he winced as he waited for Kase's argument. He didn't know Oliver; he didn't know how he would take that kind of reaction. Maybe it would only make him more angry, and he would rush out after them. Or maybe he would just go on sulking. Or maybe he would finally jab that knife of his through their flesh rather than the tabletop. The image of the blade sliding through Tobias's chest made him shudder.

A beat passed. Oliver never came out after them. Tobias sighed in relief, exhaling the tension that squeezed his limbs.

"Well, there goes that plan," Kase muttered, kicking a stray pebble in his path. He paced away from the door, raking his fingers through his hair. "Sorry. I had no idea I'd screw this up too. I knew he was upset last time I saw him, but this is beyond what I had imagined."

Tobias shook his head. It wasn't really Kase's fault—as far as Tobias could tell, anyway. Oliver's bitterness almost seemed self-imposed, possibly from months of solitude, locked in his own thoughts. If anything, Tobias pitied him. He knew what that felt like, only his attention was always snatched away by work or the book.

Even so, he couldn't let this chance slip away. He lifted his gaze to the forest beyond the borders of the town. The brown and red canopy of leaves stuck up above the red roofs surrounding him—a sea of scarlet that collided with the brilliant azure sky.

"You didn't screw anything up," he said. Pushing himself away from the door, he walked forward to stand at Kase's side. "We're going to get the Beast Master's aid, just without Oliver."

"Huh?"

Tobias pointed toward the forest, ignoring how every part of his mind screamed that this was a horrible idea. The more it sank into his head, the more it set his body on edge. Oliver's fear should have been enough proof that the Beast Master was not to be messed with.

But Kase seems to know her, a tiny voice whispered. *He can probably find her, and she should recognize him. He's less ornery than Oliver so she shouldn't have a reason to attack him.*

Red flags waved in his mind, but he shoved them aside and clung to the tiny voice instead. This was what Talia would have done, he was certain. She would have taken any steps necessary to get the book back had it been stolen from her.

"We're going on our own. She shouldn't be hard to find; the forest didn't look that big when we were walking toward it.

Plus, it sounds like you're familiar with her." He turned to Kase, faltering slightly at the look of complete disbelief that painted his face. It put a chink in his plan, but he shook it away. "If she knows you, we're less likely to get shredded, right?"

Kase inhaled sharply through clenched teeth. Awkwardly, he rubbed the back of his neck as he looked away from Tobias. "We'll go with that, for now."

Tobias winced at the uncertainty in Kase's voice, but the slim chance of success was all he needed for the moment. Wiping the sweat from his palms onto his pants, he straightened up. It was his idea. He couldn't state it and then back down. It was their one shot of getting a flawless tracker that would lead them straight to Eira. He had to at least try.

He started down the path toward the forest. Kase followed close behind, allowing Tobias to lead the way for the first time since they'd met.

They weaved in and out of the streets and soon emerged onto the dirt path winding its way toward the Beast Master's Forest. The sun was high in the sky, driving out the chill that nipped Tobias's skin. A shiver trailed down his spine all the same.

With each step he took, another bolt of uncertainty stabbed through his resolve. The logical voice wriggled free, screaming at his stupid thoughts. Oliver was *frightened* by this Beast Master. What reason did Tobias have to believe she wouldn't scar Kase in the same way? Moreover, what reason did he have to believe that she wouldn't leave Kase unharmed and attack Tobias instead? She didn't know him. She wouldn't have any reason to trust him.

He glanced to the side at Kase, whose expression had shifted from fear to determination. His dark eyes didn't waver as they faced straight ahead. Despite this, his hand had drifted to his pocket and the dragon keeper pin he stored there.

The dirt path ended at the line of trees, revealing a wild,

overgrown forest ahead of them. Rays of sunlight filtered softly through the trees, dappling the ground with patches of warmth. Due to the cold bite of Xenah—leaking in early, as the warm season of Deiah had yet to end—the greenery had withered and turned brown. The leaves overhead bore striking ambers and reds, similar to the oak tree Tobias had spent so much time under at home. He knew as the cold grew harsher and the seasons dipped into the time of Sefah, the leaves would fall away, leaving their trees bare and empty. Perhaps if he had come while the trees were skeletal rather than fiery, he wouldn't be paralyzed at the foot of the forest.

The forest was red that day, too. The day his mother was murdered.

Tobias's breath hitched. Instinctively, his hand shot toward the key hidden beneath his tunic: the one thing that linked him to home. This wasn't about his mother. He didn't have to think of her. She had nothing to do with Ruber and its Beast Master. His fear had nothing to do with Oliver's. But still, his legs refused to move.

"Kase," he started, stumbling back. "I think…"

The dragon keeper had already stepped into the forest without waiting to hear the end of the statement. His form was quickly swallowed by thick undergrowth, and he vanished. All that gave him away was the shifting of his white cloak as he weaved in and around trees.

The heavy knot of fear twisted his gut more. Tobias swallowed thickly, gripped his sword tight, and forced himself to follow Kase. *It's just a forest,* he told himself as his foot crossed the line into the Beast Master's territory. Shadows loomed over him as the sunlight was blocked by the thick canopy of leaves overhead. *There's nothing to fear. This place is different. There's nothing to fear.*

Sticks and leaves crunched beneath Tobias's boots. With each step, his pace quickened. He sped forward to catch up to

Kase, following the white of his cloak until the rest of him came into view. Kase walked calmly, stopping every once in a while to check the forest around him. He stooped beside a tree—one which had lost all but a handful of its leaves—and ran his gloved hand along the gray-brown bark.

Kase examined the bark closely. "Oliver isn't the only person who can find her, but he hates for people to go looking for her alone." His fingers brushed across a tiny arrow carved into the bark of the tree. A slight smile curved at the corners of his mouth. "I know her habits. I can find her."

"Are you afraid she'll hurt you?"

Kase rose to his feet again, dusting his hands against each other. He angled himself in the direction of the arrow, narrowing his eyes to peer into the distance. Tobias followed his gaze, but he couldn't see past the overgrown bed of ferns.

"I think there's been a misunderstanding," Kase said calmly. "I made a mistake, yes, and Oliver has every right to be mad at me, but... he's connecting things that don't need to be connected."

His words meant nothing to Tobias though he scrambled to put them together with what little he knew. When the picture came back incomplete, he pushed his shoulders back and met Kase's eye. "Why does Oliver hate you? What did you... what did you make him do?"

"I gave him something to take care of." Kase walked away, taking slow steps in the direction of the arrow's head. "He didn't hold on to it."

Tobias furrowed his brow. This time, he was not quick to follow, but hung back for a moment. If Eira wasn't the only thing that put a rift between him and Oliver and Arayna, then what else had?

Uncertainty bubbled to the surface, and he eyed Kase's back.

He shook his head. He could worry about that later. Kase hadn't done anything malicious so far. He had been nothing but helpful since Tobias ran into him the day before. He trusted Talia and the dragon keeper pin she had given to Kase. She was no fool, and he was confident he could have faith in her choice.

Pushing through the undergrowth, Kase made his way deeper into the forest. Tobias ran after him, not willing to be left behind. He studied Kase's expression, wondering how he could so quickly bury his nervousness and fear. Though Oliver's words had clearly cut him, he kept going. Tobias was still unsure why Kase seemed to think that the book would bring back his Mage, but his dedication to her was touching. Perhaps that was what allowed him to brave the forest.

Something crunched beneath his boots. Tobias froze in place, holding his breath as his entire body went rigid. It gave off a different sound than the sticks and leaves, a deeper sound which carried more weight as it echoed in his mind. Biting the inside of his mouth and clenching his fists, he tilted his gaze downward as he lifted his foot. Bits of bones were scattered in the dark brown grass, snapped by his steps. He swallowed hard.

"Kase—"

The dragon keeper pressed a finger to his lips, his eyes fixed on a clearing just beyond the brush where they had stopped. Fallen leaves and more bones lay scattered among the cropped grass. The clearing was devoid of the trees and bushes that crowded the rest of the forest. Only when the chittering of animals was gone did Tobias realize it had been ever-present throughout the walk toward the clearing. In the resulting silence, the pounding of his heart filled the air.

In the clearing, seated on a mossy tree stump with her chin on her knees, was a girl. A pair of furry red ears stuck up from her cinnamon-colored hair, twitching in sync with her matching red tail. A tan-colored coat of fur cloaked her shoulders and chest, and a pair of worn, black shorts covered her. Her back faced them, but she was angled in such a way that he could see the countless numbers of scars upon her exposed arms and legs.

The Beast Master, Tobias's mind whispered. At the sight of her, he instinctively drew back a few steps.

Kase took a deep breath, his lips pressing into a thin line as his brows drew together. He lifted his hand for Tobias to stay put as he stepped forward.

Tobias hesitated. *Wait, was it a "stay put" signal or a "follow me" signal?* He took a step forward, and another bone snapped beneath his foot. At the sound of it, every inch of his body froze.

The Beast Master's head jerked up, her ears pricked. In a flash, she spun around, dragging up leaves and strands of grass as her feet scraped against the ground. Her gaze landed on the two of them.

Without waiting for an explanation, she drew her lips back in a snarl to reveal a set of canine fangs. She leapt from her tree stump with a howl, lunging for Kase first. He reached for the sword sheathed at his back, but stepped out of her way instead of drawing it. Yelping, she landed in a patch of thorns across the clearing, writhing and squirming as she tried to pull free.

While she was stuck, Kase rushed forward and took hold of Tobias's arm, yanking him away. His grip was hard enough that Tobias's arm ached, and the dragon keeper might have pulled it straight out of its socket if Tobias hadn't followed his tugging. Tobias jerked his arm free and made a mental note to himself not to fight Kase hand-to-hand. Or at all.

"This didn't go as I hoped it would!" Kase yelled, breaking into a sprint as they raced back into the dense forest.

"What did you think was gonna happen?"

"I don't know—what were *you* expecting to happen?"

Tobias didn't answer, shoving his expectations out an imaginary window. The plan had been half-baked from the start. It sprung from impulse and, normally, he would never have considered it all. Being away from home—strung on emotion and stress—was messing with his head.

His feet pounded across the forest floor as he ran, struggling to match Kase's pace and not daring to look back. Even when the Beast Master howled again, he just focused on the next tree to pass, the next step to take. The cry echoed through the silence, hinged on that lonely pitch a wolf carried. Tobias poured all the fear into running, pushing himself to go faster.

His foot snagged on a root, and his chin collided with the ground. Pain spiked in his jaw, and the faint taste of blood flooded his mouth. Dazed and dizzy, he lifted his head slowly. Embarrassment burned the back of his neck as Kase skidded to a halt, looking back at him, his face twisted into something unreadable. Tobias pushed himself upright with a grunt, scrambling to catch up to Kase.

With a roar, the Beast Master tackled him, flipped him on his back, and pinned him to the ground. The back of his head knocked against another protruding root, sending a bolt of pain through him. He gasped, black spots dancing in his eyes. She bared her fangs as she snarled, and her grip tightened on his shoulders, her ears flattening back.

"Arayna!" Kase shouted. His arms wrapped around her waist and hauled her away from Tobias. "Stop it! We're just here to talk!"

She growled and thrashed in his grip, kicking and twisting until she finally sank her fangs into his arm. He yelped, dropping her and stumbling back. Tobias gritted his teeth and pushed himself to his feet, grabbing hold of his sword as Arayna whirled around to face him again.

She wiped a smudge of blood from the corner of her mouth, her ears pushing back farther. Then she paused, her eyes widening. She spun around to face Kase again, her red ears lifting and her tail falling still.

"Kase?" she whispered.

His eyes lit up and he stood up a little straighter, a smile breaking out across his face, the attack and his wound forgotten, it seemed. "Yes! It's me, Arayna. It's Kase."

She tensed, her hands curling into fists at her sides. Biting her lip, tail swishing behind her, she drew a deep breath through her nose. The silence of the forest made her wordlessness press heavier on Tobias's anxious mind, but he remained frozen in place, waiting.

Arayna didn't get a chance to say anything else. An arrow whizzed past Tobias's ear and struck the ground right next to her foot. The shaft glowed blue for a moment before ice crawled up her leg. She yelped as she tugged against it, but the ice held firm. With a growl, she twisted to peer back the way the arrow had come.

Axel burst from the underbrush, soon followed by Oliver, who had his bowstring drawn back and another arrow notched against it. The wood of the bow turned blue, matching that of the arrow's fletching. A cold aura surrounded the hunter as he drew nearer. It danced and sparked with magic but didn't seem to cling to him.

"Oliver!" Arayna shrieked. "I haven't done anything! Let me go!"

He ignored her. Lowering his bow, he marched straight toward Kase, his lip curled. His steps halted when he was toe-to-toe with Kase. He glared up at the other man, gripping his bow so tightly his knuckles turned white.

"I told you *no*," he ground out, his voice dangerously low.

"It wasn't his idea," Tobias interjected, surprised at the sound of his own voice as he leapt to Kase's defense. "It was mine. Listen to me: I *need* Arayna's help. I *need* to get my book back."

"What for?" Oliver hissed. "You're better off without it."

Frustration curled Tobias's fingers into fists at his sides. The cut on his chin stung as he clenched his jaw, biting back the retort that rose to the surface. *You don't know that,* he wanted to say, but the anger died away as quickly as it had come. Deep down, he knew Oliver was right.

Behind Oliver, Arayna tilted her head to the side, her eyes wide. "My help? For a book?"

"*No*," Oliver snapped, shooting her a look over his shoulder.

Arayna lifted her chin and turned her face away, muttering to herself as the ice crawled farther up her leg.

Kase pushed past Oliver, ignoring his burning stare, and made his way to Arayna. She looked up at him, curiosity swirling in her gray-blue eyes. She leaned forward impatiently.

"Arayna," Kase said softly, bending down so he was at her height. "Do you remember Eira? And Aviva?"

She recoiled—as best as she could with ice halfway up her thigh—hissing and narrowing her pupils like slits. Her ears flattened back, and her lip curled. "I could never forget that *thief*."

Casting a quick glance back at Oliver, Kase sighed and placed his hand against the ice. A warm light encircled his palm and a steady flow of heat seeped into the air. Slowly, the ice began to melt.

"She stole something from Tobias," he said. "Something that was very important to Aviva. I need to get it back from her as soon as possible, and I need your help to do that."

Arayna glanced between the two of them. Tobias held his breath, waiting for her response. His head throbbed painfully, though he couldn't tell if it was from anxiety or the tree root. He winced as the ice finally melted away. Arayna muttered her thanks as she wiped excess water from her leg. She cast a quick glance at Oliver, who shook his head firmly.

Arayna lifted a hand, and a red glow encircled her wrist. She brought her fingers to her lips and whistled, similar to the way Kase had done to call his dragon. The glow transferred to Kase's wrist, wrapping around it and solidifying into the image of a wolf. Then, when the marking faded into his skin, she turned to Kase once more.

"My place is here, and I don't want to see Eira. But I can give you my beast spirit, Ahtella, to find her. She'll sniff out the thief and take you to her," she said, her voice marked by an accent Tobias didn't quite recognize. Biting her lip, she looked back at Oliver. "That's all I'll do, but you were once a close friend. I can't just ignore you."

Tobias opened his mouth to thank her, but she had already turned and—with a quick pat to Axel's head—dashed off into the forest again. When she vanished from sight, the chirping of crickets picked up once more, and the evening calls of birds began again.

In the light of the setting sun, the Beast Master's Forest seemed a little less ominous than it had before. Warm rays of sunlight spilled into the forest, slipping past the maze of trees surrounding them. Even as the light faded, the darkness didn't press up against Tobias. He finally took a deep breath as the knot of anxiety in the pit of his stomach began to unwind. That was, until Oliver sighed loudly and returned his arrow to his quiver.

"It's getting late, and it would give people the wrong image of me if I sent my cousin and his friend off on their way without offering them a place to stay." Oliver stepped past Kase and Tobias, snapping his fingers for Axel to follow. The dog padded happily after him. "Come on. You can stay the night and leave in the morning."

Like Arayna, he didn't wait for his thanks before setting off. Tobias followed, though he noticed Kase lingered for a moment longer, staring down at his hands.

But the moment passed and, with a hopeful smile on his face, Kase picked up the pace and followed after Oliver and Axel, leaving Tobias to wonder what had made him linger in the first place.

6

A SECRET AND A FRIEND

IN THE MORNING, Tobias awoke to the sound of hushed voices whispering downstairs. Bleary eyed, he sat up and tried to focus on the words being said. They floated up the open staircase, but his tired mind slurred them together, unable to process their meaning. Eavesdropping from a distance had never been one of his talents. He stood up, brushing aside the blankets of his makeshift bed on the floor, and made his way to the stairs. Hovering on the top step, he could hear a little more clearly.

"...sent him away to the Dragon Rider school," Oliver was saying, his voice low. "He had the potential for it, and the Head Dragon Rider there would know better what to do with him. Besides, I couldn't keep him around here. He would've piqued Arayna's interest, and you and I both know how she feels about… his *kind*."

Him? Tobias straightened up, taking a step down the stairs and pleading that they didn't creak like they did the night before when he went up. *Talia's school?* He bit the inside of his mouth, briefly wondering if this was the same "him" that Eira had mentioned working with. The mere thought of his sister in danger chilled him to the bone.

He quickly waved it away, promising himself again that he wanted to trust Kase. So far, he had shown no signs of working with Eira and her mysterious supporter. Even if he was, what would be the purpose of sticking with Tobias and helping him catch Eira? If they were working together, wouldn't he want to deter Tobias?

Kase sighed. "I… guess that's understandable. I didn't mean to just dump him on you."

"And yet, that was exactly what you did."

"I already apologized. Do you think you could stop biting my head off all the time?"

A pause followed, in which Axel whined. Someone stood up, their chair scraping across the wooden floors. Tobias held his breath, freezing. He had been caught eavesdropping before, and it never ended very well. He didn't intend to have it happen here. He waited, but no footsteps ever came toward him.

"Sorry," Oliver muttered, so quietly Tobias had to lean forward and strain his ears to hear. He cleared his throat. "So, have you brought this issue with Eira to the attention of the High Summoner? If that book turns out to be the one you think it is, this could get messy."

"I won't know for certain until I see it, but I'm almost positive. Why else would she want it?"

"Who knows? Maybe she suddenly discovered the wonders of literature."

Kase snorted with laughter. "Yeah, right. She would never."

When their conversation lapsed into silence again, Tobias left the stairway. He knelt down beside his pallet on the floor and collected his satchel and his sword. Quickly combing his fingers through his hair, he made his way down the stairs. Kase and Oliver each greeted him with a nod, though their expressions were stern as if they were both still caught up in thought. Kase was seated at the table while Oliver stood beside it, leaning against the back of his chair. Axel lay at their feet, watching the door eagerly. Neither said anything—Axel didn't even bark—while Tobias made his way past them to fetch his boots. The tension made him want to hit his head on something. Shoulders tense, he shoved his boots onto his feet.

He stood upright and turned to face them. "You're both chatty," he said, prompting them to speak again.

All it did, however, was make Kase chuckle, a smile spreading across his face. As if to hide this, he raised his cup to his lips for a drink. Oliver frowned, his eyes narrowing. Tobias began to wonder if he ever smiled, or if Kase smiled too much. Looking at the two of them side by side, they did appear to be complete opposites. Despite that, there was years of familiarity between them. *Maybe their family is close-knit.*

With a sigh, Oliver pushed away from the chair. Silent as ever, he disappeared down the hall. Axel rolled over and jumped to his feet, eagerly padding after his master.

Kase cleared his throat and set down his cup. He stood up just as Oliver returned with a sack in his hands, which he dumped into Kase's arms with a huff.

"Something to eat on your journey," Oliver said. "I don't know exactly where Ahtella is going to take you, but I imagine it'll be far. Do you know how to call the beast spirit?"

Kase frowned, looking at his wrist as he shifted the sack to one arm. "Nope, but it can't be that different from calling Smoke, right?" His words oozed with a confidence that made even Tobias lift his brow in disbelief.

Oliver blinked, folding his arms over his chest. "You tell me. Just tap the runes on your wrist and Ahtella will come."

"Right." Kase lifted a hand, hesitated, then gave Oliver a firm pat on the shoulder. That same warm smile returned. "Thanks for your help."

"Don't count on getting it again. This really is the last time," Oliver grumbled. Kase waved and joined Tobias by the door, adjusting his cloak around his neck.

When he was ready, Kase took a deep breath before opening the door and stepping out. Tobias stood a moment longer in the doorway, turning to face Oliver. He dipped his head in thanks, his words having caught in his throat.

Oliver seemed to understand, as he managed a slight smile. "Good luck." Raising his voice, he called, "And think about what I said, Kase."

As Oliver began to walk away, Tobias pulled the door shut with a soft click. On the other side, Oliver's footsteps faded as he disappeared farther into the house. Axel barked once from the other side of the door, wishing them luck as well—or so Tobias assumed. This time, the closed door felt a little more welcoming. While he couldn't say everything had been resolved, he did breathe more easily knowing no one had been stabbed or clawed to death. It had taken a bit more push than he had expected, but the result brought a proud smile to his face all the same.

Kase grinned back, holding out the small sack of food for Tobias to take. Tobias slid it into the satchel at his side for later. With his hands now free, the dragon keeper brushed back his long sleeves to reveal the red markings from Arayna's spell on his wrist.

"I'd say this was a successful endeavor."

Tobias rolled his eyes. "I'm not sure your definition of successful is entirely correct, but I'm glad it worked out in the end."

"If no one dies and the goal of the trip is achieved, I call that successful," Kase said, tapping on the runes with two fingers.

A flash of red appeared, and a whisper that resembled a howl drifted through the air. Seconds later, a ghostly red wolf emerged from a nearby street, her dark brown eyes shimmering as she came and stood before them. The sunlight peeking through the overcast skies lit up her brilliant red coat, though she cast no shadow upon the packed dirt road. Her ghostly form appeared transparent, but her eyes peered straight into Tobias's own. Even so, he couldn't bring himself to look away or step back from her.

"Ahtella." Kase greeted her with a bow. "Can you take us to Eira?"

The wolf dipped her head in a nod. With a swish of her tail, she took off, leading them down the winding path that would take them away from Ruber.

~

AFTER TWO HOURS of walking and several failed attempts to summon Smoke, Kase groaned and kicked up a cloud of dust. "Honestly, what use is having a dragon if he doesn't come when I call him? He probably took a nap somewhere and forgot all about me." He put his fingers to his lips and whistled again.

There was still no response.

"Smoke!" he called, coming to a standstill in the middle of the road. "Get your lazy lizard butt over here! If you keep ignoring me, I won't give you any more head scratches!"

Tobias pulled another slim piece of dried meat from the sack Oliver had given them and bit into it. He turned his eyes away from Kase to the direction Ahtella was going. A mountain stood in their path; its peaks barely reached the thick collection of clouds overhead. The Mountain of the Wyrm, he remembered his sister telling him. Surely the foreboding behemoths weren't where they were headed. Eira couldn't want anything more with them than Tobias did. But if she did...

Tobias winced imagining the laborious climb.

He finished chewing and swallowed, turning to Kase again. "Are you any good at climbing?"

"Hm?" Kase looked over his shoulder and Tobias gestured toward the mountain and Ahtella, who kept pointing at it with her snout. Kase's frown deepened, the crease in his forehead becoming more evident. "Luckily for us, that mountain isn't hard to climb. It's more like a… steep hike. But it would still be much faster if Smoke would *hurry up and get over here.*"

Tobias clicked his tongue and shoved the sack of food back into his satchel. "I know you're frustrated. My sister gets that way when her dragon ignores her too." *Although Sikii's attitude has never been as awful as Smoke's seems to be.* He paused for a moment to think, wondering if there was some way to get Kase's mind off his frustration for the rest of the walk. Otherwise, it would start to weigh on Tobias—and he already had enough of his own thoughts to drag him down.

He mulled it over for a moment as Kase resorted to whistling again. This time, barely a sound came out. Kase sighed, glaring at the sky.

"What were you and Oliver talking about this morning?" Tobias started, wincing at the admission to his own eavesdropping. When Kase shot him a puzzled stare, he cleared his throat and rolled with it. "When I woke up, I heard talking. Just curious about what I was missing."

"Oh." Kase cast one last look at the blue sky before turning away and jogging to catch up to Ahtella, motioning for Tobias to join him. When he slowed his pace again, just a few steps behind the wolf, he continued, "Just some stuff about Eira. He thinks I should tell High Summoner Maven about the theft."

Tobias's lips twitched as he bit back the urge to frown. *I meant the other, more sketchy topic, but I guess I'll pass on that for now.* "What makes him say that?"

High Summoners were the rulers of the Navaric kingdom, and the keepers of the borders between Hybrid Territory and the other kingdoms. They were powerful magic-users or people born into the family of the original Summoner. They were said to be the strongest magic-users in all of Anticuus. Because of this, they were called on to deal with matters of high importance or danger. Tobias wasn't entirely sure how the theft of a book qualified as that, which must have been why Kase hesitated as well.

And yet, several times, Tobias had heard it might be a spellbook. If it was, could it be worth the attention and help of the Summoners? Would Talia have alerted the Summoners right away?

Tobias's gut twisted. What if he had done the wrong thing by not taking it to them first?

Kase must have noticed, as his expression softened and a half smile made its way to his face. "Don't worry about it. I think we're okay on our own for the time being. We'll get your book back, and if things start to go downhill, then we'll contact a Summoner. Maven is probably busy with that disappearing Mage case. I don't want to bother her if I don't have to—especially not if this is something we can do on our own. Sound good?"

Nodding, Tobias looked ahead. The mountain drew nearer with each step he took, looming overhead like a massive beast. He lifted his hand and rested it against the hilt of his sword, curling his fingers tightly around it. What would he do when he finally came across Eira again?

He shot a glance at Kase, who was fiddling with his silver dragon keeper pin again. For the first time, Tobias turned his eyes from the pin to the sword handle sticking out from a sheath at Kase's back. The ornate hilt was wrapped in thick red cloth with a gold-colored guard. A flicker of surprise sparked in his mind. He had yet to see Kase draw it, and the only time Kase had reached for it was in Arayna's forest.

And yet it seemed funny to him that it had never caught his eye before. Had he noticed the sword and just forgotten? Had he been much more focused on Kase's dragon than his sword? It wasn't unreasonable for Kase to be in possession of a sword— most people carried one at all times due to the lingering fear of the Draconic people—and yet the idea had never once crossed his mind.

The image of the red-bound hilt felt familiar, along with the memory of a dusty book he would drag with him to bed every night as a child. Though many of the words were faded from age, the pictures in the book remained vibrant and bold.

Tobias pointed toward it, and Kase startled. "Your sword," he said, "I think I've seen it before. Not with you, I mean, but in a book."

Kase pocketed the pin and turned his head to look at the sword. "Oh, you have? It was given to me when I became a Mage Guardian. The Summoners told me it has some fancy name and an old heritage, but I can't remember any of that stuff." He frowned. "Oliver probably remembers. He's always been better at keeping track of things than me."

Tobias scrutinized the sword. It brought a name to mind, drifting through his thoughts along with the broken pieces of the story his sister had worked so hard to put back together for him. Now, it all slipped through his fingers like water.

The memory danced out of his reach, and he finally gave up on it with a sigh. It itched at the back of his mind, but he ignored it. *It isn't important, anyway*, he told himself whenever he thought of reaching for it again. It was just a topic of conversation to keep the awkward silence at bay.

Soon afterward, the mountain loomed in front of them. The sun began to set, taking away the light of the bright afternoon and leaving them with a dull evening. Luckily, Ahtella's red coat glowed brighter the darker it got, and she guided them patiently up the mountain. Kase had been right about the climb, however. The incline was slight, and a path of packed dirt wound up to the top. Brush clung to the mountainside in sparse patches, brown from the oncoming cold.

Tobias followed slowly behind Kase and he kept his eyes glued to the rocky, dirt-covered path beneath him. Each step drove an aching pain into the soles of his feet, racing all the way up his ankles and calves. He bit down on his tongue to push back the temptation to look down. His head spun at the mere idea; he couldn't imagine what he would do if he caught sight of the ground far below.

Somehow, it was more nerve-wracking than flying. Perhaps because flying came with a thrill, while hiking only served to exhaust him.

Rocks tumbled past his feet, clicking and clacking as they rolled down until he could no longer hear them. The thought of falling made his palms sweat, and he wiped them on his pants several times.

"Kase," he called up to where the man and Ahtella had found a ledge they could rest at for a time. The sun had long since disappeared, leaving Tobias shrouded in darkness. "How much farther is it?"

Without saying a word, Kase's hand reached down and grabbed the back of Tobias's tunic. He hauled him up onto the ledge with a grunt of effort. Dirt and rocks scraped Tobias's knees, but he muttered his thanks when he could finally collapse on a bit of solid ground.

He knelt there, panting until he got his breath. Then, he lifted his head and came face to face with the mouth of a cave. Darkness covered the entrance, blocking the inside from his view. It felt like a hollow, empty void.

Tobias swallowed hard. "Is this it?"

As if to answer, Ahtella dipped her head to them and vanished in a flash of red. As soon as she was gone, Kase peeled back his sleeve to peer at his wrist. The runes were gone, too. He inhaled sharply and fixed his sleeve again. "It must be."

Tobias gulped and pushed himself to his feet. He had come to the final step, and his thief waited just beyond the mouth of the cave.

His fingers curled into a tight fist. *Eira is waiting.*

7

MOUNTAIN OF THE WYRM

THE DARKNESS OF THE CAVE MOUTH stretched on endlessly, like a void that beckoned to Tobias's very soul. He slipped behind Kase for cover. Even the dark of night seemed more welcoming than the mouth of the cave.

"You go first," he said, prodding Kase with his elbow.

Kase glanced back, concern twisting his features. The look didn't last long before it was replaced with a confident grin—though it didn't quite reach his eyes. "Alright, alright, I'll take a look."

Tobias nodded and gripped his sword, attempting to draw comfort from the feel of it in his hands. All it did, however, was make his palms sting. Uncertainty writhed within him as Kase stepped forward, and he couldn't suppress it. Even as Kase steadily approached the mouth of the cave, Tobias's feet remained frozen in place.

Coward, whispered some hidden part of his mind. Tobias gritted his teeth.

Kase stood in front of the cave for a moment, his arms folded over his chest and his shoulders tense. He inhaled like he was going to say something, but his words were lost as a flash of movement from within the cave grabbed hold of him and dragged him down into the void. His cry cut off suddenly, as did the scraping of his sword's sheath against the rocky ground. A numbing silence hung in the air.

"Kase!" Tobias rushed blindly in after him, stumbling over his own feet as he plunged straight into the dark.

Cold washed over him like water; any light from the outside world vanished in an instant. A static, ringing sound settled over his ears. Clenching his fists at his sides, he risked a quick glance back. Now, a solid stone wall stood where the entrance had been, shrouded in black. Panic clawed its way up his throat, cutting off his air.

He poured his fear into his sword, drawing it easily from the sheath and holding it aloft. Darkness pressed against his vision, rendering his eyes useless. He turned, desperately skimming his surroundings for a flicker of light or a sign of Kase. Nothing but the same emptiness greeted him, sending shivers crawling down his spine.

Sharp pain raced up his arm, and the sound of his sword clattering against the stone reached his ears before he could process the absence of its weight in his hands. Something shoved him; he landed on his back against the stone with a grunt. A light from a small lantern appeared, brighter than any flame he had seen before—or perhaps it was his eyes attempting to adjust. He blinked, lifting his arm to shield his face from the light.

A man stood holding the lantern, his eyes a bright gold color. Tangled, dirty black hair spilled into his face, parted on one side so that it kept out of his eyes. He looked to be around the same age as Kase, nearing or having just entered his twenties. A wide grin spread across his face.

Tobias froze under the sharp, golden gaze. Briefly, he

glanced to the side, catching sight of Kase leaning against the wall to his left. Blinking rapidly, he seemed just as puzzled as Tobias felt.

"Look who it is," the golden-eyed man said in a smooth voice. "Finally decided to leave Floridus, Kase? Or did you get kicked out for causing a racket with your dragon buddy?"

Kase rubbed his eyes. "Uriah," he muttered. "Fancy seeing you here."

The man—Uriah—pulled back, kicking Tobias's sword toward him. It skidded across the floor, the sound grating against Tobias's ears. When it landed in his hands again, relief began to thaw out his frozen limbs. Keeping his eyes locked on Uriah, he rose to his feet.

"Came here to kill the wyrm that was bothering everyone," Uriah started, "Seemed to bother 'em quite a lot so I even had to use protective wards to seal this place off. If you're here for the beast too, don't bother." He lifted his lantern higher, shedding light on the body of a wyrm behind him, blood still oozing from a massive wound in its neck.

Tobias shuddered and shrank back, covering his nose to block out the stench that wafted over him. The massive, limp body sprawled across the back of the cave, blocking the tunnel that led farther inward. Glassy eyes stared blankly forward, and its tongue lolled out the side of its mouth. Scales lay strewn across the stone floor, thoroughly soaked in the wyrm's crimson blood. Tobias didn't know how he could have missed it. It was as if it didn't exist until Uriah drew attention to it. *The spell, perhaps?*

Uriah's grin spread wider across his lips. There was a gleam in his golden eyes, a touch of madness, as he said, "It's already dead." As if that wasn't obvious.

Tobias tightened his grip on his sword, though he kept the tip pointed downward. The last thing he wanted was for the tall, bulky man before him to think he was being threatened. Despite the anxiety swirling in his gut, his mind buzzed with sarcasm. *Funny that we would run into yet another person from Kase's past in the exact same place we were told to come to in order to see Eira,* he thought bitterly. The anxiety formed a tight knot.

"Relax, Tobias," Kase said, resting a hand on his shoulder. Tobias jolted at the contact, his head snapping around to meet Kase's eye. "This is Uriah. He's... an old *friend.*" Uncertainty crossed his face, and his tone took a bitter note at the end. With the shake of his head, he cleared the uncertainty from expression and lifted his face to meet Uriah's waiting stare. "We're not here for the wyrm. We came in search of Eira."

"Eira." Uriah folded his arms over his chest and cupped his chin in one hand. "Haven't heard that name in some time. What'd she do this time? Stab another friend of yours?"

Kase bristled, his lips twitching downward. His fingers curled at his sides, and a slight glow enveloped his hands.

Noticing this, Tobias quickly sheathed his sword. They didn't need to both be potentially aggravating Uriah. "She stole something of mine," he said. "Kase offered to help me find it when I ran into him."

Uriah blinked, looking down at Tobias in bewilderment. He lifted a finger and pointed at Tobias, his gaze shifting back to Kase. "Who's this? Looks like a mini version of that Dragon Rider woman. You know the one?"

I can speak for myself. Tobias gritted his teeth. "I'm Tobias. You're probably referring to my sister, *Head* Dragon Rider Talia." He met Uriah's golden gaze with a firm glare.

Uriah's face twisted, scrunching up his nose as he turned away and set the lantern down. The metal base clinked against the stone. "Right. I always forget Riders adopted Draconic terms for their ranks. How ironic." He sighed and stretched before bending down to examine the wyrm's body. "That's great and all, but it doesn't really explain what you're doing here. Kase *never* leaves Floridus, especially not to meddle with Eira. So what's different about this hunt? Or is it just that Talia told you to follow her little brother around?"

Tobias shot Kase a look, opening his mouth to ask if this was true, but he shut it again immediately. Kase had zeroed in on Uriah, his lips pursed and his eyes narrowed. "It's about—"

"Oh, that's right," Uriah said, suddenly sitting up straighter. "Don't tell me—I just remembered I don't care."

Kase reached back to grab his sword hilt, his eyes flashing. "If you don't care, then don't ask. And you're the one who dragged me in here anyway!"

Uriah barked a laugh as he spun around to face them fully. He doubled over, his hands on his knees. The sound echoed in the silence of the cave, but it didn't put Tobias's heart at ease. If anything, it made him more wary.

"That's right, I did do that, didn't I?" He laughed, wiping his eyes. "You were standing there, looking dumb. Thought I'd test you a little. Your face was priceless!"

Red tinted Kase's cheeks; if possible, his expression darkened. Tobias inhaled sharply, shaking his head when Kase finally met his eye. Desperately, he hoped to convey a *don't do it, he isn't worth your time* message.

It seemed to work. Kase's shoulders drooped and his angry expression melted away, leaving only a weary one behind. He took a deep breath, and finally his hand dropped back to his side. "It's… about Aviva, Uriah. I think the thing she stole from Tobias is connected to Aviva."

Uriah's laughter cut off suddenly, and his head snapped in Kase's direction. His eyes widened slightly before they narrowed again. Their angled, cat-like shape made him look even more frightening in the dark. His expression hardened, and his joking demeanor vanished. "There you go again, off on another deluded fantasy," he spat.

"It's not delusional!" Kase cried, stepping forward. "It's true! I saw her that day; she vanished from my arms. She isn't dead—she's alive somewhere, and I have to find her!"

"Let it go, Kase," Uriah snapped, his voice sharper than Oliver's had ever been.

Kase flinched, lowering his head. The shadows blanketed his expression, concealing it from Tobias's view. Kase remained stiff, frozen in wait.

Tobias looked back at Uriah, who was studying Kase's face with a tight frown on his lips. With a sigh, Uriah turned away. "She's dead," he finished.

"Do you think I would make up something like this?" Kase snapped. "You were her friend as well. You know what she's capable of. Of all people, you should be able to believe me when I say she's still alive!" He raked his hair back from his forehead, and Tobias thought he caught a glimpse of tears welling in his eyes. As if to hide this, Kase threw his head back and pressed his fists to his eyes, hissing in another breath through clenched teeth.

Clenching his fists, Tobias spun to face Uriah. Anger welled inside him, burning away his wariness and fear and driving out the cold of the dark. All he wanted to do now was draw his sword and protect his friend. But his hands remained frozen at his side, away from his sword. Still, he gritted his teeth as Uriah's uninterested stare landed on him.

"That's enough," Tobias ground out. "Is this really how you would treat an old friend?"

Uriah grinned, revealing wrinkles beneath his eyes, dark with the shadows cast by the lantern. "Who said we were friends?"

"Is Eira here or not?" Tobias bit back, his voice strained. If Eira wasn't in the cave but Uriah was, why had Ahtella led them there? Had Arayna sent them to the wrong place by accident? On purpose? Was Eira just leading them in circles?

He glanced over his shoulder at Kase, who still stood frozen, his fingers tangled in his hair. Or was he being manipulated by Kase?

No. He shoved that thought away. Kase wasn't pulling any strings. If anything, he had the answers to what was really going on, and Tobias would have to ask him for the full story.

After he caught Eira and managed to get the book back.

Uriah clicked his tongue, shrugging as he turned back to the wyrm. Tobias stiffened, his gaze slipping to the dead body. He swallowed hard to rid his throat of rising bile. He wasn't sure what Uriah found so interesting about it, but the very thought of it being there made him sick.

Uriah stepped closer and bent down. He scooped up a large ax, buried in the neck of the wyrm, and rested the handle of it against his shoulder. The movement drew Tobias's eyes to a pin embedded in Uriah's shirt. It was the same as the one that kept Kase's cloak together, only gold instead of red.

Recognition sparked in Tobias's mind. "You were...?"

Humming, Uriah looked down at the pin, resting just above his heart. He reached up to brush his fingers across it.

A Mage Guardian pin. Tobias bit down on his tongue to stop himself from saying anything else. Uriah must have been a Guardian for the same Mage as Kase, yet he seemed far less hopeful.

Before he could ask any questions, footsteps sounded from the back of the cave, beyond the wyrm's body. A woman's voice sighed, muttering to herself. Her words mingled together as they echoed in the silence. All three froze, spinning around to face the source of the new voice, reaching to draw their weapons.

Stepping carefully around the wyrm, her face melding into a look of disgust as she avoided a puddle of blood, Eira appeared. A satchel hung at her hip, held together with crude stitches.

Through a hole in its side, Tobias caught a glimpse of the white book hidden within.

She lifted her head, blinking in surprise as she spotted them. Her gaze met his; she hesitated a moment, and then a wide grin spread across her lips.

"Ah, the oblivious guy," she said with a chuckle. "Persistent, aren't you? Did you come all this way after me? I have to admit, I'm flattered."

For the first time since Tobias had met him, Kase drew his sword. The blade flashed, illuminating the entire cave in a brilliant green glow. Eira stepped back with a gasp, reaching for the knives at her waist and shifting her stance. In the light of the sword, surprise and fear danced beneath her confident smirk.

"Kase, Uriah," she greeted in a silky smooth voice, brushing her hair over her shoulder. Her tone carried none of the fear on her face. "Come to join the party? I must admit, I overheard a small portion of your conversation. If it's all the same to you both, I have something to contribute to it."

"The conversation ended," Kase spat, pushing past Tobias to get to her and pointing his sword at her face. "Hand over the book you stole. It doesn't belong to you, and you know it."

She lifted a curious eyebrow, frowning. "I'm a thief, Kase. Taking things that don't belong to me is what I do. And I think you'll like what I have to say."

With a shout, Uriah swung his ax. Eira leapt nimbly out of the way, taking cover behind the wyrm. The heel of her boots clicked against the stone, splashing in the pool of blood. She cursed under her breath. The ax cut into the scales of the body, slicing a chunk of flesh clean off. Sickened, Tobias turned away and covered his mouth with his hand. If the cave didn't already smell of blood and dead wyrm, it did then. The foul stench crept up his throat and lingered in his nose, making him bite his tongue to keep his food down.

"Energetic as always!" Eira taunted, her voice ringing clear over the sound of Uriah's ax crashing into the stone.

With light steps, she landed in front of Tobias. Her eyes flicked from Uriah's ax to him. She rushed forward, prying him into the open and pulling him between her and the other two. In one smooth motion, the blade of her knife landed against his throat. He clenched his jaw, holding as still as possible to avoid digging the blade into his flesh. As a stinging pain trailed across his neck down the length of the blade, he got a sinking feeling of familiarity.

Kase faltered and lowered his sword. Uriah gritted his teeth. He lifted his ax and stepped forward, only for his Kase to block him, throwing his arm out over his chest. When Uriah's gaze snapped toward him, he shook his head patiently. That patience vanished as he turned his attention back to Eira.

"Eira," Kase snapped, voice low and threatening. "Let him go."

Eira's knife pressed harder against Tobias's neck, making him wince. "Aviva is alive," she whispered, ending her statement with a hum. She tipped her head to the side, her light brown hair spilling over her shoulders. "Don't you want to know what else I have to say to you?"

Again, as he did almost any time Aviva was mentioned, Kase froze, lowering his sword further. The emerald-colored blade shimmered, and the glowing aura around it faded. Even Uriah hesitated this time, his eyes flicking toward Kase and then back to Eira.

"How do you know that?" Kase rasped, a tremor in his voice.

Tobias felt Eira shrug, the pressure on his neck loosening slightly. As the blade pulled away from his skin, the sting diminished, but she didn't let go. An idea wormed its way to the front of his mind, dragging the image of the book to the forefront of his thoughts. Holding his breath, he tilted his head downward to the satchel at Eira's side. It was within reach. Slowly, he stretched his hand out, hoping she was more focused on the threat Kase and Uriah posed than on the careful movement of her human shield.

"That's a secret," she replied, chuckling to herself.

Tobias almost smiled but forced it down. She was oblivious.

Before she could tease them any more, Tobias pried the blade away from his throat and stuck his hand into her satchel —much the same way she did to him that day. His hand closed around the book's spine and he jerked it free, jumping back just in time to see her wide-eyed look of surprise. A flicker of pride stirred in his chest, and finally brought a smirk to his lips.

"You—!" she gasped, her voice tinged with anger and that girlishly high pitch. Her tanned face flushed red; her brows knitted together as she glared at him.

"That's right." He waved the book in her face, smiling proudly. "Me. I really took your words to heart. Maybe it's time *you* paid more attention to what's going on." Giddiness mingled with pride, throwing him back to his childhood for a moment. It almost felt like he was the victor of some game. If it weren't for the slight pain in his neck, he might have forgotten the truth of the situation altogether.

With a growl, Eira pulled a second knife from the belt around her waist. "I was willing to give you bumbling idiots the information you wanted, but it seems my kindness was wasted!" With the flick of her wrist, she flung the two knives directly at Tobias.

Fear quickly overtook his pride. His heart pounded wildly in his chest, but his feet remained rooted to the stone. Without thinking, he threw his arms up to protect his face and squeezed his eyes shut, bracing for impact.

But it never came.

With a sharp ringing sound, the knives clattered to the ground. Puzzled, Tobias forced his eyes open and lowered his arms.

Kase stood in front of him, his green sword having transformed into a shield-like blade, wide enough to protect both of them from Eira. When the danger subsided, the blade of the sword shrank down again, returning to its natural size as a broadsword.

Eira stood across from them, dumbfounded. Her fingers twitched, reaching for her belt again, but closed around nothing. She gasped, shooting a glance at her empty sheaths.

"The book doesn't belong to you," Kase said. "It never will. If what you say is true, I'll find Aviva without your assistance. Now *go*, before I decide to run you through."

Gritting her teeth and narrowing her eyes, she growled, "You should have, Kase. You should have killed me while you had the chance." She let her glare linger for a moment longer before turning and leaping over the wyrm's body. Her footsteps faded as she dashed deeper into the cave and disappeared into the shadows.

When she was gone, Kase relaxed and exhaled deeply, brushing his hair back from his face again.

"Why did you do that?" Uriah snapped, resting the blade of his ax against the floor as he glared at Kase. "Why would you let her go?"

A pause followed, in which some small part of Tobias wondered the same thing. Looking at Kase, however, he thought the answer was clear. He gripped the book tighter in his hands, staring down at it and wondering why it had to cause so much trouble.

"I don't know," Kase finally said. Exhaustion hung from every word, dragging his voice down until it was almost too quiet to hear.

Silence fell over them, and Tobias left it at that. In the quiet, his mind began to whisper. *You have your book,* the nagging voice said. *It's time to go home.*

But he didn't move. He wasn't really done. Eira's fearful blue eyes had been burned into his mind, and her surprise at seeing him again didn't sit right with him. Didn't she say she had heard their conversation? If that was true, why did she seem so surprised to see him and the other two? He frowned down at the book, mulling over it in his mind.

Something wasn't right, and he had a feeling there was more to the story than just a book and a thief.

PART TWO

THE THIEF'S MESSAGE

"In order to divide and conquer her targets,
a good thief must know how to manipulate their actions."

8

WARNINGS

Kase hid his trembling hands by burying them in his pockets, gritting his teeth as tears welled in his eyes. He tried not to let it get to him, but Eira's taunting laugh repeated over and over in his mind. Was she just teasing him, trying to poke him into acting foolishly?

Or did she believe it, too? That Aviva didn't die that night, that she was still alive and out there somewhere.

Aviva. He reached up to grip the pin that held his cloak together and certified him as her Mage Guardian. The smooth surface of the gem was warm, bringing him comfort and security despite the thick fog of his thoughts.

"Kase." Tobias waved his hand in front of Kase's eyes. He flinched at the sudden motion and jumped back. Tobias then sighed, holding tighter to the book he had recovered from Eira. Concern darkened his green eyes—always focused and curious like those of a child. Whenever any sort of attention fell on him, however, that gaze would flick away and his hand reached for a thin cord hanging from his neck.

"I've been trying to get your attention for nearly two minutes," he said. "You okay?"

"Huh?" As soon as the word left Kase's lips, the meaning behind Tobias's words finally registered. Kase shook his head and brushed his hair back from his face, suppressing his thoughts for the time being. "Oh, yes. Sorry. Just... lost in thought."

He looked past Tobias to Uriah. He had a puzzled frown etched into his face, his eyes narrowed and his chin cupped in his hands. Kase released a deep sigh. Despite the resistance from Smoke's end of their bond, he cleared his throat to catch Uriah's attention.

"Uriah," he began. "Thank you for your help there. Eira... always did know how to get under my skin."

What help? Smoke grumbled, his deep voice slithering down the bond with a note of bitter sarcasm. *You were the one restraining him.*

Kase waved him away impatiently. *You ignored my summons. You don't get to give me sass now.*

Obediently, Smoke withdrew, though not without mumbling to himself until his voice faded completely from Kase's mind.

Uriah lifted his head, hand lingering in the air for a moment before dropping to his side again. Kase knew it meant he had been thinking hard—which was almost always dangerous when it was Uriah doing the thinking.

"You're going after her again, aren't you?" Uriah asked, lifting a questioning brow. "I'll come with you."

Out of the corner of his eye, he caught a glimpse of Tobias bristling and reaching for his sword. Inwardly, he bit back a laugh. Tobias's hand was almost *always* against his sword. If it wasn't reaching for the sword, it reached for whatever object dangled from the cord around his neck.

"Don't give me that look, whatever-your-name-is. I know her just as well as Kase, and the two of you are going to need help if you plan to keep being so… dense," Uriah said, waving at Kase as he said the word *dense.*

Kase narrowed his eyes. It didn't help that Smoke chortled on the other end of the bond. He pictured himself shooting a withering look at the dragon, but met a wall instead. That old fart sealed it off on one side. Sighing, Kase dragged his thoughts back to the topic at hand. "I don't know what we're doing next. Tobias?"

Tobias stared up at him, his brow furrowed. As always, he seemed so much younger than he actually was. It became harder and harder to remember he was only a few years younger than Kase himself. If it weren't for his memories of Talia telling stories about her brother, Kase might have assumed he was closer to the age of sixteen than nineteen. He gritted his teeth. Maybe he was seeing too much of his own brothers in Tobias. Or, even more bewildering, maybe he was seeing too much of that kid in him.

That thought twisted a tight knot in his heart.

"Me?" Tobias asked, his voice underlined with weariness. It gave away the dark rings beneath his eyes and the slight droop in his shoulders, signs that snatched Kase's breath away—no matter who he saw them on.

"Yes," Kase replied, forcing an easy smile. "I came with you to help you get your book back. What do you want to do now?"

Tobias turned his gaze away. He hesitated for a moment, though it felt like an eternity in the painful silence. The lingering stench of wyrm blood in the air didn't help speed things up either. Then, finally, Tobias looked back at Kase and held out the spellbook.

"I think you should have this, and I think we should find your Mage. You and Eira both said she's alive, right? It can't be a coincidence—that and this book," he said, lifting the spellbook up higher when Kase didn't move to take it.

Kase stared at it, his throat constricting as memories flooded over him. The way Aviva would hold that same book, the way she would smile when she proudly showed him her newest spells, the way her deep, forest-green eyes sparkled when she laughed at his confusion. *"It's a simple spell, Kase. Want me to walk you through it again?"* she would say, a hint of pride to her voice.

Aviva. His eyes watered again as he reached to take the book, feeling the smooth leather cover in his hands. Hot tears rolled down his cheeks. He quickly swiped them away, sniffling as he tried to bury it with a nervous laugh. Rather than face Tobias, he traced the smudges of dirt left behind on the white cover. It dragged a smile to his lips. He wiped his face again before he lifted his head. "Sorry, I… thank you. You don't know what this means to me."

Tobias patted his arm awkwardly, a sort of half-smile on his face. The gesture was strikingly similar to something Talia would have done.

"It might not be a coincidence," Uriah cut in. "But it could just be another lie."

"That's why we'll confirm it first. I just… have to know if she really is alive," Kase said. For years, he clung to the idea that Aviva was still out there, unsure if it was true or not. He held her in his arms that day, cradling her as she faded to dust. The more time passed, the more he began to wonder if it was a delusion. Perhaps holding her, his hands soaked in her blood as he tried to patch up her wound, was too much for him. But hearing the words from someone else prodded the embers of hope in his chest. Maybe it really was true. While he had been torn between the two thoughts for years, it had only taken a little nudge to send him tumbling down.

Be careful, Master, Smoke added. The bond opened up between them, and all joking tones had vanished from the dragon's rumbling voice. *I have told you my thoughts on the matter. As much as I hate to agree with him, Uriah could very well be correct.*

I have to look into it, Kase replied, tucking the book under his arm for safekeeping. With one last glance back at the wyrm—breathing shallowly to avoid the stench that hung in the air—he turned toward the exit. A faint red mark guided him through the pressing darkness toward the mouth of the cave. He clung closely to it, silently thanking Smoke for casting his magic to aid him, and hoped Tobias and Uriah would both follow him. He wasn't sure if Smoke would bother to share the mark with anyone else.

Cold, night air rushed toward him as the ledge overlooking the cliffside came into view. With a slight pop, sound filled his ears once more. The wind rustled his clothes, and a stream trickled softly nearby. Moonlight greeted him, bathing the plains far below in an ethereal silver light. The rocks beneath his feet were more uneven than the smooth surface of the wyrm's cave, but it was a welcoming feeling. The cave made his skin prickle with distrust, but the air outside was fresh and clean.

I know you believe you do, Smoke whispered, continuing the conversation. *But I think it is unwise. You will only run into more disappointment, and what would you even say to her if you found her? Perhaps she left you for a reason. Perhaps she does not want to be found.*

Hesitating, Kase pressed his lips together. Doubt and fear clashed at the back of his mind, slipping down the thread that connected him to his dragon. From the warmth that welled inside, he knew Smoke was trying to comfort him. It didn't help. The feelings continued to grow, until he finally pushed past them with a sigh.

"I have to see for myself," he said.

"See what?"

Kase leapt back, reaching for his sword. Recognition passed through him, and embarrassment warmed his face. Tobias and Uriah stood in the entrance, both looking at him with puzzled and amused expressions. At the back of his mind, he could hear Smoke laughing too.

Not funny, he bit back.

You must admit, it was.

Dropping his hand back to his side, Kase straightened up and cleared his throat. "Just talking with Smoke about something. Trying to figure out what to do next."

"Doesn't Uriah do magic?" Tobias asked, glancing at him with a pointed frown. "You made the cave spell, didn't you? Locating your Mage should be no problem."

Uriah snorted and rolled his eyes. "That spell was conjured using protective charms." He dug around in his pocket and pulled out a slip of paper, covered in runes. Smudges of blue clung to the paper's edge like frost, but it seemed normal otherwise. "All it did was seal off the cave to confuse the wyrm and keep it locked up while I dealt with it. My brother made them for me. I can't use magic, and I can't locate Aviva."

This is a first, Smoke muttered through the bond.

Kase narrowed his eyes. "Your younger brother, right? I didn't know he could use magic."

"I try not to go around spreading that information, so don't repeat it," Uriah growled. Taking the paper in both hands, he tore it in half straight down the middle. "He doesn't want to buy into the Summoners' goofy magic hierarchy, so I don't want them to catch wind of his power and force him into becoming a Mage. He's happy practicing magic alone. Don't drag him into this." He ripped the paper another time, glaring at the shreds in his hands. "And no, he can't locate Aviva either."

"We could ask for help from the High Summoner then?" Tobias tossed out, looking between Kase and Uriah. Uncertainty quieted his voice, pitching the end of his question a bit higher than normal.

Kase hated to admit it, but the thought had never crossed his mind. Even when Oliver had mentioned it, he didn't really consider it. While Uriah's statement of dislike towards the Summoners rang with hostility, Kase couldn't help but share it. The Summoners had always had a way of trying to control every little thing, and he was reluctant to put himself in their hands again. But now, things had changed. His head was full of new questions and possibilities.

Could the High Summoner find Aviva?

He looked down at her book in his hands. *Perhaps with this they could...*

What happened to saving that as a last resort? Smoke said, puzzled. Immediately after the question had passed through their bond, the dragon's confusion vanished. Magic sparked in their bond, tinting the edges of Kase's vision red. Before he could ask, an overwhelming feeling of danger cut through the haze of his mind, making the hairs on the back of his neck stand up.

Someone is coming.

Kase gritted his teeth and turned to report the same to Tobias and Uriah, but another voice made the words die in his throat. A familiar voice, just beyond the ledge where he was standing.

"I'm telling you, Arayna. You're probably overreacting. I'm sure they're fine."

Two red ears appeared over the edge of the cliffside just before Arayna's head poked up and her gaze met Kase's. Her face lit up; she hauled herself over the edge and rushed toward him.

"Kase!" She crushed him in a hug, driving away Smoke's feelings of wariness. With a childish squeal of delight, she squeezed him tighter, drawing out a laugh from him. Grinning ear-to-ear, she let go and stepped back.

"Arayna," he greeted, taking a deep breath. A slight sting around his midsection reminded him of the bear-like strength she possessed, despite her small size. "What are you doing here?"

Oliver appeared next, pulling himself up onto the ledge with much more effort than it had taken Arayna. He knelt there for a bit to catch his breath, and then he rose to his feet. Like always, he met Kase with a glare, his amber eyes narrowed. The look sent a shiver down Kase's spine, but he couldn't help the nervous smile it dragged to his face either.

Arayna looked back at Oliver, folding her arms over the tan fur coat draped across her chest. She chewed at her lip, her ears twitching like they did when she was uncertain of something. "Well…"

"Ahtella returned with her tail between her legs," Oliver said when she fell silent. "Like something had happened. It takes a lot to frighten her, so we came to see what the cause was, and… I think I know what it might be."

Kase followed his gaze to Uriah, who grinned and waved. Inwardly, Kase winced, dread knotting in the pit of his stomach. Ahtella had never liked Uriah. Because of that, Arayna often avoided him. But the beast spirit had never been *afraid* of him, so why would she be now?

"I'm not sure it was Uriah she was running from," he murmured, too quiet for anyone else to hear. The only one he knew had heard him was Smoke, who tugged at the bond to signal he believed his master.

"Arayna." Tobias stepped forward, coming to meet her on the ledge. She tilted her head as he came closer, but she didn't flinch away like she did around some. Ever since her curse took effect, she had become wary around others. Kase couldn't blame her. It didn't take much for the people of her own hometown to turn against her.

Tobias gripped the hilt of his sword like he always did, pushing his shoulders back. "I think we need you to find someone for us again."

Smoke snorted in the back of Kase's mind. *Did he not want to go to the Summoners?*

Hush. Kase wasn't going to argue with pushing that plan aside now that Arayna had arrived.

Arayna frowned, pushing her brown hair out of her eyes. She cupped her chin in her hand. "I think I might be able to try. Eira again? Did she get away?"

"She did," Uriah said. "But we want you to find Aviva."

Hushed silence spread over the group like a thick blanket. Kase held his breath, curling his fingers tighter around the book and looking anywhere but at Oliver. Even without looking, he could feel Oliver's stare drilling holes into the side of his head. He gritted his teeth and reached for Smoke, grounding himself in their bond. As he often did, Smoke only suggested running Oliver through with his sword. Kase dismissed that idea, biting down on his tongue to keep quiet.

"Aviva is dead," Oliver ground out. "I made my opinion on the matter very clear before."

"Eira said she wasn't." Uriah shrugged. The same nonchalant, uncaring attitude lingered in his tone, making Kase's skin prickle. "Kase just wants to double-check, and I do too. It's the smart thing to do. After all, Kase and I are her Mage Guardians. Isn't it natural for us to want to look for her?"

Except that he did not want to just moments ago, Smoke growled. *I am coming to you, master. Something is not right; I cannot seem to make these pieces fit.*

Oliver stepped forward. "But she—"

"It's not up to you to decide," Kase interrupted, returning the hunter's stare with a firm glare. "It's up to Arayna. She came all this way to check on us, and it would be a long way back home at this hour. If Arayna can't find her, then..." He trailed off. Then what?

He couldn't give up, not when he had the spellbook in his

hands. Not when someone else—someone he never expected to weigh in—had confirmed his suspicions.

Unless, of course, Eira was lying. She couldn't let the book go that easily, so she was trying to manipulate him again. It wouldn't be that strange for her. She had manipulated him in the past, separating him from his Mage when Aviva needed him most. Because of her, Aviva was...

Kase shoved the thought away. *I have to check that what she said is true. That's all.*

"Then," Tobias continued when Kase fell silent. "We'll call for a Summoner. Missing Mages, thieves hunting spellbooks, and... I don't even know what else, but it sounds like something worth telling someone higher up. A person who can help us unravel this."

"See? A plan," Uriah said with a smirk. "What's-his-face is good for something after all!"

"It's Tobias."

Arayna's ears twitched as she listened to the conversation around her. Despite that show of curiosity, her brows were drawn together and her eyes narrowed. Kase recognized that thoughtful, nose-scrunched look. When they were kids, Oliver would tease her that it made it look like thinking was too hard for her. Now, he said nothing about it when she glanced back at him. He only shook his head, as if he already knew what was on her mind.

Turning back to the group, Arayna lifted her hand in the air. Red runes glowed around her wrist, and Ahtella reappeared in a flash of light. Smiling softly, Arayna stroked the wolf's head. "I'm not hunting Eira, but if Aviva's alive... I want to know, too." She met Kase's gaze. The confidence swirling in her eyes was a world of difference from the frightened, cursed girl he remembered. "I'll see what I can do."

A weight vanished from his shoulders, allowing him to stand straighter. "You're staying, then?"

Arayna looked back at Oliver with pleading eyes as if silently voicing the same question. The hunter sighed heavily and massaged his temples. "Fine. But for now, we're going to sleep. It's late."

"Sleep time," Tobias murmured as he stretched. "My favorite time."

Kase rolled his eyes, a slight, amused smile pulling at the corners of his mouth. Arayna burst out laughing, soon followed by Uriah. Tobias stared at them blankly. At the sight of his confusion, even Oliver chuckled a little to himself, though he hid it behind his hand. His gaze lingered on Arayna and Uriah, though, as if he was laughing at them instead of Tobias.

The moment provided a brief respite, and Kase couldn't help but feel drawn to the sound of the laughter. It didn't last long, as Smoke tugged faintly at their bond, a gentle reminder that he couldn't lose focus. Something wasn't right, and he didn't know how much longer they had to enjoy their time together.

9

CURIOSITY

As much as Tobias had wanted to go to sleep, he couldn't. He tossed and turned, trying to find the most comfortable position on the ground. Grass kept tickling his ear, and the flat earth pressed his arm uncomfortably against his side. Laying on his back was no better, as it revealed that the ground was not entirely flat but was littered with hidden bumps and dips. When standing, it never occurred to him that it would be so uncomfortable. The soles of his boots must have absorbed most of the horrors.

Eventually, he gave up trying and sat up. The sun had barely begun to rise in the distance, setting the sky on fire as it crept above the horizon. He frowned. Nighttime seemed to last much longer when he was restless and jittery.

As if to agree with his discomfort, the shallow cut in his neck began to ache. He winced and brought a hand to the spot. For the second time, Eira had gotten the better of him. The thought made him sick, and the aching in his neck stirred the irritation buried in his gut. He would be happy if her blade never touched his skin again.

Looking to the left, his gaze landed on Kase, who was sound

88

asleep several feet away. He had tucked the white book against his chest, arms curled protectively around it. Tobias heaved a sigh, shaking his head. In fairness, he had snatched the book back in the end. Knife or no knife, that was what he wanted. That was what he set out to do. A flicker of pride stirred beneath his frustration.

Then why did I give it to him? he asked himself. The pride withered. *You were the one that wanted it. Why did you hand it over?*

"Because it belongs to him," he whispered back. He pushed to his feet, brushing grass from his clothes. His shoulders remained stiff from being pressed against the ground. Muttering to himself, he rolled them and swung his arms until the feeling diminished. Satisfied, he picked up his sword and tied it to his waist. He needed a walk to clear his head, and the brilliant pastel hues of the sunrise beckoned him toward the horizon.

A little farther from where they had settled down for the night, a river wound its way down the rocky mountainside. The crystal-clear water pooled at the foot of the cliff, forming a basin deep enough to reach Tobias's elbow when he stuck his hand in. Oliver had declared it was clean enough to drink the night before, and Kase had given Tobias his spare flask. At that time, there was nothing on Tobias's mind but sleep and he had gone to bed without refilling it. Now, his mouth was sandpapery and his throat dry.

He knelt down beside the water, taking out the flask and dipping it in. Cool water brushed the tips of his fingers, bringing with it the same chill that lingered in the air. The water reflected the image of the sky; oranges, pinks, and reds painted over the deep violet of night as the sun rose higher. Only a few stars remained visible, and Tobias tilted his head back to gaze at them. They had names, ones his sister would have immediately recalled. Unlike her, he drew a blank.

He looked away and pulled the flask out of the pool. As he

drank, the cold water washed away his worries. Rising, he looked around for somewhere else to wander until the others woke.

"You're up early," a voice greeted.

Tobias whirled around, hand flying to his sword. He froze, straightening as he came face to face with Arayna. Her head was tilted, her ears pricked in what he assumed was curiosity. She hardly flinched when he reached for his sword, but her body tensed, and she squared her shoulders. Offering her a slight smile, he released his sword.

"I didn't sleep much at all," he said, stepping aside so she could get to the pool. "In fact, I'm really not sure I ever went to sleep."

She crouched, cupping her hands in the water and splashing her face with it. Flecks of scarlet magic clung to her wrists, glittering in the early morning sunlight. Shaking her head, she looked over her shoulder at him again. "I've been up for a while now trying to locate Aviva. No luck. As far as my power is concerned, there is no Aviva. She... clearly doesn't want to be found."

He sank to the ground beside her. "Are we going to call for a Summoner?"

"I'd have to ask Oliver." She rubbed her wrist until what remained of the runes dissipated. "So, what's bothering you? Was the ground too uncomfortable or are you upset about something?"

"A little of both. I think I'm starting to get homesick." Tobias drew his knees up against his chest, wrapping his arms around them. "It probably sounds stupid, but I miss my sister. I miss..."

He trailed off. Sighing, he buried his face in his knees. It probably all sounded dumb to her. He was certain there were many things she had lost when she became... whatever it was she had turned into. All of them had more reason to complain than he did. His fingers curled around the key hidden beneath his shirt. Was it even truly a home if he was there alone all the time?

The grass shifted as Arayna sat down; the water splashed as she stuck her hands in it again. "It does sound dumb, but that doesn't mean it won't hurt you. I miss a lot of things that sound stupid to other people. I miss being part of human society. I miss not having to rely on Oliver to keep me safe from others—from what *I* could do to *them*." She chuckled a little to herself, though the expression she wore was dark. "I miss looking normal, as ridiculous as that sounds. But that doesn't stop me from feeling sad. You know? It's funny, it's such a human concept. That idea that you must be pathetic because you feel sad, or that your sadness is somehow less than someone else's."

Tobias lifted his head. "What does that mean?"

Arayna shrugged, sipping water from her cupped hands. When she finished, she wiped her hands on the front of her fur-covered tunic and smoothed her matted brown hair back from her eyes. "I don't know. I can't explain it. But I don't think you should feel ashamed." She offered him a fanged smile. "You could have gone home already, but you decided to stick around."

"Yeah," Tobias muttered, jerking his gaze away. "I started this whole mess because I was desperate to understand that book—it consumed my life, honestly. If we're going to meet Aviva, I want to ask her about it." He chuckled as he lifted his head to face her. "Besides, I think I'm invested in the book's backstory now. I guess you could say I'm here on behalf of my curiosity."

She blinked, her ears flattening back. Her eyes dulled for a moment, and she bit her lip as she turned her face away. He winced. Maybe he shouldn't have mentioned the past again. She had already shared more than he expected her to. It wasn't fair to try to wring something else out of her.

She shook her head and rose to her feet, dusting herself off. "If that's what you like," she said. "I'm sure Aviva will be happy to answer your questions, if we can even find her." Doubt hung on every word, but she didn't linger to allow for conversation. By the time a response came to mind, she had already left.

WHEN THE SUN rose above the mountaintops, light spilling over the vast empty plains below, a flash of red scales descended from the clouds. Upon spotting the figure in the sky, Kase pressed his fingers to his lips and gave a shrill whistle. With a roar to respond, Smoke landed in the grass, folding in his wings once his talons touched the ground. Kase raced toward his dragon, shouting as he checked the saddle strapped to his back and peered into the bags attached to its sides.

"What took you so long, you stupid beast?" he snapped as he rifled through the saddlebags. He shot Smoke a withering look. "I told you to stay nearby in case I called you. I've been trying to call you for an entire day! What part of my simple instructions did you not understand?"

Smoke snorted, blowing smoke from his nose. Kase pointed an accusing finger at his dragon, continuing to spout all kinds of insults—many of them in the same nonsensical vein as "three-legged chair." Uriah keeled over from laughter. Kase's face flushed, and his mouth clamped shut as his hand fell back to his side again.

"Anyway!" Arayna dug around in Oliver's knapsack, ignoring the amber glare he shot her, and pulled out a jar of silver dust that sparkled in the light as she held it up. Ground-up dragon scales, Tobias realized with a jolt.

She pried the lid off and licked her fingers before sticking them in the jar, ignoring Oliver's cry. She pulled back her hand, now coated in the glittering dust, and bent down to trace a rough circle in the grass.

"Time to call for the Summoners," she muttered, half to herself and half to the others.

"I take it your skills didn't cut it?" Uriah teased. "So there *are* things even the great Beast Master can't find."

Oliver scooped up a rock and flung it at Uriah's head. Uriah caught it with ease, grinning proudly down at the hunter. Glowering, Oliver snapped his gaze back to Arayna. "Shut up," he snapped. "It's not like you offered to do anything."

"Maybe I prefer to get there using the power of others. You know, like the Summoners?"

Oliver made a show of rolling his eyes, but he didn't poke the subject anymore.

The dust left a shimmering trail behind, glowing when the two ends of the circle met again. Arayna brushed the remaining specks of dust off her hands and stepped inside the circle, sitting with her legs crossed and her back straight. She laced her fingers together and rested her hands in her lap. Her eyes slid shut as she inhaled deeply. The glow from the circle increased, giving off a low hum as power stirred to life in the air around Arayna.

Hushed silence fell over the group, painted over with the thick aura of magic. No one moved for several seconds. Not wanting to risk disturbing her, Tobias stood as stiff as a statue, his hands curled into fists at his sides.

The stillness was broken when Oliver sat down in the grass, just outside the circle Arayna had created. He screwed the lid back onto the jar and stuffed it into his backpack. "You don't have to just stand there," he said, his tone flat. "It's going to be a while. As long as you don't touch the circle, it'll be fine."

Tobias shot a glance at Kase, who had already plopped down in the grass and cracked open the spellbook. He flipped through the pages one at a time, his eyes scanning the contents slowly. Tobias couldn't tell if he understood what the book said or not, but a smile appeared on his face regardless. He wondered if it made him think of his Mage, just holding the book and looking at it.

You did a good thing, he reminded himself. *This was the right thing to do.*

Still, some inkling of doubt clung to the back of his mind, desperately reminding him of the fact that the book had fallen into *his* hands. The overwhelming emptiness that stretched within him during its absence buzzed with uncertainty. Clenching his jaw, he reached up to rest his hand against the key. The cool metal pressed against his chest, and its presence brought him some semblance of comfort.

Uriah yawned and stretched. "Well, if it's gonna be a long time, I'm gonna take a nap."

Tobias frowned, dropping his hand to his side. "But you just woke up."

"So? Doesn't mean it can't be nap time." Uriah flopped down and rolled over onto his side. Before Tobias could argue, his eyes slid shut and his soft snores joined the sound of birdsong—a rather unpleasant symphony.

"Unbelievable," Tobias muttered, picking up his satchel and scooting farther away from Uriah. He sat down beside Oliver, whose gaze was fixed on Arayna.

Strangely enough, a sort of smile made its way to Oliver's face as his gaze slid past Arayna to Uriah. For the first time since Tobias had met him, his expression softened—a mirror of Kase's easygoing smile. It was the only time he looked even remotely similar to his cousin, jolting Tobias with the reminder of their relationship.

"Sleep always comes as easily as breathing to Uriah," Oliver said. "I suspect it's how he deals with things, in his own way."

Tobias fiddled with his fingers in his lap, biting down on his tongue. It wasn't his place to poke Oliver with more questions, and yet the perfect opportunity had just presented itself. Throwing his anxious thoughts aside, he faced Oliver square on. "What things?" he asked. "If you don't mind, I'd like to know more about what happened between you and the others. About Eira, and this Mage we're going to find."

Oliver raised a questioning brow. His smile vanished as quickly as it had come, reverting to his usual disapproving frown. It was a wonder his face wasn't permanently stuck that way. He pursed his lips as he thought, plucking at the grass. It went on long enough that Tobias considered giving up and moving on to pester Kase instead. Then, finally, Oliver straightened and combed his fingers through his black hair.

"Alright," he sighed. "I guess it won't hurt anything. Just know that none of us like having it brought up, and Eira's reappearance is… I don't know what it is, really. Stressful or painful, maybe. Most likely both."

Tobias nodded. It wasn't like he really needed to be told—their avoidance of the topic was as obvious as the sun in the daytime.

"When Eira was little, her parents were killed in an accident of some sort. She lived on the streets in a town near the outskirts of Calistie," Oliver began. "That's what she always said anyway. I don't remember how it all happened, but she left the town and went off on her own. She sort of made us into her family. Me and Arayna, Kase, Uriah, and their Mage, Aviva." He pulled more grass from the ground and let the wind carry it away. He focused his gaze on Arayna and rested his hands in his lap. "It was good for a time, but like all good things, it came to an end."

Tobias leaned in closer, intrigue winding its way through his bewilderment. "What happened?"

Oliver shrugged. "I was young; the memories are in pieces. Arayna and I were still just kids. The only reason we got to tag along was because Kase is my cousin. He would watch us during the day while my parents were out. It was a mock adventuring game when it started—harmless and entertaining." He wrapped his arms around himself. "One day, Eira suggested we turn our game into an actual adventure. We went after some magical treasure and were attacked. Eira turned on us and killed Aviva. The change was sudden and without reason. Arayna didn't take it well at all."

The story resonated in Tobias. He had never heard someone's words ache so much.

Oliver sighed deeply and his shoulders drooped. "But I should have seen how hurt Kase was. His Mage was gone, and I... didn't do anything to stay by his side. I was too worried about Arayna, and I just abandoned him." He grabbed a fistful of grass, his eyes narrowing. "But I was just a kid. What was I supposed to do? How was I supposed to know?"

Tobias looked at Kase, who was still entertained with the book. "Eira killed Aviva?"

"I thought she did. Kase seems to think otherwise." Oliver groaned and flopped backward, lying on his back in the grass. He covered his face in his hands, smearing dirt across his cheeks. "It's all so stupidly confusing."

Tobias's gut twisted. The pieces did fit together, but Oliver was right. Something seemed out of place. Why would Eira betray her friends? If she had worked so hard to build a family with them, why tear it down? Moreover, why did Oliver believe she had killed Aviva while Kase was sure of the opposite?

"I guess," he began, "we'll just have to hope the Summoner can help clear up this mess."

"I'm certain she can," Oliver murmured, draping his arm over his eyes. "I'm just not sure I want her to. I don't want to see Arayna hurt anymore."

Looking at Arayna, sitting peacefully in her glowing spell circle, Tobias thought back to their conversation from that morning. The story dragged up memories from his meeting with her and Oliver, reminding him of how adamant Oliver had been about not getting involved. If it really was all because he worried so much about Arayna, then maybe he wasn't as much of a jerk as he originally thought. Maybe a little jaded, but he was soft deep down.

"Still, I don't think you have to worry," Tobias said. "Arayna will be just fine."

Oliver said nothing for a moment. Then, flatly, "I'm sure you're right."

Tobias picked at a loose thread dangling from the hem of his tunic. "If you don't mind me asking, how does that boy fit into all of this?"

Oliver frowned. "Boy?"

"The one you were discussing with Kase. I overheard your conversation that day and I've been wondering about it."

"Ah." Oliver turned his face away. "That's not for me to say. You'd have to ask Kase about that."

Disappointment settled heavily in the pit of Tobias's stomach. Getting that information out of Kase had already proven to be difficult, and he had hoped Oliver would be more open to the idea of sharing. Yet, it seemed both were set on leaving him to drown in his own ideas. He gave the thread a sharp tug. Maybe he would have to try asking Kase again.

With a jolt, Arayna leapt to her feet, her ears pricked and her eyes wide. The glow from her spell vanished. She scuffed a crack in the circle and stepped out, hauling Oliver upright. Smiling widely, her tail wagging like that of a proud puppy, she said, "I managed to get through to her! High Summoner Maven is on her way here now."

Oliver returned her grin, his face lighting up in a way that Tobias hadn't seen before in his expressions. "Excellent. Do we wait then?"

She nodded and sat down next to him, drawing her knees up against her chest. "We wait."

IO

SEARCH FOR AVIVA

For the umpteenth time since Arayna had announced Maven was on her way, Kase looked up at the sky to check the time. The sun had drifted to the middle, marking it as noon. He frowned. It had been several hours already, and still no sign of Maven. Impatience gnawed at the back of his mind. He could only stare at the spellbook so many times before his heart began to ache.

Please hurry up, he begged the Summoner, knowing she couldn't really hear his thoughts. The only one who could was Smoke, and he proved his unhelpfulness by laughing again.

She will get here when she gets here, Smoke said, stretching his neck forward and resting the very tip of his chin against Kase's knee. Warmth flowed from the dragon's scales, calming his frazzled mind at least a little. *Try not to fret so much. It interrupts my thinking.*

Sitting in the plains at the foot of the mountain, Smoke stood out like a sore thumb. The grass was golden and brown, pressed against the ground by his massive body. Sunlight reflected off his brilliant red scales, revealing a slight mirage of heat around his body. Despite that, he was never uncomfortable to be around. His body carried a flame that touched his scales, yet he regulated it well. It was most obvious when he brushed up against Kase, leaving only a faint touch of warmth rather than a sharp burn.

Kase snorted, rolling his eyes and setting the book aside in the grass. He patted Smoke's massive head. "What sort of thinking is it this time?"

Thinking about what I want to eat for lunch. Currently, I think I would like a deer. Maybe several deer.

"Then go get one."

No, I think I would rather pester you with complaints and thoughts about deer, Smoke said, looking up at him with a teasing shine in his old amber eyes. Just as he had said he would, he sent only thoughts of deer down their bond. Deer wandering in a forest, deer stopping to drink water from a stream, deer standing there minding their own business. It wasn't long before Kase was drowning in thoughts of deer and the anxious bouncing of his leg came to a stop.

Kase huffed and smacked the dragon, closing off his mind to the deer-thoughts. "You're an absolutely useless dragon. You're more like a chipped porcelain teacup."

Smoke blinked, lifting his head to peer at Kase. Thick tendrils of smoke drifted from his nostrils as he exhaled. *How does that make any sort of sense?*

Kase shrugged and picked up the spellbook again. "I don't think insults have to make any sense."

That explains much about you, Master. Smoke turned on his side, tucking his nose under his tail like a giant, scale-covered puppy.

No sooner had he opened the book yet again than Arayna was on her feet and pointing off into the distance. Her ears pricked, and a wide grin formed on her face. "I see her!" she called. "I can see the Summoner!"

Kase leapt to his feet and looked around. He scanned the

horizon for a glimpse of her, straining his eyes but to no avail. Arayna's sight had always been far better than his, but he faced the same direction as her and peered into the distance. Drawing in a deep breath, he exhaled slowly to calm his racing heart.

Smoke? He mentally quested toward his dragon, grabbing hold of the thread that bound them.

The dragon didn't respond with anything more than a grunt. Magic greeted Kase's touch and flooded through him, warm and familiar. He blinked several times, his vision tinted with red as he looked through Smoke's eyes.

Sure enough, the Summoner had come into view, though still several miles away. She rode atop a strangely draconic-looking horse, crossing the distance at an unmatchable speed.

A kirin, Smoke supplied for him. *The beast is called a kirin. They are not related to the dragons, but they do share similar traits. If anything, they are more similar to the extinct unicorn species than dragons.*

Kase squeezed his eyes shut, rubbing them until they ached. When he opened them again, Smoke's vision left him and he was once again stuck with the view of a distant speck to mark the Summoner's approach. He turned to Arayna, just as Oliver picked a rock up from the grass and threw it at Uriah's head. Tobias flinched at the action, though the corners of his mouth twitched up.

"Get up," Oliver snapped, rushing toward Arayna. He straightened the front of her coat and combed his fingers through her tangled hair to get rid of some of the knots. It was mostly unsuccessful. His fingers ended up caught more times than they detangled themselves. "Let's try not to embarrass ourselves in front of the High Summoner."

Arayna licked her hand and reached toward Oliver's hair. He yelped and jumped back, swatting her hand away. With a smug smile, she wiped her hand on her pants and shook out her hair again. "The only one likely to embarrass us is—" She paused, cutting off her sentence mid-thought. Her gaze shifted to Uriah, who was just sitting up and yawning. She snorted. "Yeah, no, I think we all know who it is."

Uriah is likely to do more than embarrass you, Smoke added, his voice tinged with something Kase didn't comprehend. It made his hands burn with the beginnings of a flame, however. He curled his fingers into a tight fist and closed off the bond, sealing the magic away with it.

The beast—kirin, as Smoke called it—gave a low whistling sound as it came into the field where they waited. It tossed its mane and slowed to a canter. It finally came to a full stop near Smoke, not even flinching as most creatures did around him. The High Summoner climbed down from the back of the kirin, brushing her long, black hair over her shoulder as her diaphanous cloak settled upon the ground at her feet. The fabric resembled a sunset, with pale pinks at the bottom blending into a deep, star-covered violet around her shoulders. A gold chain held it in place. Dressed in deep purple robes and adorned with silver and gold jewelry, she stuck out like a queen among commoners. Her skin was the color of honey and her eyes silver like the moon.

Kase stared at her, bewildered. He guessed she couldn't have been older than fourteen, judging by her round face and short stature. Still, the aura around her danced with overpowering magic, leaking into the very air around them. The feeling of it was light and free, easy to breathe and it calmed Kase's restless thoughts. The tension in his shoulders relaxed.

That calm is a part of her magic, Smoke said. *There is no malice in it though. She seems sincere. I can cut it off if you would like me to.*

No, Kase replied. *It's alright.* His head was clear. If anything, it was pleasant to be able to relax for a moment. If she meant no harm by it, then there was no reason for him to cut himself from a moment of peace, something he rarely got from his own head.

She dipped her head, her jewelry sparkling in the sunlight as she moved. "Greetings," she began, her voice no louder than a whisper in the wind. "I am High Summoner Maven Astraela. I was called on by a user of Beast Magic. What might I do to assist you?"

Kase glanced at Tobias, who was staring back at him with the look that he had come to know well: he was waiting for Kase to do something. Kase squirmed uncomfortably in his head. How was he supposed to address someone at the top of the chain of command? He had never been good with words, and now he was expected to use them in conversation with the most powerful and influential person in the Navaric kingdom.

It is your Mage, Smoke said.

And his thief, Kase added. It was a lame excuse, but he couldn't scrape together anything better.

Smoke didn't argue with that. He withdrew back into himself, leaving Kase's mind strangely empty without his presence. Gritting his teeth, Kase took hold of the book and approached High Summoner Maven. Her kirin nickered and stepped back, allowing her to fully turn her attention to him.

"We need you to locate someone for us. A Mage who has been missing for... a long time." He lifted the book, holding it out for her to take. "You're the only person who can find her."

Maven looked down at the spellbook, her silver eyes widening. "There have been many reports of missing Mages lately, but this book... You must be looking for Aviva."

Kase nodded slowly. His heart snagged on the name. Some part of him almost didn't want to believe Eira's words, but he couldn't risk abandoning Aviva if she truly was alive. He was left with only one option, no matter how painful it was.

Maven smiled softly, meeting his eyes. "My mother, the

previous High Summoner, was the one who mentored her and assigned her Guardians. I had heard Aviva died, but…"

"That's the thing," Uriah spoke up, coming closer. The kirin kicked and paced the closer he got, nickering and whistling like it had when it arrived. Uriah ignored it, but it didn't stop until Maven grabbed hold of the reins and pulled.

"Sorry," she said, tucking the book under one arm. Her face flushed slightly. "He doesn't usually act like this."

Uriah blinked, his gold eyes growing duller for a moment. Then he shook his head and the moment passed as he plastered a grin on his face. "It's fine. I've never been great with animals. Anyways, there's something strange about it. We thought Aviva was dead too, but… well, something happened, and we don't know anymore. We need you to search for her to confirm if it's true or not."

"It's *not* true," Kase snapped. But even he had uncertainty squirming at the back of his mind.

Maven looked between the two, confusion creasing her brow. "Well, I'll see what I can do. I won't be able to locate her if she truly is dead—I search by aura, and a dead person has no magic aura surrounding them. And if she's dead, she's dead. I didn't come here to bring her back: that's a forbidden art that *no one* should ever practice. Are we clear?"

Kase bowed to her. "Of course, High Summoner Maven."

A handful of seconds passed, in which Maven fixed Uriah with a firm stare. He hesitated, his lips pressed into a thin line. Kase clenched his jaw, mentally begging Uriah to bow and save them all the embarrassment of his disobedience.

Finally, with a resigned sigh, Uriah bowed low. "Yes, High Summoner Maven."

Her expression softened, and she motioned for both to stand upright once more. Lifting her hand, she traced a diamond-shaped symbol in the air and reached inside it, pulling a long staff from seemingly nowhere. The length of the staff was red, wound in a gold metal trim on the top end, where an opal-like stone rested. She twirled the staff and let the flat end touch the ground. "Then it is settled. Please step back so I can have space to perform the spell."

Kase nodded and stepped back, whistling for Smoke to follow. The old red dragon jerked his head around to look at him, exhaling a cloud of smoke through his nose before opening his wings and pushing off the ground. Kase stumbled back, buffeted by the wind. When he looked up again, he caught sight of Tobias's gaze locked on the dragon, following him upward until he disappeared into the clouds.

I am going to eat, Smoke said by way of explanation. His tone came across as matter-of-fact, but there was an underlying level of annoyance to it. *I shall return when the spell is complete.*

I hope you catch a nice deer, Kase said.

Smoke responded with another mental image of a deer—a strong buck this time.

Maven twisted the staff, pushing the end deep into the soft ground. Her kirin nudged her shoulder before moving several feet away. She held the staff in one hand and the book in the other, taking in a deep breath and sliding her eyes shut. As she began to murmur the words to her spell under her breath, the opal gemstone on her staff began to glow with a white light, growing brighter as she spoke more of the spell.

It had been a long time since Kase had seen anyone perform magic—or at least, magic that wasn't Draconic or connected to his bond with Smoke. Watching her made his chest tighten with longing. He reached up to touch the pin in his cloak, the one that connected him to Aviva.

"Watch carefully," Aviva would say, twirling her staff over and over in her hands. It was her way of showing off, and she would giggle with a proud smile on her face when she did it. Once, she smashed the gem on top of her staff that way. She twirled it less after that.

Kase shook the memory away. *I'm watching, Aviva. Watching and waiting. Where are you?*

Maven knelt down and laid the spellbook on the ground, leaning it against her staff. With her free hand, she traced the letters of her spell through the air. The symbols glowed with the white light from the gemstone. When she was done, she snapped her fingers, and a red light began to bleed into the white. Wind stirred around her, and the sky darkened. The humming of her magic in the air turned to a low growl.

At that point, her eyes opened, and she grabbed hold of the red letters suspended in the air. They formed a scarlet string in her hands, connected to the gem on her staff. She pulled on the string until a massive claw emerged from within the stone, followed by the deep growl of a dragon.

Kase took another step back, throwing his arm up instinctively to protect Tobias and Arayna behind him. The wind grew stronger, clawing at his clothes and hair, pulling him toward where Maven stood. She seemed unbothered by the wind, tugging harder on the string until the claw angled downward and touched the spellbook. It was disproportionately large compared to the opal on her staff—which wasn't much bigger than Kase's fist. He had never seen a Summoner's magic before. It was fascinating to watch.

Immediately, the claw retreated, and the dragon-like beast within the stone gave a shrieking cry. The red light vanished, along with the string which Maven pulled, and the wind died down once more. Quiet settled over the group as they stared at the Summoner in confusion and awe.

"So… was the shrieking a good thing?" Tobias asked as Maven studied the opal stone with a thoughtful frown.

She picked up the spellbook and brushed the dirt from its surface. As she held out the book for Kase to take, her frown lessened. "Yes. It means she is alive, though quite far. I will guide you to her."

"What *was* that beast?" Arayna asked, pushing past Kase to get to the staff still sticking out from the ground. She pressed her hands to the gemstone, peering at it like she could see the beast inside. Her ears twitched, and her eyes sparkled with awe.

"A wyvern. This one lives in the void I call from and easily locates the aura and souls of others. It's an elaborate way of tracking someone down." She waved her hand to dismiss the subject, holding out one hand. Her staff flew into her hand, settling into her palm easily. She snapped her fingers, and it vanished, back into the nothingness from which she had pulled it from earlier. Or so Kase assumed.

"It will be several days on foot," Maven went on, drawing a map in the air for them. Shimmering white lines settled into the image of the sprawling mountains and valleys that made up the Navaric kingdom. She pointed to a forest, far to the west of the mountain of the wyrm. "Shall we start heading that way now?"

Kase tugged on his bond with Smoke, a slight smirk finding its way to his face. "I have a better idea." He whistled, calling for his dragon the way Talia had taught him to.

For once, Smoke answered back immediately. From the clouds overhead, he emerged and descended, landing gracefully in the place he had been before—or as gracefully as a creature of his size could be. Kase made his way toward him, placing a hand on his warm red scales. *Showing off for the Summoner, hm?* he teased.

Smoke flicked his tail. *I did not even get to hunt, so I would appreciate if you refrained from sassing me right now.*

Sorry. You'll survive. Kase gave Smoke one last pat before turning his gaze back to Maven. "Smoke can take us there much faster. Just tell us where to go."

Maven blinked, her silver eyes shining. Childish glee dragged a wide grin to her face; for a moment, she seemed to have forgotten all about being a high and mighty Summoner. "I've *always* wanted to ride a dragon."

Kase couldn't help the laughter that slipped from his lips. "Then today is your lucky day, I suppose."

His heart had never felt lighter. He held the spellbook close to his chest, smiling brightly. He was a mere flight away from Aviva.

Finally, he would see his Mage again.

II

REUNION

A ROUGH SHAKE of his shoulder yanked Tobias from sleep. Cold wind rushed past him, smacking him in the face. He sat bolt upright and blinked away his exhaustion.

The sky still bore the violets and blues of night; it was a blanket dotted with thousands upon thousands of stars. The steady sound of Smoke's wingbeats provided a break from the constant whistle of the wind. Tobias's legs were starting to ache from sitting so long, but he knew trying to speak his complaints would be useless. The wind would carry his voice away before it ever reached the others. Not to mention that complaining would have no practical use in conversation and would only frustrate those around him. It was one thing he could remember clearly that his father had told him—that he was prone to complaining and it was exhausting to the whole household.

He shook the memory away and looked over his shoulder, wondering who had woken him from his sleep. Arayna sat directly behind him; she was pointing ahead of them in a silent signal. Confused, Tobias faced forward again and gasped.

A large forest stretched for miles below them. Smoke's shadow flew over it, a massive, dark stain on all the vibrant green—and yet there was still more of the canopy left untouched by his form. So far from the mountains, the cold had lessened slightly, as if the territory was suspended in the proper warmth of Deiah unlike the rest of Floridus and the surrounding areas, which were making an early shift into colder weather.

Tobias rubbed his eyes. Were they supposed to find Aviva somewhere in there? He inwardly groaned. *That's going to take us days!*

Smoke folded in his wings slightly and angled downward. Tobias gripped the leather saddle beneath him, biting down on his tongue to keep his mouth shut. The wind whipped past him, stinging his eyes and raking through his hair.

Then it stopped. Smoke's feet touched the ground, and his wings closed against his sides. At the base of Smoke's neck, Kase was the first to slip down. He swung himself over to one side and dropped to the ground—this time, he landed on both feet. Tobias followed his lead, pushing off of Smoke and landing in the grass below. His legs wobbled from the long flight, but he gritted his teeth and stood firm.

"She's in this forest, you said?" he asked, turning to Maven. He held out a hand to her, which she accepted with a smile. Gently, he helped her down from the dragon's back.

Maven looked at the entrance to the forest. She tapped the opal on her staff, causing a red light to ripple across the surface. Nodding, she turned back to him. "Yes, she is."

"But this is the forest where she lived before. The one where I met her," Kase said, his voice pitched low. His eyes darkened and he looked away. "I came here already to look for her— several times, in fact. She wasn't here then."

Maven looked from him to the forest, tightening her grip on her staff. "I can only tell you what the wyvern tells me, and it senses her presence here." She straightened her spine and twirled her staff before it disappeared from her hands again in a flash of pale pink sparks. "Although, it does appear to me that there is some kind of spell over this place. It's likely that it was a kind of confusion enchantment where the forest moves to keep something hidden from you, or where you are turned around before you can get far. Something along those lines."

Tobias swallowed hard, gripping the hilt of his sword. Was Aviva that worried about being found that she would even hide herself from her friends?

Uriah landed behind Tobias with a thump, lifting his ax up onto his shoulder. He inhaled deeply, his eyes fixed on the forest. Tobias followed his lead and looked at the forest, just as everyone else did. No one said a word, but he had a feeling they were all thinking the same thing.

What was she hiding from? What was so frightening that she had to fake death to get away from it?

"I can attempt to dissolve the spell," Maven said, drawing another set of runes in the air with the tip of her finger.

This time, the runes formed a pale blue thread that wound around her fingers. She pulled the thread taut, exposing a thin veil hanging over the line of trees. A concentrated frown knitted her brows together as she tugged harder.

The air seemed to groan, and the veil stiffened, refusing to move as she tugged against it. She tried to jerk it free, and the thread snapped. The force rebounded against her and sent her stumbling back. Uriah snagged her wrist and hauled her upright again.

"Thanks," she murmured, giving her head a quick shake.

Uriah didn't respond. He released her and stepped toward the forest, holding out his hand as if to touch the barrier. The air shimmered around his palm like heatwaves rising off a path in summer, but it never landed against anything solid. "Interesting. Did you manage to undo it?"

"No." Maven smoothed back the loose strands of hair that

had fallen in her face. "I think it needs some sort of key to get through. Did she leave you with anything else?"

"Only the spellbook." Kase sighed heavily, rubbing the back of his neck. He cast a longing glance at the forest. "Is there no way to find her without getting through this spell?"

"You won't find her unless she wants you to," Maven said. She hung her head slightly, her silver eyes darkening. "I'm sorry."

Arayna hummed to herself as she drew closer to Tobias. As her gaze slid over him, her lips pursed and her brow furrowed slightly. Grabbing hold of his arm, she lifted it high as she turned to face Maven. "What if Tobias is the key?"

Tobias's blood ran cold as he stared blankly at Arayna. The back of his neck burned as everyone's curious stares turned to him. He cleared his throat. "What?"

"Think about it." Arayna dropped his arm and stepped away, rejoining Oliver's side. "Sounds like something Aviva would do: leave her spellbook with someone Eira wouldn't know or think to go looking for, then make that same person the key to her magic veil thingy. Tobias has a surprisingly blank and invisible aura. Maybe that has something to do with it."

Tobias tried to ignore the slight, underlying jab in her words —she probably didn't mean it that way at all—but a disapproving frown rose to his face anyway. *What's that supposed to mean?* "Even if that's true, how does that fix anything? I can't use magic, and my standing here doesn't seem to have solved the problem."

"Well..." Maven approached him slowly, her gaze shifting between him and the forest beyond. "To make use of a key, you must first insert it into the lock."

She stood at the foot of the line of trees, gazing up into their branches. Bathed in pale moonlight, the silver glow further enhanced her regal appearance. The violet night sky matched her robes, and the stars glittered like the silver that lined her cloak. When she turned to him, he stiffened under her gaze. She only offered a soft smile in response before extending her hand to him.

"It's worth a try," she said. "Come stand beside me and put your hand in mine. I'm going to try the spell again and see if I can make Arayna's theory work."

Holding his breath, Tobias cast a quick glance at Kase, who nodded encouragingly. Ultimately, he was doing this for the dragon keeper. Aviva was his old friend, and it made his chest ache to think about the suffering Kase had been through—the years of not knowing whether she was truly alive or not but desperately clinging to the hope that she was still out there. He had tried to imagine that pain but could only come up with the engulfing lone-liness he found himself stranded in while his sister was busy at the school. That probably didn't compare at all, but it was enough.

If he could do something to ease that pain, he would.

He gave a firm nod and placed his hand in Maven's. Her hands were tiny, almost entirely engulfed by his own. He had never thought of himself as tall either until he was standing beside her, with her head just barely coming up to his shoulder. Looking at her, it was hard to believe she was the High Summoner, the young heir who would rule his kingdom, and the one who oversaw the border of Hybrid Territory.

Maven drew in a breath through clenched teeth, her face screwed up in concentration. She lifted her free hand, her pointer finger extended as she began to write out the same runes as before. Standing close while she worked, Tobias could feel the steady drop in pressure in the air around her as magic filled the air. His ears popped, and he cringed. Before long, the blue thread was winding its way around her fingers once more.

She squeezed his hand at the same time as she pulled on the thread, muttering faintly under her breath. This time, the veil tore, as if Maven had found a loose thread in the seam. She gave another sharp tug, and it ripped open, exposing the vibrant green forest within. Now torn, the veil quickly began to dissolve, leaving Maven's thread slack until she released it.

"What do you know, Arayna's instincts were right." Uriah folded his arms over his chest, regarding the scene proudly.

Maven stepped away from Tobias, sending another smile his way. "You have a gift," she said.

Before he could ask her to elaborate, she turned away and made her way toward the forest, cutting the conversation short. He bit back a sigh, reaching up to touch the key that hung around his neck. Thinking about it now, he never intended to get himself tangled in the spellbook's history, though he had always been somewhat curious about its owner. He was mere steps away from her now, and his legs had turned to lead. The thought of going forward made him tremble. Who was Aviva really? Why entrust her book to him? Why make him the "key" to her barrier?

Before anyone could move, the underbrush shifted. A shadow darted out from the line of trees, vanishing deeper into the forest with the rustling of branches. Kase stiffened. Then, without warning, he dashed after it.

"Kase!" Tobias called, rushing after him, swerving around a tree in his path. "Don't go off on your own!"

"That's her familiar!" he called back, leaping over the trunk of a fallen tree. He quickly grew farther and farther away, his form swallowed by the shadows of the trees.

Tobias cursed under his breath, forcing his legs to move faster. His feet pounded against the dirt. He leapt over the foliage in his path. It wasn't long before he caught up to Kase again, skidding to a halt just before he collided with his back.

Kase had come to a standstill at the edge of another line of trees. In front of him stood a small cottage, surrounded by an array of ferns and flowers and lined with the cut stumps of trees. White flowers grew like crawling ivy along the walls, shimmering like pearls in the moonlight.

But it wasn't the cottage that brought Kase to a stop.

Stepping around him, Tobias spotted a young woman in a white cloak standing at the other side of the clearing. Her arm was outstretched, a winged snake-like creature curled around it. Iridescent green scales covered the creature's body, and a forked tongue flicked in and out of its mouth. The woman inclined her head toward the snake as if listening. With a gasp, her head snapped in Kase's direction. Her eyes narrowed and her lips pressed into a tight frown. Blonde hair tumbled down her shoulders in even waves, interlaced with tiny braids and white-and-pink flowers. In her other hand, she held a white staff with a clear crystal situated at one end. A thin chain hung around the crystal, two charms attached to it. One red, one gold.

"Aviva," Kase breathed, taking a cautious step forward. "Aviva, it's you, isn't it?"

The snake hissed at him, but she waved it away. Its form disappeared in a shower of green sparks, returned to the magic that surrounded her.

She stood straighter, lifting her chin. Several seconds passed, in which Tobias held his breath. What if it wasn't her? What if she really was dead and it was some kind of trick? What if Eira had fooled them?

What then?

Dropping her staff in the grass, the woman ran to Kase and threw her arms around him with a cry of delight, her facade crumbling. He scooped her up in his arms, planting a kiss on her cheek as he laughed.

Tobias blinked; his worry vanished, carried away by the breeze. The knot in his gut untangled itself, and a soft smile found its way to his face as he stepped back from the two of them. All his anxiety seemed so distant, quickly dissolved by the relief that she was alive and well.

"I knew you were still out there," Kase murmured, setting her down on her feet again. "I never gave up on you."

Aviva cupped his face in her hands, standing on the tips of her toes just to reach him. "I knew you wouldn't."

"Iila still doesn't like me?"

Aviva laughed. "I hate to say it, but your luck with scaly creatures is quite poor."

Kase rolled his eyes, though a playful smile remained on his face. "Is Smoke the exception or the rule?"

"Ah, yes. I believe he should be the exception."

Leaves rustled as Arayna burst from the undergrowth. She stopped short, just as Kase had, her ears pricked and her tail twitching. Her eyes widened and her hands flew to her mouth. Aviva and Kase both turned to look at her, and another smile lit up Aviva's face.

Arayna rushed toward the Mage and enveloped her in a hug, pulling Kase in too. Laughter drifted through the air, pleasant and happy despite all that they had been through to arrive. Oliver swept past Tobias, following Arayna's lead and joining the hug. Kase ruffled his hair affectionately, and for once, Oliver responded with a wide grin—that, or Tobias had finally lost his mind.

Finally, Uriah emerged from the forest with Maven a few steps behind. Uriah laughed the loudest as he joined them, pulling Aviva from the center of the group and crushing her in a hug of his own. Next to him, she really was tiny. Her head barely reached his shoulder. She stiffened at first, but quickly relaxed into his embrace and wrapped her arms around him to return it.

"It's good to see you all," Aviva said as she broke away from the hug, offering Uriah one last pat on the arm before she turned to the other three again. "You look like you're doing well."

Arayna clasped Aviva's hands in her own, her lips quivering

as she examined the other girl's face. "Aviva… we really thought you were dead!"

At that, Aviva's shoulders drooped. "I know; I'm sorry I lied to you. But—" She cut herself off, glancing over her shoulder. Tobias froze when her gaze landed on him, and his hands curled into fists at his sides. Aviva seemed to notice this, but she turned back to her friends for one last word. "Another time."

With that, and one last look at Kase, she slipped out of their crowding semi-circle and collected her staff from the grass. Her steps were slow but deliberate as she came and stood before Tobias and Maven, and she dipped her head to both of them. "High Summoner Maven," she began. "I understand you are the one that brought them all here? My familiar also tells me you made use of my key I left with Tobias to get through the barrier."

Tobias bristled. *I haven't introduced myself yet. How does she know my name?*

The question died on his tongue before he could voice it as Maven raised a hand in a silent acceptance of Aviva's words. "Your spell was quite strong. I could not break through it on my own. That said…" She flicked her wrist, summoning the threads of her magic. It took only a simple jerk to bind Aviva's wrists and haul her forward. "I'll need you to come with me."

Tobias stepped away from Maven, his hand landing against the hilt of his sword. Unlike him, Kase didn't hesitate to draw his blade against the Summoner. Arayna followed suit with a low growl.

"What are you doing?" Tobias snapped. A clouded mix of anger and hurt rippled through him, burning the back of his throat. Uriah's bitter words about the Summoners echoed in his mind. Shame coiled in the pit of his stomach. *This is my fault.*

"Calm down. Lower your weapon, Kase," Aviva said softly. She held Maven's stare calmly with her head high and her shoulders pushed back. The aura of her magic curled tightly around her as if it was mimicking her snake familiar. "The High Summoner is not at fault."

Kase froze. When Aviva shot him a pointed glare, he gritted his teeth and slid his sword back into its sheath. At his side, Arayna curled her lip and lunged towards Maven with a growl. Oliver caught her wrist as Uriah jumped between her and the Summoner. She fought and screamed as they wrestled her to the ground. Maven watched silently, with one brow raised and her lips settled in an unmoving frown.

Tobias turned away. His fingers curled so tightly around the hilt of his sword that his knuckles began to ache. Several seconds passed before Arayna quieted again, but he refused to look at her.

"Mage Aviva," Maven went on when the silence settled over the group. "You have broken our code of conduct by hiding yourself from the world, withdrawing this location from our sight, and teaching magic to an unregistered apprentice. You will return with me to the palace and face punishment for these crimes. If there are no objections, I will seal your magic."

Kase rushed forward and grabbed hold of Aviva's arm. "Hold on. There must be some mistake. Aviva would never break the code unless she had a good reason. A-and there has never been an apprentice. There's no one else here. Right, Aviva?"

"There is no one else here, yes," Aviva replied, keeping her gaze locked on Maven. "But I did take on an apprentice while I was alone. I sent her to deal with a task of her own." With a sigh, she added, "I had to stay *dead*. I couldn't register her with the Summoners."

Maven narrowed her eyes and tugged on the threads. They tightened, pulling Aviva closer. "It is forbidden to teach magic without license from the High Summoner."

Tobias frowned, glancing between the two. Something itched at the back of his mind, burrowing deep into his thoughts. There was conviction in Kase's voice and sincerity in his eyes as he defended the honor of his Mage. Even Uriah seemed doubtful: his brow was furrowed, and his lips were pursed.

Clearing his throat, Tobias stepped forward. "Mage Aviva, did something happen? You separated yourself from your friends, left your spellbook in the hands of a stranger, and sealed yourself away. If you knew these things would break the code of conduct, why would you go through all the trouble? You have nothing to gain from this."

Uncertainty crossed Maven's gaze and the threads of magic went slack in her grip.

Aviva stiffened, her viridescent eyes darkening. Her focus slid to Tobias again, nearly jolting him out of his skin. When she looked at him, the aura of magic around her stirred, reaching out to him curiously. He gripped the hilt of his sword tighter, though he never drew it from the sheath.

"There must be a reason for these actions," he went on. "High Summoner Maven, please release her until she can explain the details to us. I believe Kase; Aviva wouldn't do these things without reason."

Maven narrowed her eyes at him, her fingers curling as she dropped her hand to her side. Finally, she sighed and turned her face away. The threads dissipated, releasing Aviva from her magic bonds. "Fine," Maven said stiffly. "I will hear you out."

Aviva stepped back into Kase's arms, dipping her head to the Summoner. Behind them, Uriah released Arayna and rose to his feet with a grunt, rolling his shoulders. Arayna glared at him as she shook away Oliver's lingering grip and shot up. She remained at Oliver's side, and the relief on his face was clear as day.

"The truth is, someone powerful is hunting my spells," Aviva began, threading her fingers together. She bit her lip and cast her gaze to the ground. "I disappeared to protect myself."

Tobias drew in a deep breath. There was uncertainty in

Aviva's face and tension in her shoulders. She refused to meet Kase's eye even when his hand brushed her shoulder comfortingly. Silence settled for several long seconds. Maven's soft, patient expression fell away.

"Why give your book to a stranger?" Tobias prodded, hoping to stir the conversation once more. He didn't know how long Maven would wait for an answer before she whisked Aviva away, taking his one chance at getting the answer to his curiosity. She was his one shot at satisfying the emptiness inside him, left behind by the book. "I'm... not anything special, and I couldn't even protect it from a thief. Why didn't you give it to someone stronger? Wasn't there someone out there more worthy of it?"

Someone like Talia.

It had chewed at the back of his mind since he learned who the book belonged to: even her Guardians knew his sister. If they knew Talia, why didn't Aviva give the book to her instead? Talia would have kept it well-guarded. Talia would never have lost it to Eira. Talia would have understood it better if she had more time with it. Talia would have protected it better than Tobias ever could.

Talia would have been a better choice.

The thought made Tobias bite down on the inside of his mouth, his hand reaching to rest against the key that dangled from the cord around his neck. Briefly, the thought of him being "the key" to Aviva's barrier crossed his mind, but he couldn't understand why that had to be him either. Was it because he supposedly had a blank aura? Wouldn't Talia's be the same?

You have a gift, Maven had said. At the time, he wanted to believe her. Now, it only felt like a gift to other people. Something they could use to their advantage. Was he simply useful to Aviva, or did she truly see something in him?

Aviva looked up. "It's not about being worthy. I entrusted it to a stranger because I knew it would take Eira longer to find it. I left it with someone unknown, someone less powerful, in the hopes that she would overlook you. It worked for a time—six years, in fact. You are the reason I could remain hidden for so long."

A thread of her magic wrapped around his finger and pulled taut, biting into his skin. When it did, a sharp ringing sound filled his mind. Within seconds, the noise diminished and a voice took its place.

I gave it to you because you are gifted, and you are a key. A key to unlocking this puzzle, her voice whispered. She was loud and clear, even as she turned back to Kase and took her spellbook from his outstretched hands. Her mouth moved, but the sound of her words in his head didn't match up with her lips. *Your aura is blank, making it hard for you to be found with magic. I went to you because someone powerful is searching for me and my spells. You are the only one this person cannot sense.*

Tobias opened his mouth, the words sitting on the tip of his tongue. Before he could get anything out, however, the thread snapped and her voice faded from his mind. The general chatter around him flooded in once more. He looked down at his hand, at the finger where the thread had squeezed his skin and then snapped. A faint mark had been left behind, along with a slight sting. Nothing else gave a hint as to what had happened.

"Why did you have to disappear in the first place?" Maven spoke up, her voice cutting cleanly through the talk and silencing it. "Why go through all the trouble of convincing everyone you had died? If you were being hunted by someone more powerful than you, wouldn't it make more sense to seek protection in the Summoners? My mother has been puzzling over it since she heard the reports, and I'm sure your companions are confused as well. You were an obedient, loyal Mage, bound to the code. What pushed you to break it?"

Tobias hadn't been there six years ago when Aviva disappeared, and he had only heard bits and pieces of the story, but he wasn't sure *confused* covered it all. Kase had been broken by it, Oliver had been hurt by it, Arayna had been scarred by it, and Uriah…

Tobias scrutinized him, frowning at the gleam in his golden eyes and the smirk on his lips. Reading him was like trying to read a brick wall. How did Uriah feel about it all? His responses to the event flip-flopped from one emotion to another without warning or reason.

Maybe confusion was the word for *his* emotion.

Aviva pressed her lips into a thin line, casting a quick glance at Kase. Finally, she faced Maven again. "Something is stirring," she said. "The world is changing, moving dangerously closer to a darkness I see no escape from. It grows worse with every year that passes, and Eira seems to have been roped into it. She tried to take my spellbook the day I vanished, and I didn't have the power to face her. So I ran away." She summoned Iila in a shower of green sparks. The snake curled protectively around her shoulders, flicking his tongue out of his mouth as he surveyed the group. Aviva sighed before continuing. "I don't want to face what's coming, but I also don't want to isolate myself from my family anymore. Maybe if I can free Eira from whatever binds her, I can bring out some good from this."

A shrill laugh rang through the quiet air of the forest, just as sunlight began to break through the canopy of trees. A shiver traveled down Tobias's spine. Without waiting, he drew his sword from its sheath and stepped between Maven and the source of the laugh.

"Free me?" Eira's voice called from deeper within the forest, followed by a dry chuckle. "How cute."

She dropped from a tree only a few feet away from Tobias, landing perfectly on her feet. Several new knives gleamed in the morning light, strapped to the belt around her waist. They looked as wicked as her smile and as sharp as her glare.

As he always did in her presence, Tobias froze up. Ice cold fear crawled across his heart, and he could do nothing but stare at her as she reached for one of her daggers.

Only then did he catch sight of it. It was faint in the sunlight, but it was still there.

The gleam of a golden thread, wound tightly around her wrist. As soon as he saw it, however, it vanished again.

He inhaled sharply. Eira was entangled in someone's magic.

12

PUZZLE PIECES AND POISON

"I'D LIKE TO THANK YOU all for leading me straight to Aviva. I must admit, I was really at a loss with how to get to her and all. Getting the spellbook was easy, but locating Aviva was proving to be too difficult for me alone," Eira taunted, drawing one of her daggers from the belt. She spun the blade around her fingers. "I suppose that's what idiots are for, isn't it? Doing the hard work for you?" Her smile grew wider as her gaze landed on Kase. "You were the easiest to manipulate. I could say anything with regards to Aviva, *and you'd believe it.*"

Pulling her staff out of the air, Maven rushed past Tobias and straight for Eira. Eira leered down at her, raising her knife, but Maven didn't even flinch. She drew a set of runes in the air with her finger, and Eira froze mid-strike. Thick silver thread wound around her, binding her hands and feet together. Maven closed her fingers into a fist around the thread and yanked on it, dragging Eira to her knees at Maven's feet.

Tobias paused, looking back at the same place where Maven had been standing only a minute before. Then he turned his focus back to her again.

She wasn't a High Summoner for nothing, it seemed. For the moment, he was glad that she had dropped her issue with Aviva.

"Eira," Maven ground out, her voice low. Magic crackled in the air around her, flashing like lightning at her fingertips. "I believe I have seen enough."

"What could you have seen from the comfort of your palace?" Eira sneered, her eyes flashing. "And what makes you think your magic can bind me?"

"My magic binds *all*."

At this, Eira barked a laugh. With the flick of her wrist, Maven's silver threads snapped and Eira leapt to her feet again. Maven stumbled back, her face twisting as if she had been struck.

"Your magic is nothing compared to that of my companion's," Eira teased. With one smooth motion, she swept the younger girl's legs out from under her.

While Maven scrambled to her feet, Arayna lunged toward Eira with a howl, slicing her claw-like nails in an arc in front of her. Eira dodged, quickly returning the strike with a swift kick to Arayna's midsection.

Eira rushed toward Aviva, her dagger raised. With a flourishing wave of her arm, Aviva summoned her staff again, holding the shaft across her body to protect herself. Eira didn't stop, thrusting her dagger forward. Kase leapt in front of her and blocked the strike with his sword. Gritting his teeth, he shoved her away and slashed in a forward arc. Eira jumped back with a gasp, just barely dodging the edge of his blade. Without giving Eira a chance to recover, Arayna tackled her and threw her to the ground, pinning her down.

Oliver fumbled with his bow, shakily aiming for Eira. He drew the string back just barely. "Hold her, Arayna."

Tobias clenched his aching jaw, watching Eira struggle and thrash beneath Arayna's grip. The thread of gold he had seen before wasn't visible anymore, but something wasn't right.

Unease hung over his mind like a heavy, gray cloud—the calm before the storm.

"You don't have combat experience, do you?" he asked, glancing at Maven.

She shook her head, tightening her grip on the red body of her staff.

Pursing his lips, Tobias drew his sword from its sheath, wincing at the scraping sound it produced. "It isn't safe for you to stay here. Take Aviva and Uriah with you and go find Smoke. He'll protect you. The rest of us can hold Eira off."

Maven hesitated. Something flickered in her silver eyes—the faintest look of defiance dancing beneath the surface—but she nodded. Turning on her heel, she dashed toward Aviva, taking her by the arm and pulling her away. Aviva's gaze remained fixed on Kase, but she allowed herself to be pulled along. Uriah followed without prompting, shepherding the two girls back to the line of trees. Tobias could only hope Maven would have the sense to refrain from trying to capture Aviva again while they were separated from the group.

Swallowing his own fear, Tobias approached Kase, pointing the tip of his sword at Eira, who struggled against Arayna's hold.

For a brief moment, Eira's gaze flicked up to Tobias's face. Her expression hardened as she looked away. She wrenched one of her wrists free, grabbing hold of her knife, and slashed the blade across Arayna's cheek. She yelped and fell backward, pressing a hand to the wound as blood oozed from it. The thief shoved herself up, but Arayna pinned her again with a growl. Blood seeped from the wound, smeared across her skin by her fingers, but the glare in her stormy eyes was as fierce as ever. Tobias stiffened even though she wasn't looking at him.

"Arayna!" Oliver cried from farther back. He pulled the string back to his jaw. "Don't move another inch, Eira."

Arayna wrinkled her nose, her lip curling slightly to reveal her pointed canines. "I thought I smelled poison," she spat. Her gaze flicked to Kase and Tobias. "One scratch from this blade and you'll be dead."

Tobias stared dumbly at Arayna, his heart leaping into his throat. "But Arayna—"

"You don't have to worry about her, *Tobias*," Eira cut in, her voice dripping with malice. "Her Beast Curse grants her immunity to most poisons—this one included. The unfortunate price is her disgusting appearance."

Arayna bristled, her ears flattening back against her head. A deep growl reverberated from the back of her throat. "Maybe I should give you a taste of your own medicine. You may look pretty, but will that protect you from your poison? Didn't think so."

"Oh, I'm not immune at all." Eira smiled sweetly.

She twisted her arm, wrenching it free of Arayna's grasp. Drawing back her legs, she threw a kick to Arayna's gut. With a winded gasp, Arayna released her, wrapping her arms around her middle as she struggled to catch her breath. Now free, Eira scrambled away and twisted, driving the blade of her dagger deep into Kase's thigh.

"And neither is he," she finished.

Eira wrenched her knife free, shooting to her feet and dancing away as Oliver's arrow let loose. It struck the ground by her foot, but she kicked it away before ice burst from the tip. Kase buckled the moment the knife was free, letting out a sharp cry as he cradled his leg. Arayna cried out and crawled toward him, tearing back the ripped fabric around the wound. Black marks had already spread out from the cut like cracks in his skin. The sight squeezed Tobias's heart, and he could do nothing but stare in disbelief and shake his head helplessly.

"Venen poison," he breathed, though his voice came out choked. "It's poison from a Celestial Class dragon." His grip tightened on the hilt of his sword, his mind reeling. The world rocked beneath his feet, despite that he wasn't the one suffering from the deadly poison.

Kase was.

With a sharp inhale, Eira backed away. She spun around and bolted into the forest.

"I'll kill her!" Arayna screeched, shooting to her feet.

Oliver caught her wrist before she could take off. "No," he snapped. "No, I won't let you. Go get Aviva. I'll stay here with Kase."

"Are you going to let her go?" Arayna hissed as she glared down at Oliver, her ears flattened against her head. "I could kill her right now. I'll tear her to pieces!"

"I'll go after her," Tobias cut in, glancing between the two of them. "Send Arayna to fetch Aviva and I'll handle Eira. We don't want her circling back around for the book."

Arayna flinched. With one last glance at Oliver, she wrenched her wrist free. "Fine." Turning on her heel, she disappeared into the underbrush.

As soon as she was gone, regret cracked Tobias's resolve. He would rather go find Aviva—the thought of going after Eira alone made his palms sweat and his hands tremble. Though there was no wound from his previous encounter with her, the spot on his neck where her blade had touched began to sting. She had tried to kill him multiple times before, and this time, she had gone so far as to stab a former friend.

His gaze landed on Kase, who pressed a thick cloth to the wound in his leg, Oliver's hand against his to add pressure. Sweat beaded Kase's forehead, and his skin had already gone pale. Blood soaked the cloth.

How fast did the poison work? How long did Kase have? Tobias wracked his brain. Though he knew the poison spread black marks across the skin as it worked its way into the bloodstream, he didn't know how quickly it did that. But he was certain time was not on their side.

Swallowing his fear, Tobias slid his sword back into its sheath before he dashed off. Eira's steps had left a trail in the soft dirt, easy to follow despite the forest growth around it. Sunlight filtered through the canopy, yet it was bleak and gray. His feet pounded against the ground as he ran, the world blurring around him as the wind whipped past. The fires of anger lit in his core, searing through the cold fear that pinned him before.

It wasn't long before she came into view. Eira cast a glance over her shoulder and caught sight of him. Her eyes widened as he threw his hand out toward her. He grabbed a fistful of her dark brown hair.

She shrieked, her foot colliding with the root of a tree and sending her falling face-first into the dirt. His grip loosened as she fell, throwing her to the ground without his support. Tobias came to a halt, looking down at his fist, where a few of her hairs clung to his fingers. He shook them away and drew his sword. Eira rolled over to face him, her eyes wide and her lips quivering. Pointing his sword at her chest, he planted his foot on her wrist as she reached for the collection of daggers at her waist.

"Where do you think you're going?" he hissed. Adrenaline rushed through him, making his hands tremble. Or maybe that was all that remained of the fear he had clung to before.

"Let me go!" she cried, her eyes flashing.

"I'm not going to do that. Don't think I don't know what you could do if I let you wander free."

Her breath hitched as tears gathered in her eyes. "What do you want with me? I don't have your book anymore."

"Come back with me," he said. "Tell me how we can fix this o-or give me the antidote."

"I don't *have* anything like that!" she bit back. "And even if I did, I can't go back there."

"You have to!" Tobias snapped. The tip of his sword touched

her chest, though his heart shuttered at the idea of piercing it through her flesh. "You have to have *something*!"

She shook her head furiously, tears trailing down her cheeks. Covered in dirt and scratches, reduced to a sniveling mess, she looked nothing like the confident thief who had swiped the spellbook from his hands only a few short days ago. Now, she was pitiful and small, at the mercy of his blade.

"Nothing," she replied, her voice breaking. "He told me to get rid of Kase!"

"*He?* Who is this person, Eira?"

Like it did the day she stole the spellbook, a golden light touched her eyes as her breathing evened out. A slight laugh tumbled from her lips and her tears stopped flowing. "Curious?" she asked. "I'm sure he'd be happy to have your assistance as well."

Tobias narrowed his eyes. Every time the gold came into her eyes, Eira changed. She went from frightened and confused to confident, cocky, and… slightly unhinged. It had been there when she broke free of Maven's spell, and it was possible it had been there when she stabbed Kase and he had just missed it.

Questions made his head spin, his brow furrowing as his thoughts slowly engulfed his mind. Slowly, without fully comprehending it, he moved his sword away from her.

She laughed. "I thought you learned your lesson already. Stay focused on your enemy in a fight, Tobias."

The meaning behind her words clicked in his mind a little too late. Her free hand grabbed hold of a knife. Narrowing her eyes, her lips set in a firm frown, she summoned the threads of gold magic to her fingertips again. An unseen force knocked him back, slamming him into a tree. He gasped as the wind was knocked out of him and dropped to his knees, wheezing.

His thoughts flickered like the edges of his blackened vision. Dimly aware of Eira still standing nearby with her dagger unsheathed, he reached out for his sword. His fingers brushed the hilt, buried in the tall grass. Grabbing hold of it, he pushed himself to his feet and faced her, stepping away from the tree to avoid being thrown into it again.

The threads wove around her fingers, sparking and dancing with the suffocating pressure of magic. Her lips curved in a smile, one that was cruel and mocking. "It's a shame really that Kase dragged you into this. He should have left you alone, and you should have let me go."

In the blink of an eye, she vanished. Only the flicker of gold remained where she had been, but it too began to fade away. Tobias tensed, searching the dense undergrowth for a sign of her. Cautiously, he stepped forward.

She appeared in front of him again, standing toe-to-toe with him. His heart leapt to his throat, and he stumbled back, but the gold threads had wound around him and pinned him in place.

"Maybe this time, you'll learn to stay away," she said, her voice low and words slow.

As soon as the final word left her lips, she plunged the blade of her dagger into his abdomen.

Pain tore through his entire body, shooting toward his chest and gripping his heart in fiery agony. He gasped, stumbling back as she pulled away and released him from the magic. He barely registered collapsing against the dirt. His vision flickered; he could do nothing but bite down on his tongue to stop from screaming.

Eira's boots scuffed as she turned, her blade sliding against her sheath as she put it away. "Goodbye, Tobias," she said, before she took off once more.

He didn't even have a chance to call out her name. Darkness consumed his vision, and his mind went blank. The agony faded out, washed over by numbing, cold darkness.

13

HEAD DRAGONBORN

Eira returned to the crumbling castle of Sheniir, glancing over her shoulder for what felt like the hundredth time. Still nothing. Her skin crawled with unease all the same. She shivered, tilting her head downward to gaze at the red blotches across her fingers and gloves. She could still feel the resistance of tensed muscles against her blade as she drove it through Kase's leg. For just a moment, there was sympathy in his face when he looked at her, as if he saw the golden threads that tugged her along.

Then there was Tobias, an innocent soul who carried a sword but had clearly never been forced to use it until she showed up. He was only a year younger than her, but there was so much light in his vibrant green eyes. Her scalp ached from having her hair pulled, yet she couldn't find the will to ignite the flames of anger within her. He was desperate to save Kase, and she knew she would have done the same.

Tears stung her eyes, and her breath hitched. She stopped in the entryway, covering her mouth as a whimper escaped her.

There could be no weakness in front of the one she served. She could show no sign that she might have strayed from him.

The mere thought of it made her throat tighten, as if his golden threads had wound around it and pulled taut.

Maybe she should have strayed. She should have run away and not come back to the castle. He had ordered her to kill Kase —once her close friend—and anyone else who would get in her way. Once, she had been willing to do anything he asked of her. Now, looking again at the red stains on her gloves, she didn't know what to do. It seemed like such a simple request when it was spoken aloud, but the action itself twisted her mind painfully.

When she had first come to him, he had only promised power in return for her help. All he asked her to do was steal, but stealing had quickly become something much darker. Something she knew wasn't right.

But she couldn't stop.

She took a deep breath and wiped her tears. Taking a moment to steel herself and regain her composure, she pushed those thoughts aside. She could sort through them later.

She picked her way across the dirty floors, littered with broken parts of the crumbling castle walls and other things she dared not ask the origin of. Wrapping her arms around herself to block out the chill of the autumn evening, she frowned and allowed her mind to drift off to distract her from the sickening red blotches on her gloves.

Why couldn't he have picked someplace warmer? she grumbled, hiding her hands from her view. The cold allowed for an easy distraction; complaining came naturally, after all. *We could set up a base in someplace with actual, functioning walls, perhaps? I really don't understand—*

"Why have you returned here?" a deep voice questioned, echoing in the expanse of the throne room. "I didn't call you."

Eira flinched. She still stood within the doorway of the room, several yards away from his shadowed form upon the throne, but even that was too close for her liking. Standing up straighter, she cleared her throat and studied the cracks that spiderwebbed the stone floor.

"I know," she said, her voice breaking. She winced at its hoarseness. "Aviva was indeed beneath that barrier, and the key to getting through it was the… invisible guy who was holding her book, as you suspected. Kase and his group are there with her. As for this Calix you seek, he wasn't with them. In fact, I haven't even heard them mention him. I'm not sure even Kase knows where he is."

She curled her fingers into tight fists. Memories flashed before her eyes, images of Kase's look of hurt and surprise when she stabbed him. She shook her head. "Are you sure that you know what you're talking about…?" she whispered, ducking her head. She twisted the hem of her blouse between her fingers. "Kase would never—"

A slam made her jump back. The figure rose from his seat on the throne, his golden eyes flashing in the dark. "I know what I'm speaking of!" he snapped. As he stepped forward, the light of the evening sun fell on his face through the cracks in the crumbling roof. Black scales gleamed in the light, covering most of his pale skin like a hideous scar. Though his face was that of an ordinary man's, most of it was hidden beneath his scales. Two black horns rose up from his head, blending in with coal-black hair that stuck up unevenly.

When he met her eye, she flinched and looked away.

"Kase isn't at all who you think he is. He's a pawn in my way, an obstacle that blocks me from my prize. He protects something that has been allowed freedom for far too long. The goddess's will must be carried out—both Kase and his traitorous dragon have stood in the way of that long enough."

Instinctively, Eira reached for her daggers. She stopped herself before she could draw one, however, knowing it would only make him lash out. Against him, she had no hope of winning. Powerful magic thrummed in the air around him, and the sword leaning against the arm of the throne gleamed wickedly in the sunlight. Instead, she kept her hands at her sides, trying to hide her trembling.

"I'm sorry. I'm the one who doesn't understand, Head Dragonborn."

The ancient creature, the leader of the servants of Selini, managed a grin. With a flurry of his cloak, he returned to the throne atop the dais. His steps echoed against the stone, breaking the eerie silence of the castle. Behind the throne, a wall of black and green scales shifted. A low rumble echoed before the monster lay still once more. Eira waited with bated breath until the dragonborn sat down again. She didn't wish to anger him nor the dragon he kept as company.

Growing up on the outskirts of Calistie, a kingdom that had always stood against the will of Selini, she had heard the stories whispered from every mouth. The dragonborn had killed countless people, nearly wiping her kingdom from the face of the earth. The castle she stood in now was one this dragonborn in particular had conquered all on his own. His sword had slain many, and his magic had thrown the castle of Sheniir into an eternity of emptiness, left to crumble slowly as the years passed by.

Yet his name… it flickered in her memory, resting just out of reach.

"You have done well so far, thief," he said, lifting a hand and combing it through his black hair, revealing more inky scales splattered across his forehead. "Though I worry about the weakness of your human heart. You failed to bring back the book, you failed to capture the Mage… but you *did* kill Kase, didn't you?"

Eira stiffened again. Her mouth opened and closed several times, but no words ever came out. She didn't want to admit it, even to herself. Her heart raced at the thought of being wrong. "Yes," she finally said. "Yes, him and the one who had the book. The brother of the Dragon Rider you worried about."

"Ah, him. I forgot about him." Humming to himself, the dragonborn drummed his fingers against the arm of the throne. "Well, I suppose you deserve a reward for accomplishing one of the tasks I assigned you."

The dragonborn lifted a hand. Gold threads appeared in his fingers, tied tightly around Eira's hands, neck, and feet. He tugged, pulling Eira forward. Her legs moved of their own accord, despite her attempts to dig in her heels.

When she reached the final step of the dais, she stopped, and the threads fell slack once more. They vanished, whisked away by the swirling black aura around the dragonborn. He grinned down at her, amusement dancing in his golden eyes.

"You've done well so far, Eira," he said. Leaning forward, he placed his fingers to her forehead.

Magic rushed from his hand into her body, coiling around her heart like a snake. Eira looked down at her hands, flexing her fingers. The same power danced at her fingertips, sparking and crackling. With a gasp, she pulled back.

Magic. She had her own magic. The thought sent a thrill through her, a warm buzzing that brought a smile to her face. Awe and wonder ate away at her fear until it slipped easily through her fingers.

"Now Aviva won't be a problem for you," the dragonborn said, his voice even and smooth. "But, to help you stay focused, I want you to take this."

Eira turned back to him, curling her fingers into a fist to stop the flow of magic. "What is it?"

He rose from his seat and held out a necklace to her, placing it over her head so that it rested against her chest. It was a thin gold chain with a rough green stone at the end. Eira blinked, looking down at it.

"Just something. A gift, you could call it," he said with a

softer smile this time, though something dangerous danced in his gaze. He sat back down again, leaning against one arm of the throne. "Now, go on. You know what to do."

Eira dipped her head to him, reaching up to grip the pendant. She made her way out of the throne room. When she had come to the castle, something dark and anxious had hung over her. Now, her mind was clear and empty of fear. He had given her a gift, and she could not fail him. Whatever the dragonborn said, she would do.

With magic in her possession, it made it that much simpler. Now, there was nothing she couldn't do.

Just wait a little longer, she promised herself, though some part of her hoped the dragonborn would hear her sincerity as well. *I'll get that spellbook back. Aviva can't hide it forever.*

Brimming over with confidence, with no show of fear or uncertainty, she left the old castle of Sheniir and made her way out into the world again.

PART THREE
THE THIEF'S FEAR

"She put up quite an impressive front,
but nothing could hide the fear she felt deep down."

14

SOMETHING MORE

A DULL THROB IN TOBIAS'S side dragged him from the darkness. His eyes fluttered open, flooding his vision with bright light from above. Groaning, he rolled over and shut his eyes. The ache turned into a sharp pain, like fiery needles stabbing through his abdomen.

Reality crashed down on him, dragging up his memories. The forest, Eira's poisoned dagger, the wound in his side. He sat bolt upright with a gasp. Sweat plastered his hair to his brow, and he raked his fingers through it. Eira had stabbed him. She got away. Kase had been poisoned.

Kase had died.

Scrambling to free himself of a heavy quilt, he swung his legs over the side of a bed and leapt to his feet. Black spots danced in his vision, and the floor swayed beneath him.

"Easy there." Hands grabbed his shoulders to steady him, easing him back into the bed. "That was quite the awakening. Dramatic, aren't you?"

When his vision cleared, Tobias looked up to see Uriah standing over him. As soon as he was settled again, Uriah released him and stepped back. Clicking his tongue, he crossed his arms and looked down on Tobias with a faint glow in his golden eyes.

"It's just a little scratch," Uriah went on to say, one brow cocked in amusement. "Not like you'll die."

Little scratch? Tobias pressed a hand to where the wound was. Needles erupted in his side again. It felt like Eira had cut a hole in his torso and left him for dead in the forest, all alone and bleeding out.

Maybe he was being a bit dramatic.

He shoved that aside. "Kase," he said, his throat and mouth like sandpaper. He cleared his throat. "What happened? What happened to Kase?"

Uriah's amused grin faltered. He jerked a thumb to the bed on the left of Tobias's own. "Kase is right there. He's fine. Maven drew the poison out of his body; Aviva closed your wound as well as his." Sighing, almost wistfully, he turned his gaze to the floor. "Having magic really is an amazing thing."

Tobias swallowed hard, the spittle scraping down his throat. Dreading what he might see, despite Uriah's reassurance, he turned his head to the left. Sure enough, Kase slept peacefully in the second bed, tucked safely under a pile of blankets. Tobias breathed a sigh of relief and rested his head back against the pillow again.

Kase was safe.

"Where are we?" he asked, finally allowing his gaze to sweep across the room. It was small and quaint. The two beds were pushed up against one wall, each with a nightstand beside them. On the opposite wall, there was a row of cabinets and a countertop. Faint moonlight drifted in through a crack in the white-curtained window.

"Aviva's cottage," Uriah replied, propping himself against the wall beside the window. "You could say this is the first-aid treatment room. It was kind of dusty when we brought you in here, but it looks nice now." He paused. "Nicer now that the bloody stuff is all gone. You bled all over one set of sheets, you know."

"Sorry." Tobias glanced down at his torso. The bandages wrapped around his wound were clean now, and it didn't hurt as much as before. If he thought for too long though, he could feel the frigid touch of her blade sliding through his flesh. He shuddered and dropped the blankets back in place.

The door opened with a click. Aviva stepped in, her staff in hand, Oliver trailing close behind her. Her gaze swept over the room, drifting first toward Kase and then to Tobias. When she met his eye, her face lit up, lifting the crease of worry from her brow. Handing her staff to Uriah, she exchanged a quick word with him before waving her hand and dismissing him. He shut the door behind him.

"How do you feel?" Aviva asked as she sat on the edge of Tobias's bed. Her hand brushed his forehead, sweeping his bangs out of the way.

He shrugged, forcing a slight smile. "I'm... not dead?"

At that, she laughed. "Well, that's good." She fixed the blankets and smiled softly. "Nothing was severely damaged—nothing I couldn't fix, anyway. I'm sure it will scar as it heals." Sighing, she said, "It's been a long time since I last used healing magic. I guess I'm a little out of practice. I didn't used to leave scars at all."

An awkward moment of silence fell over the room. Tobias barely even dared to breathe in case it disturbed the thoughtful, forlorn look on her face. In the back of his mind, he knew it would be right of him to say something, but nothing came to mind. Instead, he fidgeted with his hands in his lap.

"A scar will be good for you," Oliver chimed in, saving him. He lingered near the opposite wall of the room, where a countertop was covered in various first aid supplies. He picked up a bowl left behind by Uriah and inspected its contents. Wrinkling his nose, he set it back down and turned his gaze to Tobias again. "Your pride may be ruined, though."

Tobias winced at the memory of Oliver's scars. A jagged mark down one shoulder, which he had intended to use to frighten them away from Arayna. Maybe he was bitter that he had failed in that regard but left both Kase and Tobias with the image of the scar in their minds anyway. Perhaps that was why his amber eyes flashed so angrily.

Aviva turned to Oliver, her lips set in another frown. "I cannot heal broken pride, so we'll hope it doesn't make him as irritable as you, Oliver."

Oliver narrowed his eyes. "What I went through was different. I have every right to be bitter about it." He heaved himself up onto the countertop and sat down, his hand finding its way to his scar again, concealed by his tunic and outer coat.

"It wasn't pride I broke," he murmured, "but trust."

Tobias sank farther down into the blankets, his mind reeling. He knew what he had broken, but he wasn't sure it was ever mended in the first place.

Picking at the blanket, he tried not to imagine what Talia would do if she saw him wounded. He could picture the worry on her face and the speech she would give him about how helpless he was without her. She would scold him for letting it happen in the first place, and she would shadow him for weeks on end. There was something painful about that thought, and he both longed for it and dreaded it.

If she happened to hear of what he had found himself caught up in since leaving home, there would be no way to put her mind at ease. His chance of proving that she didn't need to put her life on hold just to watch over him would be utterly destroyed.

The fact that Aviva leapt to defend him from Oliver pricked his heart. Once, he had the wit to defend himself—wit enough to spare, Talia would say. But there, as Aviva and

Oliver continued to exchange jabs with each other, he knew. He couldn't even muster a bit of wit anymore. Not that he really needed to. Wit wouldn't protect him from magic and daggers.

But it was how he shielded himself from others.

Aviva straightened and folded her hands together in her lap. She turned back to Tobias, ending her conversation with Oliver despite his indignant look. Tobias stamped out the sulky feeling and faced Aviva with a neutral expression, hoping his weariness didn't show through.

"High Summoner Maven returned to the palace," she said, as if finishing her report of what had passed while Tobias was unconscious. "She's worried about how easily Eira broke away from her magic, and she thinks it's connected to the forbidden arts. To dark magic. It seems that, for the time being, she has decided to let me off the hook."

Tobias sat up more, ignoring the pain that spiked in his abdomen. "You think she's right, don't you? About these... forbidden arts?" The idea of it sent a shudder crawling down his spine.

She hesitated. Weariness seeped through her expression. Her skin had grown paler, her gaze duller than when he first met her. Dark circles hung under her eyes, and her hands trembled ever so slightly when she lifted them. Tobias was not an expert in magic—in fact, he knew next to nothing about it—but even he could guess Aviva had used a lot of it to heal him and Kase. His chest tightened and he sucked in a breath.

He had been careless when he rushed after Eira. If he had only been more aware, none of this would have happened. If he had only been *more* than what he was. Perhaps if he had magic of his own, he wouldn't have been so easily fooled. If he had more experience, Eira wouldn't have gotten the better of him.

With a soft sigh, he turned away. Frustration made a tight frown on his lips, nagging him with the same repeated thoughts.

He should have been *more.* More useful. More careful. More aware. More prepared.

Aviva lowered her head, pressing a fisted hand to her forehead. "I'm so, so sorry," she whispered. "I dragged you into something you had no part in, without a reason or even a good excuse. I was a coward, and now I've hurt you and Kase. All because I wasn't enough."

Tobias jolted in surprise, puzzled to hear his thoughts mirrored in her words. Slowly, his frustration ebbed away as he looked at her. When she was hunched over, her eyes screwed shut and her blonde hair in a tangled, unkempt mess, she seemed small and pitiful. Even her magic shrank back from the air, its presence nothing more than a faint brush against him.

How could a Mage have the same doubts that he did? How could someone so powerful be so fragile?

Oliver grunted as he pushed himself off the countertop. "If you're so ashamed that you brought him here, it's time to send him home. He could have been killed, and things are only going to get worse if we pursue this."

Aviva's head shot up, throwing a glare in his direction. He merely shrugged, his expression flat.

Stiffly, Aviva rose from the bed. As soon as her feet touched the ground, The iridescent green snake appeared loosely curled around her neck, its wings folded against its body. It flicked its forked tongue at him. *Iila*, he recalled.

Aviva stroked its head before glancing at Tobias again. "Get some rest. You'll need to regain your strength."

He nodded as she began to walk away. He caught a glimpse of her when she stopped at Kase's bedside and bent down to press a kiss to his hand. Iila hissed in protest, but she ignored the snake and straightened again. As she opened the door, urgency welled up inside Tobias and he sat up straighter. "Aviva?"

She paused in the doorway and glanced back at him. Oliver slipped out of the room alone.

He swallowed hard, twisting the blanket between his fingers. "I saw these… threads around Eira," he said. "They were gold, barely visible unless I caught them at certain angles. I—I think they were magic. She was tangled in them like some kind of… *puppet*. Do you know anything about that?"

Darkness crossed her expression as it pulled down into a tight frown. Pressing her fist to her lip, she turned to the door. "I will look into it. Thank you."

Tobias rolled over to face the wall, his wound aching in protest. Soon afterward, Aviva blew all the candles out. She left silently, though the thoughtful look on her expression as she turned away was enough to make his chest ache. If even Aviva was disturbed by what he saw, he was in over his head.

Moonlight washed the room in a soft, silvery glow. Tobias glared at the wall across from him. The floral-patterned wallpaper seemed too elegant for the raging storm in his mind. Bitterly, he knew Oliver was right. It was time for him to go home. It had been silly to think he could do something more. To think that he could both return the spellbook and catch his thief was ridiculous. The least he could do was pass on what he knew, but that wasn't enough to fix anything. Aviva and Maven were wrong—he wasn't gifted.

Without meaning to, his mind drifted to his sister again, and he buried his face in the pillow. He hated that he always went straight to her but still didn't look to anyone else.

All he wanted in that moment was to hear her voice—even if she would only scold him for being stupid. He needed to be told.

"Tobias," he remembered she would say, with an edge to her voice like no one else's. In the memory, she stood over him with the blade of her sword pointed at his chest, narrowing her emerald eyes as she stared down at him. Her pale face flushed

ever so slightly in anger. *"You're too quick to give up on things. If nothing ever challenged you, how could you learn anything new? How do you expect to be something more if you don't even try?"*

But I did try, he'd argue.

Even without her there, he knew what her retort would be. *"Not hard enough."*

He frowned, hating that she was right. He fumbled for the table beside him, patting the smooth, wooden surface until his fingers brushed against the key that normally hung around his neck. He scooped it up and brought it closer, running his thumb across the jagged teeth. It smelled sharply of metal, though it looked as if it had been recently scrubbed down. *I guess I got blood on this, too.*

"Do you intend to sulk forever?" the memory of Talia continued. She stepped away from him, dropping her sword. *"What, because you screwed up, you think that's it for you? You have to learn somehow, don't you?"*

In the memory, he knew he was staring down at the blisters on his hands, crying over the weight of his sword. He shoved it aside. There was no comparison between blisters and thieves who liked stabbing old friends and new enemies. If he went home, he would be wrapped in the safety of familiarity. No magic could touch him there, and there was nothing to fear except the distant howl of the dragonborn.

He wasn't like Talia. He wasn't like Kase. He wasn't even like Aviva, who shared similar doubts and fears.

He was just the stranger who happened to pick up Aviva's book. He wasn't a key to anything, nor gifted with any useful power.

And he certainly wasn't someone his sister could be proud of.

15

A PROMISE OF PROTECTION

A FEW DAYS PASSED with the same routine: Tobias drifted in and out of sleep, only awoken whenever Aviva came in to check on him or when someone brought food to him. Sometimes, Arayna would come and sit beside Kase's bed, but she never said a word. At one point, Aviva's snake familiar, Iila, kept watch over Kase and Tobias. Its narrowed eyes never left him. He didn't sleep much that day and instead often found himself staring back at the snake to show he wasn't intimated. He could only entertain himself that way for so many minutes, though.

For the most part, he found himself constantly replaying Eira's attack, analyzing it from every angle. Some days, he gripped the key to his house so hard that his hands began to hurt, but he desperately clung to the reminder of home. If he left now, he would never have to deal with Eira and her magic again.

And yet, the more he thought about it, the more he was drawn to the panicked fear in her expression. There was real desperation in her voice when she claimed that someone else had ordered her to kill Kase.

"Do you intend to sulk forever?" the memory of Talia asked once again.

He still had no response.

Finally, Aviva dismissed him from bed. His wound had completely healed, leaving behind only a faint scar as proof that it had ever been there at all. When he rose to his feet, he stood easily on his own. He turned to Aviva. "I can't thank you enough," he said, dipping his head in a slight bow to her. "I'm sorry to have caused you so much trouble."

Aviva chuckled, a sheepish smile finding its way to her face. "It was no trouble at all. Truthfully, I should be the one thanking you. The others would never have been able to get here without you. I heard from Maven that she had to use you to unlock the barrier, but there's a bit more to it."

Puzzled, Tobias sank back onto the bed. "There is?"

She nodded. "No matter how much anyone searched, they would never have been able to make it here without you."

"Right." His heart sank a little, and he clasped his hands together in his lap. "Because of the book."

"Because of you." Before he could argue anymore, she turned away to check on Kase. "The world of magic is complicated. Try not to let yourself get too worked up over it."

She was no longer looking at him, but he nodded intently anyway. "Of course," he murmured as he made his way toward the door. "Thank you."

He cast a passing glance at Kase as he came to the door. Same as ever, Kase slept soundly, his expression wrapped in an eerie sense of peace. Throughout the whole time Tobias was recovering, Kase had only woken once or twice, but he was hardly even *awake* then. It was more like sleepwalking, only he never left his bed. He would shoot upright, muttering to himself about nothing in particular. Each time, he was quickly soothed back to sleep by Aviva's magic.

Today, the state of deathlike sleep remained.

Aviva looked up and, upon catching him staring, gave one of her reassuring smiles. "He just needs more time to rest," she said. "He'll be alright."

Tobias chewed the inside of his cheek, inhaling a deep breath through his nose before exhaling slowly through the mouth. "How much longer?"

At that, Aviva looked away quickly. She squeezed Kase's hand. "I don't know for sure. It's beyond my power at this point. Smoke is asking to keep him asleep while he mends the bond." Sighing, she released his hand and rose to her feet, smoothing down the front of her forest green blouse. "I'm leaving that to Smoke. I don't... I don't really know anything about Riders and dragon bonds."

"I know some," Tobias said, turning away from the door. Despite being consistently rejected by the dragons his sister offered him, Tobias's fascination with dragon bonds had never slacked. "Talia says that Riders or dragons will sometimes temporarily close off their bonds if one party is experiencing pain. It's to protect the other from harm. I guess if it was cut off hastily, it could have been damaged." *That doesn't explain why Smoke would ask for Kase to remain unconscious though.*

Shaking his head, he gripped the doorknob and twisted it, pulling the door open. "Well, I'll get out of your way," he said, dipping his head slightly. "Thank you again."

Aviva offered a wave but said nothing more, her brow furrowed in thought. Satisfied to have been able to help explain, he closed the door softly. With a sigh, he sank back against the wood.

A heavy knot formed in his chest, one thick with worry and too stubborn to be untangled by anything but Kase's recovery. Was Kase afraid of the poison hurting Smoke? Or was Smoke trying to prevent it from damaging their bond? Or was there something else—maybe something connected to the magic he didn't understand—going on behind the scenes?

Glancing down at the key in his hand, Tobias pushed away from the door. He tied the cord of the key around his neck and tucked it back under his shirt. The knot would unravel with time. Hanging around the room would only put him in Aviva's way, which was the last place he wanted to be. He had caused enough trouble for her already.

When his thoughts were settled and neatly shoved into the back of his mind to be unpacked later, the sound of chatter drifted toward him. He had stepped out into an open study area with windows lining the opposite wall allowing sunlight to flood the room. A desk was situated near the windows, nearly buried beneath scrolls, papers, and books. Much of them were bound in the same dyed leather as the spellbook he had held for so many years. Curious, he approached the desk and flipped through a pastel blue book perched near the edge of the desk. It was written in the same delicate yet meaningless symbols, though every other page revealed an illustration of a different flower. After flipping through a few, he set the book down and closed it.

Outside the window, a garden stretched from the edge of the house to the line of trees. An array of flowers populated it, in all different colors and shapes, yet he didn't know any of their names. His gaze drifted across the garden, eventually landing on the source of chatter that floated toward him

Arayna stood by herself outside, laughing and calling back to the forest. Bewildered, Tobias left the cluttered study and headed outside. The door creaked on its hinges as it swung open, and Arayna immediately spun around.

"Tobias!" She ran to greet him, crushing him in a tight hug and lifting him several inches off the ground. He gasped at her strength, attempting to wriggle free. With a laugh, she set him back down again, bouncing on the balls of her feet. "It's good to see you awake and moving again," she said, grinning up at him.

He matched her smile as a bit of warmth began to spread

over the worry that clung to his heart. "I'm glad to be out of bed too." He gave her a pat on the shoulder, wincing at how awkward and stiff the motion was. She laughed again, her ears twitching slightly.

Oliver and Uriah emerged from the forest, pushing and shoving to get ahead of each other. Leaves and bits of mud clung to Uriah's hair and clothes, and his golden eyes flashed wildly as he barked a laugh. With one quick shove, he pushed Oliver down and sprinted through the line of trees. With a shout, he pumped his fists in the air.

"I told you I could find my way back here first! I win the race. You owe me ten silvers." Grinning, he spun back around to Oliver and held out his hand, palm up.

Oliver rolled his eyes and shoved his way through the last of the brush. He buried a small object into his pocket as soon as he was free of the underbrush. "It's not a race, Uriah. You were supposed to be keeping watch. You know, looking out for Eira?" he muttered, picking a stray leaf from his hair. "But if it was a race, Arayna beat you. Don't you owe *her* ten silvers?"

Uriah glanced over his shoulder at Arayna, who had turned to face him. His gaze slid quickly over Tobias before he looked away. Hooking his arm around Oliver's shoulders to pull him in close, he dropped his voice as he continued. "Arayna doesn't understand money and numbers and stuff," he whispered, though it was loud enough that Tobias could hear it.

Arayna frowned and bounded over to Uriah, elbowing him harshly in the side. With a yelp, Uriah stumbled back. He tripped over his own feet and landed unceremoniously on his backside. Arayna stood over him, planting her fists on her hips. "I do understand money!"

"Oh yeah?" Uriah pushed himself upright, grinning up at her through his tangled, muddy mess of black hair. "How much is ten silvers worth then?"

"It's worth ten silvers, of course." Pride gleamed in her eyes as she lifted her chin high.

Oliver looked on from the distance. He arched his brow, narrowing his eyes as he folded his arms over his chest. "Maybe I should get the money," he said flatly. "I'm the only one of us that knows what to do with it."

Tobias bit down on his tongue, covering his mouth to stifle his laughter. It still spilled from his lips. All three looked up, their eyes locked on him, but he didn't mind it for once. He doubled over, trying to catch his breath between laughs.

"Breathe, Tobias, breathe!" Uriah called, struggling to get to his feet. Arayna gave him another shove, planting her foot on his chest to keep him grounded.

Oliver looked down at him again. A slight smile twitched at the corners of his mouth. "I think that counts as another loss for you. What are we at now? A total of thirty-two losses out of thirty-six rounds of spontaneous wrestling?" He tsked and whipped out a paper and pencil from a pocket in his coat. "You're really going to let a little girl beat you up like this?"

"Hey, you know better than I do that she's not just some little girl." Uriah rolled over to off-balance Arayna and sent her tumbling to the ground. He pushed himself to his feet and brushed the dirt from his clothes. "Besides, I've been going easy on her. Want me to get serious now?"

"Please do. My tally sheet is looking rather uneven."

Arayna jumped to her feet. "That would be more fun," she chirped.

When Tobias finally caught his breath, he circled around to stand with Oliver, who had backed up a few paces to give Uriah and Arayna space to play. Tobias sat down in the grass, crossing his legs and resting his elbows on his knees. Normally, he wouldn't have been as entertained with the childlike jeers and the play-fighting. At the moment, however, it was better than letting his mind wander. It gave him something to latch onto—

something that pointed away from Talia, from his dad, from home, from Eira.

"What do you think you're going to do?"

Tobias jolted, head shooting up to follow Oliver's gaze. The hunter didn't even look at him, his eyes glued to the fight and his fingers holding tightly to the paper with his tally marks. Even without meeting Oliver's eyes, or waiting for further explanation, Tobias knew what he meant. His thoughts immediately leapt back to the other day. Oliver had been quite adamant about Tobias returning home, and the more he thought about it, the more Tobias found himself agreeing. It didn't help that he had tripped himself up so much that he was having imaginary conversations with his sister, who was miles and miles away from him. She probably wasn't even thinking about him. She had students to teach, a wedding to plan, and a life of her own to live.

Yet he was using her to convince himself of his uselessness, as if she was an excuse to set him back on the path that led home.

He wrapped his arms around himself, balling his sleeves in his fists. It was strange how easily he could slip from the pleasant, light feeling of laughter. He fixed his eyes on the grass, watching as the wind toyed with it. He couldn't face Oliver anymore.

"I don't know yet," he said plainly. The truth left a bitter taste in his mouth. He hated how often he sat frozen with indecision.

Oliver crouched beside him. "Take this in the best way, but I think you should go home. You don't exactly seem..."

"Fit for adventure, thief-catching, and magic stuff?" Tobias scoffed, rolling his eyes. He rested his chin in his hands. "Yeah, believe me, I know that already." *I'm not my sister.*

Uriah screeched in defiance as Arayna pinned him again, grinning. She turned to Oliver, raising a proud thumbs-up. He smiled back at her before marking another tally on his sheet and returning his attention to Tobias.

"That's not exactly what I meant," Oliver said. With a sigh, he sat down in the grass and crossed his legs. His hand drifted to his pocket. "Is anyone ever really up for… thief-catching and magic stuff?"

Tobias opened his mouth to say that yes, some people obviously were. Like Talia, Kase, Uriah, Aviva, Arayna, and even Oliver himself. Thinking about it some more, he put Smoke and Maven on that list.

The deeper he dug into his memories, almost desperate for more he could add to the list, the more buried thoughts stirred. Old memories, steeped in blood and ringing with his screams, surfaced. Dragonborn lurked in the shadows of his mind, their eyes glowing in the dark, their fangs stained crimson. Magic flickered wildly in the air around them, tainted black with the evil that lingered in their hearts. Fear drove Tobias to take up the sword—the weapon he had never brought into a fight yet carried with him always.

He was a writer, a man who puzzled over words all day. Of course he didn't fit on that list.

He clamped his mouth shut, swallowing hard. Quickly, he smothered the thought again, hoping to bury it so deeply that it would never return. Perhaps he was projecting that horrifying image where it didn't belong.

Yet it was the reason for everything.

He ran a hand through his hair. He knew his list of people really weren't ready for it either. In the face of the dragonborn from his memories, Talia could do nothing but tremble and hide with him. In the present, Eira had proved to be one step ahead of him and his friends from the very start. She dragged them around in circles like dogs chasing after a treat in their master's hand. Neither incident was a good judge of what he could and could not handle, were they?

Oliver frowned. "What are you thinking about? I wasn't really asking for an answer, you know."

"But you're right." Tobias sat up, brushing his hair back from his face. "Aren't you trying to say nobody is ever ready for what life gives them? If that's true, then why should I be so worried about it?"

He wasn't sure he agreed entirely, but from Oliver's perspective, perhaps there was nothing to worry about. Kase was fine, the spellbook was back in Aviva's possession, so what had Tobias so riled up if not the longing for home? If he looked at it that way, Eira wasn't some impossible obstacle. She wasn't comparable to the bloodstained memories that lurked in the back of his mind. He was the one pulling himself in circles, comparing things that didn't need to be compared and stacking himself against people he shouldn't compete with.

"Because worrying and overcomplicating things is apparently what you do—and don't try to argue with me, you're doing it right now," Oliver said.

Tobias winced. "How can you tell?"

"You make this expression when you think." Oliver scrunched his face up into an exaggerated thoughtful frown. He held it for a moment before he relaxed back into his neutral disinterested expression. "Like that."

Ignoring the mockery, Tobias puzzled over the original statement. Did he overcomplicate things? Looking back at the deep hole he dug himself into, he knew the answer was clear. He shook his head. "What did you really mean, then?"

Oliver sighed and leaned forward, marking yet another tally on his sheet as Arayna threw Uriah to the ground and danced around to celebrate her next victory. Tobias winced at the shaky way in which Uriah rose to his feet.

"Look," Oliver said, "what I meant was, I don't think it was right for Aviva to drag you into something that doesn't concern you. I don't understand her twisted, backward reasons for it, even if in her mind, it makes sense. If the problem isn't yours, you shouldn't be trying to fix it. That's my thought on the matter."

"But Aviva—"

"You asked a question, so listen to the whole answer before interrupting." Oliver shot him a look. Then, satisfied, he turned his head away again. "But you're not me. I don't know what you're thinking, what you want, or why you are the way you are. Think about where your limits are and remember not to overstep them. Does that make sense?"

Tobias nodded slowly, yet the motion was numb and distant. While he appreciated the way that Oliver tried to view the issue, it wasn't that simple. It was a deep-rooted habit that he had grown up with: always measuring himself against another's accomplishments, always discounting himself for his failures. It was simple to say, but it was difficult to practice.

"*You have to learn somehow, don't you?*" Talia's voice spoke again in his mind. She looked down on him in the memory, but there was gentleness in her eyes. This time, her voice turned soft as the memory played on. "*What are you trying to accomplish, my knight of dreams?*"

"*I want to be like you,*" he said back then, his voice choked with frustration. "*I wish to protect the people I care about, so that no one will be hurt the way that... so that no one will be killed the way that mother was.*"

"*That's an admirable goal,*" Talia had said. "*But it's nearly impossible to accomplish. People are going to be hurt, and people are going to be killed. That's part of life, Tobias.*"

Tobias pressed his hand against the key, balling his fist around it. Protection. That's what it was.

He failed to protect Kase from Eira, and he had even failed to protect himself from her. He had forgotten that was the reason he took up the sword. It didn't start as a selfish fear or a need to be someone he wasn't. It started in memory of his mother, the one who was killed in front of him. The one who was killed protecting him.

But if he was trying to protect Kase, then why was it Eira's face that lingered in his mind? When he confronted her, hadn't she been trembling? Didn't her voice shake when she mentioned the other person she was working with? For just a moment, didn't she seem small and fragile?

The threads of gold came to mind, wound tightly around her wrists. They were positioned to control her, not to be controlled by her.

"There's something that doesn't add up," he finally said. "About… Eira and this partner of hers. The magic, too."

Oliver glanced back at him, his eyes narrowing as he frowned in thought. "What about her?"

Tobias focused on Uriah and Arayna's mock fight. This time, it was Uriah who triumphed, pinning Arayna face down and twisting her arm until she yelped. He immediately backed off, but his grin never faltered. When he caught Tobias staring, the look in his eyes shifted back to the glimpse of madness he had seen back in the cave.

His eyes shimmered with flecks of gold—that same other-worldly, glittering look as Eira's did when she summoned her magic.

It was only for a moment before Uriah looked away again, but Tobias couldn't help but shudder. It was faint, but the air around Uriah shifted with the sharp pull of wrongness.

"Before I go home, I think I deserve to put everything together," Tobias said. Slowly, his grip on the key began to loosen, his fingers aching from how tightly he had been gripping it. "It doesn't sit right with me, and I can't drop it so easily. Especially not when Eira was practically begging for my help."

"She's a thief," Oliver muttered. "She lies and steals, Tobias. She's probably trying to get something from you."

"I have a feeling there's more to it than that, and I want to understand why."

The past she shared with the group always puzzled him. If she was so close, why would she betray them? Why did they believe she had killed Aviva—and why did Aviva let them believe that? On its own, the incident made no sense.

However, if someone was pulling the strings, then it would make sense that everything they had fell apart at the seams. If that was true, then perhaps Eira never truly betrayed the people she cared about so much.

Turning his gaze toward the horizon, where the endless blue sky met the canopy of trees, he couldn't help but recall the old stories of a black-scaled dragonborn who manipulated golden strings. If Eira had found herself tangled in his web, then she was the same as that image left behind in Tobias's last memories of his mother.

She was someone to protect.

16

IRIDESCENT BLUE

THE FIRST THING Kase saw when he awoke was the ceiling. Some part of him expected never to open his eyes again or to open them to the afterlife. He at his eyes, trying to clear his vision. The same ceiling remained, with dark wood paneling and a small lantern hanging from a thin silver chain. A flickering flame behind the glass of the lantern bathed the room in a soft, yellow glow.

It wasn't the dark that had whispered to him in his dreams. It wasn't the vision of bloodstained walls and dust-covered stone floors. It was light, peace, and security.

Tears rose to his eyes. *That's right. I'm still alive.*

Kase, Smoke's voice greeted him with a sigh of relief, the bond between them thrumming with excitement. *You are not dead.*

Laughter broke from Kase's lips, his shoulders trembling with the force of it. His leg ached, but it no longer felt like it was being burned from the inside out, eaten away by the poison of Eira's blade. Beneath the blanket, his hand brushed against the bandages wrapped tightly around it.

I guess I'm not, he replied. With a groan, he pushed himself upright and fixed his pillows against the headboard. Sighing, he sank back into their comfort. *Does anyone know yet?*

It appears Aviva is on her way now, Master. I am certain Iila is with her as well.

Kase furrowed his brow. *Can you tell that snake to go away? I don't feel like dealing with his pointed stares right now.*

No, Master. The snake stays. Besides, Iila is a coatl, not a snake.

Hush, you.

The door swung open as soon as the last thought traveled down Kase's bond. Aviva stepped in, her staff in hand with Iila coiled around the top of it. Her gaze snapped toward him immediately, and she gasped. Dropping her staff, she rushed to his side and threw her arms around him, pressing a quick kiss to his forehead. As she pulled away, she smiled warmly and perched on the edge of his bed. She squeezed his hands, her magic seeping through his skin to clear away the last bit of aching in his leg.

Behind her, Iila hissed, clearly displeased as he flapped his feathery wings and gently leaned her staff against the wall. Kase couldn't help the smug smile that rose to his face as the snake's piercing gaze landed on him.

"How do you feel?" Aviva asked, voice barely above a whisper. Her voice had always been soft, but now, it trembled ever so slightly with fear; it was as though she were afraid to break him if she spoke too loudly.

His heart leapt in his chest, and his skin prickled where she had touched him. He cleared his throat. "All healed, I would guess. It doesn't hurt, and my head feels clear, and I can breathe again. So pretty good, all things considered."

She chuckled, leaning her forehead against his. "I'm glad. You really had me worried there."

"Psh, I'm much harder to kill than this. A little poison won't stop me."

You were on the very brink of death for several hours. It was my power that sustained you until Maven and Aviva could heal you, Smoke said with a snort.

Kase's smile dropped into a frown. *Shut up, cracked vase. I was being sarcastic.*

Aviva's smile faltered, her green eyes growing duller. She pulled back from him and sat up straight, brushing her loose blonde hair back from her face. There were no pink-and-white flowers in it this time, and it was uncharacteristically unkempt and tangled. He couldn't help but notice the dark, weary circles under her eyes, and it tightened the knot in his chest.

"Eira is serious about this, then," she murmured, fiddling with her diaphanous sleeves, the freckles across her pale arms visible underneath. With a heavy sigh, she rose to her feet. "She really tried to kill you."

Kase froze. Eira's face flashed through his mind, bringing along with it the fiery pain of her knife plunging into his thigh. He exhaled through his nose, looking toward the window. Sunlight filtered in through the curtains, stretching across his blanketed form and granting him a bit of warmth from the outside. The delicate brush of light was welcoming—too gentle for the tension in his muscles.

"Yeah," he finally said. "Yeah, I guess she did."

"It's not her. It can't be. But…" Aviva gestured to Kase with the sweep of her arm, her lips pursed. "I guess now she's changed. She's trying to kill you. She hurt Tobias as well, and it's…" She dragged her fingers through her hair, moving to the empty bed opposite Kase's. "It's not her at all."

Kase looked down at his hands folded in his lap. It was true that when they were young, Eira had never hurt them. In fact, she had done everything she could to avoid it. Though she was the same age as him, she tried to play the role of leader and mother. She brought them together and gave them a place to belong. The pieces didn't fit right. Even if Eira was hungry for power, or obsessed with climbing to some new status, it wasn't like her to turn on her friends, the kids she had watched over for so long.

Then it hit him. Tobias had mentioned to him before that Eira claimed to work with someone else, and he was almost certain he had heard her say it herself. Frowning, he turned to Aviva and lifted his head to meet her gaze. "You believe it's some kind of corruption, don't you?" he asked.

She faltered, but finally nodded stiffly. "I do," she said. "Tobias mentioned these threads around her and…" She took a deep breath, smoothing her skirts out over her knees. A moment of silence settled between them as she frowned thoughtfully at the tips of her boots. Putting her head in her hands, she murmured, "I think I made a mistake somewhere."

Kase pulled the blankets back and lifted his legs over the edge of the bed so he faced her.

She shot him a warning look but continued speaking anyway when he didn't stand. "I shouldn't have run away that day. I shouldn't have hidden myself. I shouldn't have placed my spellbook in Tobias's hands. I should have dealt with this myself, but I didn't because I was afraid." She buried her face in her palms, her hair spilling over her shoulders. "I was weak."

"What does that have to do with Eira's corruption?"

Aviva dragged her fingers through her hair, raking it back from her face. "If I had stayed—and if I had been paying more attention back then—I could have prevented it. I would have seen it coming."

"You still don't get it," Kase said, shaking his head. "You didn't have to do it alone if you were afraid. That's what I'm here for, as your Mage Guardian. And so is Uriah."

"I know that, but the point is still the same." She stood up, staring down at him with that dull, weary look in her pale green eyes. Shaking her head, she crossed to the door, where Iila had propped her staff up against the wall. The snake flew over to her shoulder, coiling loosely around her neck. When he was settled,

Aviva took her staff in her hands again. She turned back to Kase, her brows drawn together in a pensive expression. "I failed to do what I should have, as both a Mage and a friend. I dragged someone into this who doesn't have a place in it. Eira is clearly after Tobias, and I think… I think it would be best if we sent him home."

A flicker of worry sparked in Kase's mind, tugging faintly on his bond with Smoke. Turning his eyes to the window once more, he ran his fingers through his hair. He could feel what Smoke's opinion on the matter was just from the way it made their bond shiver. The dragon's touch oozed with faint remnants of his magic, which latched onto the choking unease that welled up inside Kase's chest. The sparks flared, igniting a small flame beneath the surface of his skin. Gritting his teeth, he quickly reined in the burst of power, shoving it back down. *Deep breath, in and out,* he told himself. *Keep the flame under control. Don't let your mind wander too much.*

Sorry, Smoke murmured. *The sleep has made your control over my magic a bit finicky.*

Kase brushed him away, and the fire soon died down again. Once the heat began to diminish from his skin, he faced Aviva again. He wet his lips and hoped his weariness and stress didn't show too clearly in his expression.

"I think you're right," he said. A slight tremor crept into his voice, and he winced at the sound of it. "He may not like it; he has been dead set on unraveling this mess since the very beginning. He's my friend, but so is Talia—his sister. I can't imagine she would be too pleased to know what I've dragged him into. More than that, I don't know what I would do if he stayed and something happened to him, and he…" He trailed off. The unspoken words hung heavily in the air between him and his Mage, but they both knew what it was he couldn't say.

To add to that, Smoke interjected, *the boy never has any clue as to what is going on, or what he is even supposed to be doing.*

Kase snorted, a faint smile lifting the tightness of his frown. In the back of his mind, he thanked Smoke for trying to lighten the mood a bit, but it did little to remove the uncertainty that blanketed his thoughts.

"Smoke again?" Aviva spoke up, cutting off Kase's reply to the dragon.

Kase nodded. "Sorry. He's being snarky again."

Am I wrong? Smoke cut in, flooding the bond with a strangely childish pride. To anyone else, it would seem out of place for the ancient, red dragon, but Kase had always known Smoke had the maturity of a two-year-old deep down. Though perhaps it was only a façade to hide the truth of *Imago*, his real self that Kase had helped him bury.

The thread of the bond snapped against him. Kase hissed in pain, pressing a hand to his temples until the faint sting began to fade. *Real mature, Smoke.*

With a final huff, the old dragon retreated into his side of the bond, pulling the warmth of his presence away.

Aviva chuckled behind her hand. "As long as Smoke isn't causing any serious damage, you're free to go see the others whenever you're ready. And…" Her knowing smile faded as she dropped her hand against the doorknob. Iila glanced up at her face, flicking his forked tongue. It took a moment, but Aviva eventually straightened up again, pulling the door open. "Please talk to Tobias if you can. He came here with you, so I think he's most likely to listen to you."

With that, she left.

AVIVA'S COTTAGE hadn't changed at all since Kase had last been there. Bookshelves lined the walls of almost every room, stacked full of books in all colors, sizes, and materials. Some proved to be more worn than others. Pressed and dried flowers hung on the pale walls wherever they weren't occupied by shelves. Tables were so buried in scrolls, papers, and pens it was hard to tell they were even tables anymore.

Kase smiled. *Cluttered* was the word that always came to mind. Cluttered but homey.

Smells too much like lavender, Smoke grumbled. *And honey.*

Kase rolled his eyes and mentally pushed the dragon away. *Then stop using my senses and you won't have to smell it anymore.*

Smoke didn't respond with any quips or retorts that time, but Kase could still feel his muttering running up against the bond. This time, his words were in Draconic: only bits and pieces made sense to Kase. He sighed and made his way down the hall to the door.

As he drifted outside, the scent of rain washed over him, which made Smoke grumble even more. Dark clouds rolled over the sun, dimming the brilliant, afternoon light. Despite this, Arayna and Uriah seemed to be engaged in a mock fight. Arayna danced easily out of the way of his slow swings; Uriah took a kick to the chest, sending him sprawling backward. Even so, he laughed as if it were the funniest thing in the world. For all Kase knew, to Uriah it was.

The door had barely even closed behind him when Arayna froze, her ears flicking upward on alert. She spun around, a bright smile breaking out across her lips the moment her gaze fell on him. "Kase!"

At that, Uriah looked up. Oliver, who was sitting in the grass, lifted his head and rose to his feet.

Kase met Arayna's attempt at a hug with a quick pat to her head. Bewilderment flashed through her eyes, but then she dipped her head and accepted the touch instead. "Sorry," he whispered as he pulled his hand away. "Maybe another time."

She grinned, needing no further explanation. Kase had suggested to her before that she had a tendency to squeeze too hard when giving hugs. Kase was tired enough without being crushed to death.

Uriah gave him a firm pat on the back, knocking the air out of his lungs. "Glad to see you on your feet again! You really had everyone scared for a bit there."

"That's what Aviva said," Kase replied, pulling the front of his cloak straight again. His fingers brushed the red pin, and he tensed. "Like I told her, it takes more than a bit of poison to kill me. I hope we all learned a valuable lesson here."

Oliver shoved past Arayna, eyes shooting daggers straight through Kase. He jabbed a finger at his chest. "You. How dare you! You really could have died!"

Kase blinked, his chest tightening. It felt like a thorn twisting in his heart. He really could have died. He almost did, in fact.

Cold seeped through his bones. He almost died.

Smoke brushed up against him through their bond, offering warmth to send the bitter fear away. This time, it came as a small, manageable flame, like the soft touch of sunlight during the warmer stretch of the season of Deiah. Kase took a deep breath and faced Oliver again.

"I could have, but I didn't. It's not like I was asking to be stabbed."

Oliver opened his mouth to argue but quickly clamped it shut again. Kase had a sinking feeling he knew exactly what Oliver wanted to say, and he was glad the hunter kept it to himself. He had heard it enough times already.

Oliver stepped aside with a huff, pulling Arayna away by the arm. Uriah muttered something under his breath, but before Kase could ask what it was, he had already walked off, leaving Kase alone.

Standing up straighter, Kase looked around again for Tobias. When Kase had first stepped outside, he thought he had caught a glimpse of Tobias's purple coat, but now, he seemed to have disappeared while Kase was crowded by the others. His fingers curled into a fist at his side.

You do not have to get so worked up about this, Smoke reasoned. *Tobias has never proven difficult to talk to.*

But if I don't get the chance to before he does something stupid, he's going to hurt himself again. I can't sit around and allow my friends to keep getting hurt. Clinging tightly to that thought, he whirled around and found himself facing the garden. There was no sign of Tobias there. He turned around a corner of the cottage. A pond glittered in the distance, and Tobias stared down into it. The tension faded slightly. *If I did, what kind of a person would I be?*

You would be just like all the other humans out there, Kase, and I do not know that I would continue to be your partner, the old dragon sighed. *The kindness of your heart is something I have never truly understood.*

Kase hesitated, watching Tobias as he settled down beside the water. *Is it really kindness to tell him to go away when he was so sure that he wanted to do this?*

I do not know. I am a dragon, Kase. Kindness does not come naturally to me.

Smoke cut off the connection for the time being. Heavy silence fell in his place; it carried a certain emptiness with it. Kase straightened his shoulders and tried not to let Smoke's usual cryptic attitude get to him. The squirming knot of unease in his chest pulled taut anyway, forming a mass of problems he couldn't even begin to unravel. It didn't help having Smoke add another layer of confusion to top things off. The dragon was supposed to be his anchor, and yet he seemed just as adrift as Kase.

Perhaps the poison had shaken him, too.

One step at a time, he drew closer to the pond and knelt at its edge. It wasn't very deep—if he stepped in, it would probably come up to mid-calf. A handful of fish swam in circles within, their iridescent blue fins flashing as the sun peeked out from behind the clouds. Visions tickled the back of Kase's mind, filled with images of shimmering azure scales and a child's bright laugh.

He shook the thoughts away.

Tobias's gaze stayed on the water as he approached. "Did you know one of the Head Dragonborn of Selini is said to watch the world through a pond just like this one? He is the eyes of the goddess; he sees everything, so therefore he knows everything."

"I've heard the story, yes." Kase crouched beside him. "Not even the Summoners can see the world as he does." Whether the legend was true or not, he chose to brush it to the side. Selini was already displeased with him for disrupting her perfect rule. He didn't need the added worry that came with being watched all the time. "What brings this up?"

"I've been thinking."

Kase snorted with laughter. "Aren't you always thinking?" Talia had said it was one of her brother's strengths—but also his ultimate downfall. She spoke of this quality with a strange mix of pride and worry swirling in her eyes.

"Yes, I guess, but I was… thinking harder," Tobias said. "Before you go on, I want to say something."

Tobias's hands gripped each other so tightly his knuckles had turned white; his lips were pressed in a thin line, and his brows had drawn together. It mirrored the look he had seen on Talia's face. With a sigh, Kase sat back on his heels. "Sure. Go ahead." What he had to say could wait if Tobias was so nervous.

"For a while, I thought about going home," Tobias said, hunching his shoulders. "I thought it would be better—technically, I have overdue work to complete and household chores to take care of. More importantly though, I felt like I wasn't doing much good here anyway. But… there's something I don't understand. I set out to reclaim the spellbook, yes, because I had this dream of unlocking its secrets all on my own. I've realized that this is beyond me and the book." He inhaled sharply, squeezing his eyes shut and ducking his head. "I'm worried about Eira. Something isn't right. It's childish, but I wish I could see her through this pond. I wish I could understand the truth. So that's why, I want to stay. For her sake."

Kase froze as Tobias lifted his head. For a moment, it wasn't Tobias's face he saw staring back at him with that determined emerald gaze. It wasn't even Talia's face, which he so often saw reflected on Tobias. This time, it was someone else's, with the same look in deep red eyes and a scarred, dirtied face. His heart squeezed painfully, and for a moment, he could do nothing but stare—and plead that the vision would vanish soon.

Tobias dipped his head to the side slightly, and the illusion subsided. Kase rubbed his eyes.

"Did you know that's what I was going to talk about?" he asked, voice low.

"You were going to talk about me leaving?" Tobias cleared his throat. "I mean, I kind of had a feeling. Did Aviva ask you to?"

Kase sighed and rubbed the back of his neck. "She did. She thinks bringing you here was a mistake, and I have to admit, I agree. A little bit."

Tobias narrowed his eyes. Though the look was pointed and sharp, there was hurt swimming beneath the surface. "Eira is suffering, Kase. There's these threads and—She's being controlled by someone else. You're not even going to acknowledge that?"

Kase swallowed thickly, piecing his words together in his mind very carefully. "Aviva mentioned that you said that. We don't have any way to know for sure that she's being controlled instead of wielding the threads. Right now, Eira is unpredictable, and that makes her a threat. It's not that I don't admire your new... determination. It's just that things are going to get even more dangerous and—"

Rather than argue, Tobias sighed, pushing himself to his feet. As he dusted the dirt from his clothes, Kase couldn't help but shrink back from the information he had dropped. He shook his head. Tobias's words echoed in his mind—that stubborn will to see something through to the bitter end, even if there was no promise that they would arrive there. *Just like...*

"Calix," he whispered, glancing down at his hands in his lap. Slowly, he reached for the silver pin he kept buried in his pocket. His thumb brushed across the surface, running along the engraved image of the dragon. "You're a lot like Calix."

Tobias paused. "Who?"

Releasing the pin, Kase lifted his head. "Nothing. Just reminiscing."

"That's him, isn't it? The boy you mentioned to Oliver," Tobias said, pinning Kase beneath a firm stare.

A nervous flutter stirred in Kase's chest. He choked out a dry laugh. "I didn't think you would remember that. Yes, that's him." When Tobias's stare didn't let up, he sighed and continued. "He's... someone I tried to protect. Despite everything he had been through, he was always stubbornly set on doing whatever he set his mind to. In that way, you remind me of him."

"I'll take that as a compliment, I guess," Tobias murmured.

"I wish I could tell you more about him," Kase admitted. "I wish I could speak of him freely. But, for his protection, that's all I can tell you."

If he could, Kase would have kept Calix with him forever. His heart ached with sympathy whenever he remembered the boy he had rescued from his fate in Hybrid Territory, the same boy he was later forced to send away. There were many things Kase could fight against, but the wrath of the dragon goddess was not one of them. It was a cowardly attempt to preserve both of them, and it would hang heavily over him forever.

Somewhere, Calix was out there, fighting to stay hidden from the Head Dragonborn, and Kase couldn't save him.

Drawing in a deep breath, he faced Tobias again. *Stay in the present,* Kase reminded himself. *Don't pull anyone else into the past.* He cleared his throat. "I'm not going to make you leave if you don't want to, but I can't say the same for Aviva. As for Eira…"

Tobias hesitated a moment longer, searching Kase's face. "I'm staying, regardless of what Aviva says."

Leaving no room for more debate, Tobias left, his fists clenching and unclenching at his sides. Kase watched him go, emptiness settling in his chest like the steady cold of the Sefah season. He reached for Smoke to quell the empty feeling, but found it resided in the dragon's side of the bond as well.

Do you miss him? the old dragon whispered.

Of course I do. Kase tilted his head back to gaze up at the overcast sky. *If only I had let Calix stay as well…*

17

EMPTY PROMISES

WHEN KASE FINALLY REJOINED the others at the front of the cottage, the threat of rain had deepened into an ominous, dark covering for the sky. Cold wind brushed against his cheek; if not for the warmth from Smoke's bond, he would have pulled his hood up to protect at least some of his exposed face from the chill.

It was puzzling. Aviva's forest had always been rather warm, even during the cold seasons. He reached out along the bond toward Smoke in the hopes of an explanation, but the old dragon had fallen silent, pondering something.

The door opened with a creak. Aviva stepped outside, gripping the spellbook tightly in one hand at her side, her face downcast. Her hair had been tied back into a tight ponytail away from her face, though it still appeared tangled near the ends.

At the sight of her, Arayna and Uriah stopped their play-fighting. Oliver looked up from what he was writing on, and Tobias stiffened a little. Even the very air had hushed, as if the whole forest was holding its breath.

"All quiet, I assume?" Aviva asked, glancing at Oliver.

"There's no sign of Eira still. However…" He reached into his pocket and pulled out a chunk of bark. As Aviva reached out to take it, he placed it in her hand. "I noticed this when I was out in the forest."

"Were you near the far east side?"

Oliver nodded.

Aviva pursed her lips and turned the bark over. Kase stood beside her, glancing at the object in her hands. It was a rough slab of wood no larger than the palm of her hand. A blackened mark consumed the face of it, glistening with the faint aura of magic. It was the same as the reports of the bodies of the missing Mages that had been uncovered—black as though burnt and sucked dry of its life. Kase recoiled as the stench of rot rolled over him. Aviva examined the bark calmly, her brow furrowed in thought.

"I think it's time I told you the truth," she said, curling her fingers around the wood. "Or at least, my thoughts on everything."

Aviva stepped forward, opening her spellbook and gesturing for everyone to gather around her. Kase offered a smile of encouragement. She looked up at him but did not return his smile, which stung worse than the poison had.

She turned to a page with an illustration Kase had seen many times before: a symbol like a crown, with jagged edges and sharp points at the corners. The words around it blurred, nonsense to him no matter how hard he focused on them. He glared down at the paper and its nonsense words.

Aviva was inhibiting his ability to read the book.

I can bypass her block, Smoke offered. Before Kase could even respond, the dragon was already readying his magic on the other end of the bond.

It's fine, Kase quickly replied. *I trust her.* Besides, he didn't want to invade Aviva's privacy if she had gone through the trouble of cutting him off from reading the words. If she wanted him to see, she would let him.

Smoke grumbled incoherently and withdrew the heat of his power. *If you say so.*

"There is dark magic involved in all of this," Aviva said, pointing to the jagged drawing of the crown-like symbol. "High Summoner Maven suspected there was, and she's right. I didn't want to admit it, but I think it's best if I say it now. Before we wade deeper into this storm." She took a deep breath and withdrew her hand from the illustration. "None of you are ready to fight this kind of magic."

Her gaze zeroed in on the figure to Kase's left. Even without looking, he knew Aviva was staring directly at Tobias. On top of that, he knew Tobias would be staring right back at her with that indignant determination. He sighed. The air between them was thick with tension.

Aviva didn't like for her warnings to be ignored, and Kase had gone and allowed Tobias to ignore them. Dread welled in the pit of his stomach. He should have fought harder to do what Aviva asked of him, but it wasn't his place, was it? Tobias looked young, but he was an adult. He could make his own choices.

He's not... The vision of those iridescent blue scales flashed through his mind again. Biting his lip, Kase reached for the Dragon Rider pin in his pocket.

Uriah, dense as ever, cut through the tension without a care. He leaned forward a bit, his golden eyes alight with curiosity. "What kind of dark magic?"

At that, Smoke hissed and drew back, huddling deeper into his side of the bond. *That is not a question he should ask. Why should it matter?*

This is Uriah, Smoke. He asks dumb questions all the time. But something itched at the back of his mind. The raw curiosity in Uriah's eyes didn't come from a place of stupidity, and neither had the question. Unease settled over their bond, leaving a sharp, bitter taste in the back of Kase's mouth.

Aviva snapped the book shut, making Kase jump. "Magic like a sickness," she said, holding up the chunk of bark. "It slipped into my forest several years ago, latching itself onto anything that lives—anything that holds even an inkling of magic in it. It feeds on the life of whatever it snatches up, but I can't tell what exactly its purpose is or what it's stealing. All I know is that nothing it comes in contact with ever lives long. It's why I took on an unregistered apprentice, it's what I sent her away to deal with. I'm not the only Mage that went into hiding because of this threat, though I am one of the lucky few who's still alive. There's no telling what else is suffering from the same curse, but I think Eira might be affected somehow. Or at least, she came in touch with something similar."

"Can you cure it then?" Uriah asked, folding his arms over his chest. "You know, purify or whatever? That's your area of magic, after all."

Hesitating, Aviva drew her shoulders back and sucked in a breath. Kase shot her a look, puzzled. In all the years he had known her, he had never seen her so unsure. Her eyes flicked down, glittering with unshed tears. Her lips quivered and her hands shook. He had always thought of her as someone who knew the answer to every problem she was presented with, and she was always eager to solve every issue that came her way.

She had never looked as fragile as she did now.

Finally, she clutched the book against her chest and pulled her hood farther down around face.

"I don't know," she whispered. "I—I don't know if I can, or even where I would begin. If Summoner Maven couldn't stop Eira, how am I supposed to? Beyond that, how am I supposed to purify an entire forest? That much magic would require the sacrifice of life, and I'm not willing to take that." Turning sharply, she threw her arm out to gesture to the forest around them. "You can feel it too, right? This place has changed. It is cold, weak, and no longer the forest of my master." When she turned back to the group, she fixed Uriah with a pointed stare. "There are limits to what I can do, and I can't overstep those boundaries or I'll be killed. Or worse, I'll be corrupted by my own magic." She hugged the book closer, voice dropping. "I don't know."

Uriah took a step forward, towering over her. "What do you mean you *don't know?*" he snapped. Aviva flinched back; Kase thrust his arm in front of her, stopping Uriah from coming closer. He didn't even seem to notice. His golden eyes flashed as he went on, glaring down at her. "You're Aviva! You're supposed to know *everything*! You're supposed to have the answers. No, you *do* have all you need. Magic is the solution, but you're simply letting your power rot because of your fear!"

"That's enough." Kase shoved him, but Uriah barely budged. Instead, his eyes flicked to Kase; their malicious look didn't match his strained, desperate tone. Gritting his teeth, Kase gathered Smoke's strength into his arm. Heat raced along the surface of his skin, lighting the fire in his chest. He pushed back against Uriah, sending him stumbling a few steps.

"Mind your place," he said, letting his arm fall to his side again. Anger made his cheeks burn, and the same heat formed in his fists as stray bits of magic slipped down the bond from Smoke. "You are Aviva's Mage Guardian, and you will treat her with respect. Or have you forgotten?"

Uriah froze, lifting his chin as everyone fixed their gazes on him. He clenched his jaw and held Kase's stare, his eyes sparking with anger. "No, I didn't forget."

Aviva laid a hand on Kase's arm, startling him out of his moment of anger. He dragged his gaze downward, shoving his concerns with Uriah aside for the time being. Like always, she didn't seem angered by Uriah's stupid actions. From the creases in her brow, he gathered she was focused more on the other problem at hand.

Kase released a deep sigh and let go of the threads of Smoke's magic. The heat in his skin began to dissipate, taking with it the suffocating anger. Uriah could be dealt with later.

"I hate to disappoint," Aviva said, "but I'm nothing special, really. I'm just another Mage. There are hundreds—thousands— out there. There's much that I still don't know." She smoothed her fingers over the book in her hands, looking down as she spoke. "This corruption, this sickness, that I'm describing to you is like nothing I've ever heard of or seen. It literally eats away at magic. So what makes you think magic can cure it?"

"If power can't fix it, what can?" Uriah spoke up again. "There's nothing that can't be solved with a little magic."

There is much that magic cannot fix, Smoke murmured. His voice lingered in Kase's mind longer than usual, like he was trying to draw emphasis to his words. *Never forget that, Master.*

Kase wanted to respond with a quip, but all he managed to send was a strangled sound of confusion. As the connection fell silent again, he glanced at Uriah. His golden eyes flashed as they met Kase's gaze, but he said nothing. The look held for only a few seconds before Uriah sharply turned away from the group.

"Whatever," he grumbled. "I respect your decision, Aviva."

Aviva's shoulders drooped slightly as she sighed. "Thank you."

"Aside from… all of that," Oliver said, glancing between the two. "You and Maven both believe this ties into Eira somehow?"

"It's a miracle she would agree on anything with you at all," Arayna muttered.

"High Summoner Maven believes it does, yes. Several years ago, when I first noticed the corruption seeping into my forest, I sent word to the Summoners. Maven was not in charge at that time and was unaware that this report was made. Back then, I was told to keep watch. But then I… well, I faked my death and couldn't report anything else. I thought that by putting the enchantment on the forest and hiding the book, I might forestall the corruption's consumption of my magic. I thought I could hide myself, teach my spells to someone else, and solve this problem on my own before it escalated to this level." She rubbed her eyes, dragging her hand along the curves of her cheeks. Pursing her lips, she tucked the spellbook away into her cloak. "When I reported it to Maven this time, she seemed to think it was similar to the magic she had sensed in Eira before. She's going to escalate the issue to the Summoner Court, but it's only a matter of time before she returns to seal my magic for what I've done. I don't want to leave you all to face this alone, but at the same time..." Aviva shook her head, squeezing her eyes shut. "If Eira is being tainted and all these things are connected, it's still something I can't even begin to fully comprehend, much less purify."

Tobias folded his arms over his chest, cupping his chin in one hand. "She did say something about working alongside another person. Could it be that this person is controlling the magic you sensed? Would that mean these instances are connected?"

"They're connected." Aviva reached up and grabbed something in the air. A black thread, tinged with gold, appeared clutched between her index finger and thumb. It stretched across the open area like a stray strand of a spiderweb, but it was pulled taut as if already attached to something else. "This magic carries a signature, like a stamp. Every person's magic does." She released the thread. "But if they *are* controlling this magic, they're not human. This is beyond the capabilities of human Mages. It's even beyond the Summoners. To corrupt an area this large takes a massive amount of power that humans do not possess—and that doesn't even account for whatever is being done to Eira."

"Maybe it's the Shadowslayer," Uriah muttered, turning to

the group again. "That old legend about the dead man who steals magic to wield for himself?"

Oliver rolled his eyes. "Be serious, Uriah."

"Hybrids then?" Arayna asked, keeping her voice low. She ducked her head slightly and her ears drooped. "Are the Draconic people making their move?"

Through their bond, Smoke sighed, pulling Kase away from Aviva's response. *I am going to open my thoughts to them,* he said. *I can explain what they do not understand.*

Kase stiffened, swallowing thickly as his heart skipped a beat. *If you do that—*

I know. The little one will hear. He may come looking for you.

You know that I want to see him—more than anything else. You know that. But he can't be dragged into this too. It's not safe for him, and if it's the Draconic people we're dealing with, then...

His thoughts trailed off. A dull ache throbbed in his chest, like an old wound opening in his heart. But he didn't need to form words for Smoke to understand, and his argument was a lost cause anyway. The old dragon had made up his mind already.

A harsh tug pulled at their bond as Smoke established a link to each member of the group, stretching a thin thread between each of them and himself. It was similar to the thread that formed his bond with Kase, only fragile and temporary. All the thread did was allow him to speak in their minds. It would break as soon as he was done with it.

Once each link was established, Smoke drew back into his bond with Kase, hesitating a moment before he began to speak.

It is not a hybrid that has tainted the thief, he promised, his voice laced with authority and power—a voice he only used when he was showing off or mocking other dragons. It took Kase a moment to recognize it, as he was still expecting the lull of Smoke's sarcastic, mocking tone. This was the voice of Imago, not Smoke.

At the sound of it, Tobias jumped; Oliver reached for a small knife at his waist. Arayna's ears pricked, her eyes darting around for the source of the voice. Aviva and Uriah, however, immediately turned toward the place outside the forest where Smoke waited.

May I remind you that hybrids cannot wield magic like humans can; they only possess strength beyond your boundaries. Selini, the goddess of the dragons, has yet to show signs of advancing on human territory in the near future. She is occupied by other things at the moment. He sighed, and Kase could easily picture the smoke curling out of his nostrils as he exhaled. *The magic Aviva senses comes from either an ancient dragon or a dragonborn. Pray that, if it is a dragonborn, it is not a Head Dragonborn—the goddess Selini's chosen disciples. For if it is, you will all perish.*

Silence settled on them once again. Smoke cut the threads and quickly withdrew, curling up safely within his bond with Kase. Puzzled by the exhaustion radiating off the dragon, Kase offered him a mental pat. *You did good, buddy.*

Uriah's mind is frightening, Smoke murmured.

Kase glanced at Uriah again. *It's a little too empty, huh?*

Smoke remained silent.

Before Kase could pursue the issue, Arayna shook herself from her stupor. A grin plastered itself onto her face, her eyes wide. "So you *do* talk!"

Laughter built up in Kase's chest before it spilled from his lips, light and easy despite the weight crushing his mind. "He can, when he needs to. For the most part, he stays within our bond. There's… something we don't want to notice us." He inwardly cringed at the word. It wasn't a *something* at all, but a child. A little boy who couldn't stay by Kase's side, though he desperately wanted to.

His smile faltered and his gaze swerved toward the horizon. *Calix…*

Smoke mentally nudged Kase back to the present. *Let them*

have courage, for I am on their side until the time comes. I will not see this world consumed by dark magic. I have grown quite fond of it, after all. I would like to die knowing it is safe.

Kase pressed his lips into a thin line, his fingers curling tighter against his palms. *You... you made that up, overgrown lizard. You never cared about humans.*

I care for you, Kase, and by extent, I care for what you care for. That is the human-dragon bond.

"Kase?" Aviva brushed a hand against his arm again. "Are you okay?"

"Hm? Oh, yes, of course. I'm fine." Kase forced a smile, combing his hair back from his face and laughing—though it sounded strained and tight this time. "Smoke is just being... Smoke. He did say that you don't need to be worried. He's on our side, and he's going to protect us."

At that, relief broke out across all of their expressions. Arayna was the first to laugh things off, wrapping an arm around Oliver's neck and muttering something in his ear. He retaliated with a shout, drawing back from her and waving her away. Tobias simply watched the two of them, his hands tightly gripped together, though his expression was masked. Aviva seemed convinced and left Kase standing there after giving his arm a quick squeeze.

The only one who seemed just as preoccupied as Kase was Uriah, who stared off into the distance. His back was turned so Kase couldn't see his face, but he didn't have time to sort through the puzzle that was Uriah.

Smoke shrank further back into the bond. *But I believe you know better than anyone that these promises of mine are false.*

The inside of Kase's mouth turned sour as he nodded. He did know, better than anyone else possibly could. All he and Smoke could do was make empty promises.

Time was short and it waited for no one.

18

SENSING DANGER

If he hadn't been listening, Calix might have missed it.

Like a whisper in the wind, it vanished as quickly as it came. Just the faintest brush of a familiar voice against his mind.

His ears pricked at the sound of it: an old voice, thick with a Draconic accent, and laced with both power and authority. A shudder traveled down his spine, sending a flash of warmth through the scales that covered his arm. He exhaled a cloud of frost, pulling back from his own dragon's magic.

"Calix?" his companion asked, waving her hand in front of his eyes. "Come on, don't get distracted. We still have a few chores to finish, then we can call it a day."

Calix swallowed, feeling his throat constrict. He twisted the cloth in his hands, wringing drops of water free. Not even Kiara's voice could motivate him to focus on chores, not this time.

Sighing, Kiara dropped her own cloth into the pail of soapy water at her feet. She wiped her hands on her pants, then bent down to pick up the bucket. Water sloshed, splashing her skirt, but she refrained from spilling it all over herself like she did the last time.

"We can take a break, I guess," she said, hefting the bucket and turning on her heels. "But only for a few minutes."

He nodded as she set off, making her way toward the river at the edge of their makeshift camp. Despite it being early afternoon and the sun shining as brightly as ever against a clear blue sky, a chill hung over Calix. It wasn't the chill that came from his dragon's ice magic, or from the shifting of seasons. It was a warning. He could feel it.

He wrapped his arms around himself, casting a glance over his shoulder. There was nothing there: nothing but his blue dragon, Stiria, rolling in the same puddle of mud that he had just pulled him out of and cleaned his scales of.

But even that seemed distant and wrong. He licked his dry lips and turned away, putting up mental walls between himself and Stiria.

"There's nothing," he promised himself, sinking into a crouch with his arms wrapped around himself. Unease slithered down his spine. "There's nothing there. It's just your imagination."

The chill shifted to a burning prickle of danger, worming its way through the dark blue scales on his arm. The burn didn't lie. It was a feeling—a hum at the back of his mind—that warned him of danger, like the dark clouds that gathered when a storm was approaching. It was a tingling in his fingers, a pressure in his head, an unnatural warmth in his body.

He squeezed his eyes shut, biting down on his lip. The feeling was too familiar. The last time it had come, he had been forced to flee from the school. The memory brought a pain to his head, a residual feeling from the ax being rammed into his skull. The Dragon Rider school was supposed to be safe. It was supposed to be the place he could stay.

But the golden eyes had followed him there too.

"Hey." Kiara's hand brushed against his shoulder, jolting him out of his thoughts. She smiled softly, her blue eyes shining.

Tucking a loose strand of cinnamon-colored hair behind her ears, she sat down with him. "Is something bothering you? Do you want to talk about it?"

His heart leapt to his throat. A pair of golden eyes flashed before his mind, paired with a sickening grin and the gleam of black scales. With trembling hands, he rubbed the cloth wrapped around his arm, which ached more than usual. His scales itched, burning the skin hidden beneath the cloth.

"I don't know," he murmured, ducking his head so that his hair fell in front of his face. "Something isn't right; I can feel it."

Kiara sat back on her heels, lacing her fingers together. Her sapphire gaze shifted away from his face, facing the open expanse of the plains in front of them. "I believe you—I promise I do—but I think you need to try not to worry. Get some rest. You're still recovering."

He nodded slowly. A gentle breeze brushed his cheek, and he lifted his head. The open expanse of blue sky above him stretched on forever without a cloud in sight. Sunlight bathed him in a comforting warmth—like the fire in the hearth, or the heat that radiated from Imago's crimson scales. *Safety. Security. Freedom.* Isn't that what he had here?

Kiara's finger turned his chin, tilting his gaze toward hers. "Promise me you won't run off and do something stupid without letting me know first?"

Calix blinked, his chest tightening as he curled his fingers around the cloth on his arm. His scales burned beneath his hand, throbbing with pain. There was no arguing with Kiara. Despite the sweetness of her voice, the softness of her expression, he knew what she could do when pushed too far. There was a fierceness that lay beneath the depths of her sapphire eyes: a wild beast that prowled around waiting to strike. Though her blade had never turned on him, and he liked to believe it never would, it was best not to cross her. More than that, she was his friend—the one and only friend he had managed to hang onto when his secret was revealed. He valued her trust. He valued her companionship.

"I promise," he said, forcing his voice not to quiver. Even to him, the words sounded empty and hollow, oozing with lies. Still, the golden eyes in his visions barred him from making any promises he could truly fulfill.

If Kiara had noticed, she pretended not to. Another soft smile touched her lips, and she leaned forward to press a kiss to his cheek. Butterflies stirred in his stomach, but even they were suppressed by his aching, itching unease. When she pulled away, she waited for a moment before pushing to her feet.

"Get some rest, okay?" she said. "And let me know if the feeling persists. It may be time for us to pack up and move on again." With one last, lingering glance, she turned and left to attend to other tasks.

Inhaling deeply, he sat back on the grass. Stiria rose from the muddy patch and padded toward him. His frosty breath tickled Calix's ear as he nudged his shoulder. Calix shifted, allowing Stiria to curl up in his favorite spot even though the dragon was going to get mud on him. Stiria flopped down unceremoniously, pressing up against Calix's back as he curled protectively around him. His head fit comfortably in Calix's lap, though it was getting a bit large as Stiria began to grow out of his adolescence. A soft purr rumbled in the back of the dragon's throat as his eyes slid shut. Carefree as always. Sleep came easily to him.

Calix chuckled, stroking Stiria's head and combing his fingers through the dragon's unruly ice-blue mane. Gaze tilted downward, he spotted several discarded scales in the grass. He scooped them up, brushing dirt from their shining blue surfaces, before sliding them into his pockets. A dragon scale would pay for their supplies that needed replacing. He frowned. Maybe it was a good thing that Stiria was growing. Kiara mentioned they would need to replace their saddles soon, and the look on her face meant it wouldn't be cheap. Expenses were a concept he still struggled to grasp, despite Kase's best efforts to teach him.

Kase. His chest tightened as he looked down at the scales.

The meaningless chatter of his thoughts faded as the faint whisper of Imago returned, like a gentle caress at the back of his mind. Words faded in and out, and he could only catch one or two.

He shot to his feet, startling Stiria awake. *Where are you?* he begged the voice, but it didn't reply.

Stiria looked up this time, his cerulean scales shimmering in the sunlight. A puff of icy cold breath left his nostrils as he snorted, shaking his head and setting bits of dirt free from his untamed mane of fluff.

Calix curled his fingers into tight fists at his sides, willing the voice to speak again. Only the wind greeted him, whistling as it rustled through the grass. The empty sky mocked him, as did the open plain. There was nothing there—nothing besides him and his camp.

I know you're out there, he told Imago. Closing his eyes, he reached out through his mind for the fraying thread that dangled in front of him. *I know you hear me. Just... please let him know I'm alright. Please let Kase know I'm alright.*

Silence.

Calix sighed and plopped down in the grass again. He should have known better than to try. Imago would have preferred it if he pretended to be dead, killed by the golden-eyed monster.

He gripped his arm again, set aflame by the memories of the golden-eyed servant of the dragon goddess Selini.

"Stiria," he said aloud, "do you sense it too?"

Stiria lashed his tail, tossing his head back. Only when Calix shot him a glare and pulled down the barriers did he close his eyes and reach out with his magic, searching for whatever it was Calix sensed. As soon as the barriers were removed, Stiria's thoughts and feelings flooded their bond. It took Calix a moment to ground himself in the wild storm of concern, nervousness, and weariness.

Stiria shook his head, sighing. *I think you're just upset, Calix. I don't sense anything at all, not even this Imago of yours—and certainly not the dragonborn, Aurum.*

Calix frowned. His senses had never been wrong before, had they?

I would suggest that you just need to sleep more, Stiria added, flicking him with the fluffy tip of his long tail. *Or maybe ask Kiara to have a look. She would sense a dragonborn as well, yes?*

Calix went rigid, his shoulders stiff and jaw clenched. He pressed his lips into a thin line before swatting Stiria's pestering tail away as it waved in his face again. "I'm not doing that unless I have to. I'm sure I'm just imagining it."

Stiria turned and paced in the grass. Then, with a yawn, he curled up and covered his face with his tail. *If you say so. Wake me if you need anything.*

"I will," Calix murmured, wrapping his arms around himself. Even with the comfort of Stiria's presence curled against his mind, the prickle of unease still slithered through his skin. He shivered, digging his nails into the cloth around his scale-covered arm as he turned away from Stiria.

As it always was, the plain was peaceful and quiet. There was no one else there but the wind that returned to dance through the tall grass. Mountains loomed in the distance, their peaks tipped white with snow. All was safe and secure.

Maybe he was just overreacting. There was no threat, no danger.

His gaze landed on Kiara beside the river, who busied herself with their chores, the ones he was supposed to be helping with. Her dragon, Faiera, sat patiently at her side, keeping watch over her as Kiara busied herself with washing their clothes.

For the moment, he pushed the fear aside. He was safe, and he was free.

No golden-eyed dragonborn would come for him now.

PART FOUR
THE THIEF'S PROMISE

"Though the thief tried, there was no gift nor promise
that could sway the heart of the man."

19

STICK CLOSE TO ME

TOBIAS HAD BEEN SO sure of himself back in Aviva's forest. But now, as he walked along the rocky path through the cliffs east of the woods, his resolve crumbled easily. Maybe it was the occasional sting of his wounds or the way that his feet ached from the uneven ground. Or maybe it was the tingle of fear in the tips of his fingers, working its way to his heart.

I want to see this through to the end, he had promised himself. Now, his heart beat frantically. Eira was waiting for them at the end of their path, and he couldn't afford to underestimate her again. The wound in his side made sure he would remember that. She was the reason he came along, and yet he couldn't help but regret the idea of putting himself in her presence again.

"Are you sure she's there?" Kase asked again, pressing close to Aviva's side as they walked. He kept leaning over to glance at her open spellbook, which now showed them a map of Eira's location rather than a collection of spells. A winding, blue thread trailed out from the image of the forest, drawing closer to the mountains in the distance.

The same mountains pictured on the map loomed overhead,

tall and daunting. Cliffs rose up on either side of them and a cold wind whipped past them. The path beneath Tobias's feet was wide enough for all six of them to walk shoulder-to-shoulder, but Oliver and Arayna chose to trail behind; they spoke quietly with each other, and Arayna's soft laughter drifted through the air occasionally. Uriah lingered awkwardly between the two at the back and Kase, Tobias, and Aviva at the front. He kept silent and stared blankly at the cliff on their left side. Ever since Kase shut him down a few days ago, he seemed quiet and reserved.

The green of the forest was far behind them, and Tobias couldn't help but look back at it. On the east side, a dark, blackened spot spread over the canopy of trees, withering the leaves. As they had walked through it, Aviva had explained it was where the corruption she spoke of was the worst. Eira must have used that section of the forest to escape, most likely knowing that Aviva avoided it. However, Eira's entrance to the forest still remained a mystery, but Aviva's face twisted whenever it was brought up.

Tobias shivered and wrapped his arms around himself. The fact that it had been so easy for Aviva to track down Eira and pinpoint her exact location made him a little uneasy. Magic seemed limitless and frightening to those that couldn't use it. The mentions of dark magic, manipulation, and corruption all twisted Tobias's chest painfully.

You have a gift, Maven had said. But what use was a gift of blankness in the face of such power?

"Yes, I'm sure." Aviva answered, dragging Tobias back into the present conversation. She lifted her head, sighing, and turned the book away from Kase. "Just trust me, okay?"

"Of course I trust you. You know I do. It's just that..." He rubbed the back of his neck awkwardly, glancing at Tobias and the others behind him. "It says she's in the old dragon hoard and, well, Smoke says—"

Aviva shot him a pointed look, pushing her shoulders back. She slipped the spellbook into a satchel at her side, gripping the strap. "I know. You've told me at least four times already."

Kase lowered his head like a wounded puppy. "Sorry."

"Kase is just afraid of all the spooky legends surrounding that place," Uriah cut in, quickening his pace so that he caught up to Aviva and Kase. He elbowed the Mage playfully. "It's too close to the haunted castle of Sheniir for his liking."

Tobias eyed Kase, furrowing his brow. The stories of the abandoned castle of Sheniir were haunting, sure, but they were meant to frighten little children. He couldn't picture Kase, a dragon keeper, frightened by a castle and a mountain.

Kase shrank back. "It's not the ghost stories I'm afraid of," he snapped. "It's the real history of those places."

"Oh, yes," Uriah said with a gleam in his eyes. "The dragons and dragonborn who have passed through, right? That was a long time ago; I'm pretty sure you've got nothing to worry about."

Tobias's lips twitched. He wasn't sure Uriah was the best source for information, especially history. He didn't seem like the kind of person who ever knew anything, but the slight difference in tone when he spoke of hybrids and dragonborn was always a little jarring. His voice dipped lower ever so slightly, and the look in his eyes darkened. It was as if there was something more that he knew about the Draconic people than he did about anything else.

Maybe it has something to do with being a Mage Guardian, Tobias reasoned, scrutinizing the sharp glare Kase sent Uriah's way. *They're picked by the Summoners, aren't they? And the Summoners keep up with the borders between the human kingdoms and Hybrid Territory.* The curiosity chewed at Tobias's mind until he couldn't stand not knowing for certain. Sighing, he gave in.

"Uriah, how do you know so much about the Draconic people?" he asked, letting his gaze rest on the man.

Uriah faltered, a thoughtful frown overtaking his usual grin. He glanced between Kase, Aviva, and Tobias as if contemplating his answer. Finally, with a heavy sigh, he looked out toward the mountain in the distance. For just a moment, he looked like someone else entirely. Then it vanished, and he straightened, turning back to Tobias with his usual grin.

"My brother," he said. "He knows a lot about them. I just listen to him."

Surprise flickered in Tobias's mind at the unexpected answer. Before he could reply, a shadow passed by overhead, blocking out the bright afternoon sunlight for just a moment. Tobias glanced up, tilting his head back just in time to see Smoke flying on ahead. The dragon twisted his neck to look down at them. As he did, Kase stopped in his tracks to look up as well, shielding his eyes from the sun.

"Smoke says we're almost there. He's going to head to the top of the mountain and wait for us," Kase said, turning back to Aviva. He tucked his hands inside his pockets, but Tobias saw him clench his fists before they disappeared into the fabric. "I guess we have no choice then, huh?"

Aviva smiled at that, straightening her satchel and clearing her throat. "We do not. Everyone, come closer. The mountain is within my sight now, so I'm going to warp us there."

Uriah leapt to take her hand first, earning a slight growl from Kase as he took Aviva's other hand. Arayna giggled and tugged Oliver up with her as she put her hand on Aviva's shoulder. Tobias hesitated, staring at them all crowded together. He had never warped anywhere before—he wasn't sure many people in all of Anticuus had.

"Come on Tobias." Arayna flashed a smile, ears perked up and eyes bright. "Aviva's gonna take care of us, don't worry."

"A little magic can't hurt you," Uriah added with a nod, like he had said something incredibly wise.

Tobias frowned but put his hand on Aviva's other shoulder. He knew for a fact Uriah's words weren't true. If anything, almost all the damage in the world had been dealt by magic. History was nothing to scoff at, and magic scarred the history of Anticuus.

As if she could sense his worry, Aviva met his gaze and held it, her eyes soft and understanding. She didn't say anything—she didn't even utter some kind of incantation. Magic flickered and hummed, gathering around her and expanding to wrap them all in its warm embrace. The shimmering veil pulled them in closer to Aviva, binding them with an unseen force.

Then, in the blink of an eye, the world shifted. The cliffs on either side of them vanished and so did the rocky path under their feet. When Tobias looked up again, he stood at the foot of a mountain, one much steeper and more menacing than the Mountain of the Wyrm had been. Its jagged peaks stretched high into the azure sky, high enough that his neck ached from looking up. Disoriented, he turned back to the narrow ravine they left behind.

"We... We really did jump," he breathed, smoothing his hair back from his face to get a better view of where they had been before. How far had they traveled? How much ground had they covered in a matter of seconds?

Flexing his fingers, he wished he had the ability to bend the flow of magic like Aviva did. So many things in life would be easier.

"Incredible." Oliver must have shared similar thoughts; he, too, was staring out into the distance with wide, curious eyes. "Aviva, you've really grown in the last six years."

Aviva didn't reply to that. Instead, she pulled back from everyone and turned to face the mountain, taking in a deep breath as she stared upward. "Do all of you promise to stay close to me?"

Tobias found himself nodding, though it took him a moment longer to actually process what she was asking. He shook his head to clear his thoughts of the wonder of her power and gripped his sword to help ground himself. Magic was something he had never had and never would. It didn't do him any sort of good to daydream about it.

Though that has never stopped you in the past, he muttered to himself.

Aviva waited a moment before tilting her head down and placing a hand on the face of the mountain. Pale light flashed in her palm, tracing a set of runes into the rocks. Aviva stepped back and motioned for everyone to as well.

A crack appeared beneath her runes, glowing with the same soft light. With a shudder and a groan, the crack stretched and opened wide enough for them to walk into the mountain. It revealed a hollow space inside the mountain, a path that cut through the cave and vanished into the darkness within.

Aviva took her staff from Kase's hands and tapped the end of it, creating a white light that illuminated the way as she stepped inside the mountain. "This way leads to the cave at the top, where the hoard is—or used to be. Stay on the path and stick close to me," she said, casting a look over her shoulder. "There are no dragons or dragonborn here, and there haven't been any since the Summoners drove them out, so don't let Uriah's teasing get the better of you."

Uriah shrugged, innocently splaying his hands. "Kase was practically asking to be mocked."

Rolling her eyes, Aviva turned away. "I don't know what Eira is doing here, but if we want to stop her, we have to find out." As she set off down the path, her steps echoing in the empty stone room, the light in her staff flickered slightly.

Kase was the first to follow her into the dark, walking side-by-side with his Mage as she ventured up the winding path. Unwilling to be left behind, Tobias raced after them and fell in step, matching his pace to theirs. He looked back to see the crack sealing itself shut again behind Arayna, the last to come in. As it closed, it cut off the last bit of sunlight, throwing the cave into darkness. Aviva's light brightened to guide them. Tobias swallowed hard and kept close to her and the white light.

Even though Aviva had said there were no more dragonborn —and therefore, no more hybrids—Tobias couldn't shake the cold feeling of dread that coiled in the pit of his stomach. He stuck close to Aviva and Kase in the hopes of escaping it, but it seemed to follow him wherever he went.

"Is this mountain hollowed out?" Tobias asked, trailing his gaze along the empty corridor carved through the stone. It seemed to go on up forever, with only the thin pathway as the way to walk along through it.

"Not necessarily," Aviva said. "It's more like a pocket of space. Dragons used this place to store treasure, so it was created to keep unwanted visitors out."

"How did you know how to get in?"

"Iila senses spells and calculates how to break them." Stretching out her hand, Aviva summoned the winged snake. Iila wound around her arm, flicking his tongue as he stared intently at Tobias. "Though he wasn't physically present, he can act through our bond," she explained.

Tobias moved closer to Kase to escape the snake's piercing gaze. "Right."

Satisfied with this reaction, Iila flicked his tongue out one more time before he vanished in a cloud of green sparks. Tobias hung back with Kase for a little longer.

Trailing his gloved hand along the wall as he walked, Kase's easygoing expression hardened into something more serious. "This cave was home to Gold and Astral dragons before Smoke came across it. Many, many years ago. He couldn't wipe the walls of their tainted magic, so he didn't stay long. But doesn't it still feel slightly *warped* here?"

"A little," Aviva admitted. She lifted her staff higher to shed more light on the path, revealing that it turned ahead and spiraled upward along the wall. "I can purify enough of it as we walk to keep the corrupt magic from spreading. It's not as powerful as the magic I sense in Eira despite coming from Celestial Class dragons."

Tobias nearly tripped over his feet, but managed to right himself before his chin met with the floor. "That's a scary thought," he said, straightening the front of his tunic as Kase turned to look at him. "That Eira holds more corrupt magic than Astral and Gold dragons."

Kase flashed one of his usual smiles. "It'll be fine. I'm sure of it."

Tobias wanted to return the smile but, for just a moment, he thought he saw it falter. Kase turned his attention back to the wall before Tobias could decipher if what he had seen was real or not. Maybe the shadows had just played a trick on his eyes.

Tobias bit the inside of his mouth and shoved the thought away, focusing instead on anything that could bury it. His steps echoed as he walked; if he listened, Oliver and Arayna's hushed conversation behind him drifted up. They were always wrapped up in their own world. It was a far cry from the state he had met them both in originally.

In that regard...

"You know," Tobias began, clasping his hands together to stop their nervous fiddling. "In a weird way, I'm kind of glad I found Aviva's spellbook. I mean, I'm not glad for the events that brought it to me, and I'm not thrilled by the thought of being dragged by a deranged thief across the continent, but I guess... I'm thankful that it brought me to you guys. I couldn't have made it this far alone."

"You wouldn't have needed to," Uriah muttered. "She wouldn't have bothered with you."

Aviva looked up from the ground and smiled, her light illuminating her face and casting shadows across her expression. "Either way, I'm glad it brought something good for you. To be honest, I..." She stopped herself, her eyes darkening. Shaking her head, she faced forward again. "Well, never mind. Another time, maybe."

With that, she sped up ahead of Kase and Tobias. Puzzled, Tobias glanced at Kase, hoping for some explanation. Kase's expression portrayed the same confusion that welled in Tobias's chest. When he finally caught Kase's eye, he merely shrugged. Frowning, Tobias jerked his chin in Aviva's direction.

It took a few seconds before the intent seemed to register for Kase. His eyes lit up when it did, and he nodded firmly. Clasping his hands behind his back, he made his way up to Aviva's side and bent down to speak to her in a hushed voice. She shot him a look and shoved his arm, but there was obviously no tension in the air between them.

Remember that you have a thief waiting for you in the cave above, Smoke's voice murmured in his mind, filling his thoughts with the buzz of the dragon's magic like it had before. *Try not to forget that, or you will be sure to fail.*

Tobias startled at the voice, only managing a strangled, *That's optimistic.*

I get my optimism from Kase, that is all. Time has not been kind to my Master, although he smiles and laughs it off. You can see it in his eyes sometimes.

Tobias reached to ask what he meant, but the dragon had already slipped away again, receding back into his bond with Kase and cutting Tobias out. A knot of worry formed in Tobias's throat, and he swallowed hard to force it down. It was the second time the overwhelming presence of Kase's dragon had cut into his mind, but he hadn't expected to experience it again. Tobias could only assume that, being as old and supposedly cryptic as he was, Smoke didn't reach out beyond his Rider unless he truly had something important to say.

Tobias gripped his sleeves as he kept on walking. The echo of his steps seemed distant and muffled as he reached out for a sign of the dragon's voice. *What's that supposed to mean anyway?*

But no answer came to him, and he was left alone again with his questions.

A THIEF'S MAGIC

TOBIAS LOST TRACK OF TIME in the dark passage, where the only light came from Aviva's staff. There was nothing to tell him how long it had been, but his feet ached as if he had been walking for hours—maybe even days. At one point, he tried counting the seconds, but the monotonous echoing of the group's footsteps made it hard to keep track, and the numbers eventually slipped uselessly through his fingers. Without them, he was stranded, once again thrown into the timeless, upward spiral toward the top of the mountain.

The path widened as they walked, and Uriah sped up to walk with Kase and Aviva. Tobias fell back to Oliver and Arayna. They had quieted since the walk started, and now seemed wholeheartedly focused on walking. Occasionally, they shared glances around Tobias, seemingly speaking through expressions Tobias didn't understand.

At first, he didn't mind so much. His thoughts latched onto Smoke's words. He found himself watching Kase's back. Pity rooted itself in Tobias's mind, pulling his expression into a thoughtful frown. Though he was conscious of Kase as a man with his own worries, he had spent so much time thinking about Eira and himself that he forgotten how painful it must have been for Kase.

Tobias dropped his gaze to the floor. What was it like to suffer the things Kase had for so long?

Not to mention... there's still that whole thing with the boy no one wants to discuss. Tobias narrowed his eyes, pursing his lips. *Why did you bring this up with me in the first place, Smoke?*

As he walked, that worry slowly began to fade, replaced by the constant ache of the soles of his feet.

A groan built up behind his clenched teeth, but he shoved it back down. He wasn't going to be the first to complain and pester Aviva when she was finally starting to seem less gloomy. She carried her head just a little higher and stood straighter as she walked.

Luckily, Arayna did it for him by throwing her head back and whining. The sound of her voice bounced around the hollow cave. "Aviva, how much farther is it to the top? And when can we take a break if it's far? My feet hurt and, like the *terrible* friend he is, Oliver says he won't carry me."

"You're not a baby, Arayna. You can walk like the rest of us," Oliver snapped back, folding his arms over his chest.

"But I'm *tired*," she whined, her ears flattening down. "We've been walking for... forever!"

Tobias wouldn't say it out loud, but he agreed with her. He didn't know what kind of magical stamina Kase, Aviva, and Uriah had, but all three of them looked perfectly fine and happy to keep on walking at their brisk pace. Oliver tried to hide it by holding his chin high, but his steps had slowed, and he had been muttering under his breath about reaching a stopping place.

Aviva came to a halt, sighing before turning around to face Tobias, Oliver, and Arayna. As soon as the group stopped, Arayna leaned against the wall with a groan.

A frown creased Aviva's face as her gaze swept over them. She glanced up at the shadowed ceiling far above them. "It's not that much farther, I'm sure. But I know you're tired. Should we rest for a moment?"

"It would be best if we kept moving," Uriah said, pointing down the path. "There's no telling how much longer Eira is going to wait around here, and we don't want to get there only to find she's left already."

"But Smoke is blocking one exit to the cave, and we're blocking the other. She doesn't have anywhere to go," Kase added. "It won't hurt to stop for a bit and rest. Besides, Arayna can't fight as well when she's exhausted. We're losing more if we keep going."

"Oh, look at you, so fancy with your *logic*." Uriah stuck his tongue out, chuckling when Kase's face flushed with anger. "Remember back in the forest? Eira was using magic. What would be stopping her from doing it again to get out of here?"

Aviva rubbed her temples, squeezing her eyes shut. The light of her staff flickered for a moment, threatening to go out. "Kase, Uriah, please stop arguing. If we're worried about Eira getting away, we can split up. Those that want to rest can stay here for a moment. The rest of us can go on ahead."

Arayna's ears perked up and she pushed herself away from the wall. "No, no no. We should stick together. I can go on; I won't drop dead from exhaustion."

Oliver heaved a sigh. "No, you need to rest. I'll stay behind with you."

"But I—"

"Absolutely not," he snapped, cutting her off with a glare. "I know what you'll do if you see Eira, and I won't allow it. Aviva and the others can go on ahead. We'll wait here."

Arayna curled her lip but said nothing. With a huff, she sank against the wall and folded her arms over her chest. "Fine."

"Then it's settled," Uriah said. "Aviva, Kase, and I will go on ahead. The three of you can wait here."

"Three?" Tobias jerked his gaze toward Uriah. "I'm not staying. I'm going ahead with you."

Surprise sparked in Uriah's eyes as he furrowed his brow. It quickly disappeared to make way for amusement, followed by a snort of laughter. "Right, of course you are. Seriously, Kase, where did you find this guy? He must have a death wish or something."

Tobias gritted his teeth. "Eira's not going to kill me, nor do I want her to. I want a chance to speak with her."

The corner of Uriah's mouth twitched up into a grin. "Right," he said in a low voice. "Come along then."

Aviva scrutinized Tobias, letting her free hand drop back to her side. The light in the staff brightened, revealing more of the rocky path to them.

"You're sure?" she asked.

He nodded.

Her gaze lingered for a moment longer before she turned away. She drew a set of runes in the air, summoning a flickering orb of light. The light drifted toward Oliver, settling in his hand.

"We'll be back soon," Aviva said.

Some tired part of Tobias's mind deflated, having been excited by the idea of stopping for a rest. He cast a longing glance back at Oliver and Arayna as they sank into a seat against the wall, huddled close to the light. In some ways, it was a good thing. Arayna's aggression toward Eira was the biggest problem. Although, he wasn't sure splitting up was the best idea, but neither was waiting too long. Uriah had a point, as much as he hated to admit it. They had to get to where Eira was before she decided to move on and make tracking her even more difficult.

Besides, he thought as they continued walking again. *Stopping to talk was enough of a rest for me, right?*

The ache in the bottom of his feet disagreed, but he ignored it.

It wasn't too much longer before the path ended at the

mouth of a cave, lit by moonlight from outside and a few scattered stumps of candles around the entrance. Wax had melded them to the smooth stone, and blacked wicks topped each of them. There were ten in total, placed awkwardly around the entrance. Tobias's heart skipped a beat.

Aviva bent down, brushing a hand across one of the candles. "These are quite recent. The wax is still warm."

"It's Eira." Kase reached for the hilt of his sword. "She's still here."

Aviva's light faded out and vanished. With the wave of her hand, she dismissed her staff, dispelling it into the same cloud of green sparks that enveloped Iila when he left her.

The four of them ducked behind the walls that made up the cave mouth, peering inside. Tobias couldn't see Eira from where he stood, but his skin crawled with unease. She had to be there.

"Is this the right place? I don't see her," Kase whispered.

"She's there." Aviva laced her fingers together, her green eyes narrowed in the dark. A slight glow emanated from her gaze as the air around her sparked with magic. "I know she is."

Uriah pushed away from the wall, grinning. "Well then, what're we waiting for?"

"Hold on!" Kase grabbed Uriah by the collar of his shirt and yanked him back, out of view from the cave. "We can't just rush in blindly! You're the one who reminded us that she has magic, remember? If we're going to fight magic, we need to come up with some kind of plan."

"I have a plan," Uriah protested in a harsh whisper. He grabbed his ax and pushed Kase out of the way. "It's called *Operation: To Catch A Thief.*"

Ignoring both Kase and Aviva's disapproving stares, Uriah maneuvered past Tobias and made his way toward the entrance of the cave. His golden eyes gleamed in the moonlight, and a wide smile spread across his face as he lifted his ax. Tobias didn't know what the look meant, but a chill crawled down his spine.

A sharp ringing filled his ears as soon as Uriah stepped through the cave mouth. Tobias stumbled back with a hiss as the ringing grew louder, his vision flickering. Searing heat surged through him, and a growl tore through his mind.

Get back! Smoke's voice warned.

A sharp pain stabbed through the back of Tobias's mind, his vision completely fading to black. *Get out of my head!* Tobias snapped back, panic clawing its way up his throat.

Something yanked him forward and his knees met the stone. Shaking his head, he blinked rapidly, and his vision flickered back, his gaze resting on the stone floor bathed in silver moonlight. Smoke vanished again, leaving a dull throbbing headache behind. Aviva was beside him, her hand against his temples and her face creased with worry. Shivering, Tobias wrapped his arms around himself, sweat beading on his forehead. What was Smoke doing in his mind?

He lifted his head to take in his surroundings. He had been pulled into the cave—the dragon hoard, as Kase called it. Moonlight spilled in through the open mouth on the far side of the cave, flooding the area with silver light. Dust swirled around him, coating the back of his throat. Coughing, he scrubbed the dirt from his face and turned toward the entrance to the passage.

Rocks sealed it off, muffling the voices on the other side. With a gasp, Tobias scrambled to his feet and raced back to the rocks. Fear seized his heart, squeezing until he couldn't breathe. Had anyone been trapped underneath?

"Kase?" he called, prying smaller chunks of rubble away. "Uriah?"

A firm hand landed on his shoulder and pulled him away from the rocks. His gaze landed on Kase—his face smeared with dirt, but he was otherwise unharmed. Behind him, Uriah was helping Aviva to her feet. Relief coursed through Tobias.

"What… what happened?" he asked.

"Something tried to kill us, or separate us," Aviva murmured, surveying the pile of rocks, her lips set in a firm frown. "There was a spike of magic in the air. You collapsed and the ceiling caved in. I think it was caused by the sudden shift in pressure."

Tobias bit the inside of his mouth, taking deep breaths to calm his racing heart. "Smoke kind of… invaded my head? I don't know what he was trying to do. He's been talking to me some ever since we entered the mountain." He rubbed the back of his head, where the pain had come from. What was Smoke trying to tell him? Frustration clouded his mind.

If he wants to say something, he should say it outright instead of talking circles around me and then stabbing my mind.

Kase frowned, turning toward the opening at the other side of the cave. Smoke circled in the distance outside, his red scales barely noticeable against the deep, midnight blue sky. "If that was supposed to be some kind of protection, it was pretty lackluster. I sort of felt him shield our bond, but he said nothing to me." He pressed a fisted hand to his lips and a distant look crossed his eyes. Tobias could only guess he had taken his complaints directly to Smoke himself.

Tobias swept his gaze around the cave, searching for a sign of Eira. A large opening sat at one side; beyond it, Smoke flew circles in the night sky. A cool breeze flowed in, relieving some of the stench of dragon that lingered in the air. The cave stretched high above his head, clusters of stalactites clinging to the ceiling above. It was large enough that a dragon slightly smaller than Smoke could fit comfortably inside. He imagined Smoke himself would have had to squeeze to get in, though.

The room was empty. The walls were too smooth, devoid of nooks or crannies where she could hide. They moved toward the center of the room together, but there was still no sign of Eira.

Licking his dry lips, Tobias opened his mouth. Before he could speak, Aviva raised a finger for him to keep quiet.

"She's here," she said, voice low. "Keep still and stay together."

Tobias drew closer to Aviva and Kase, gripping his sword so tightly his knuckles turned white. He glanced toward Kase, who had reached back to grab the hilt of his weapon. Uriah pressed close as well, though his stance didn't reflect the same tension Tobias glimpsed in both Kase and Aviva.

The silence in the cave felt thick, making it hard to breathe. A million anxious thoughts flashed through Tobias's mind, and some part of him begged Eira to show her face so he could stop imagining worst-case scenarios. His skin prickled with unease. The seconds dragged by.

He bit the inside of his cheek and swept his gaze over the smooth walls another time. *Where are you, Eira?*

As though his thoughts had summoned her, Eira's laughter rang through the still air. "How perceptive of you, Aviva," she teased. "I should have known better than to expect that I could hide myself from you. I was hoping you would blunder about in search of me for a while longer, but I guess you're done playing that game now?"

Kase growled, his dark eyes flashing red. "Why don't you cut the act and show your face, coward?"

Eira clicked her tongue. "You lack tact, Kase. Still all brawn and no brains, it seems. I see you did escape death, though."

Drawing his sword, Kase rushed forward and took a swing at the empty air in front of him. Eira only laughed. He gritted his teeth and turned, slicing through the emptiness again. Tobias winced, wondering if Kase would act this violently if he could really see Eira.

Aviva gasped. Kase immediately froze and spun around to

face her at the same time as Tobias. An invisible force had latched onto her satchel, pulling the spellbook out from it. Aviva summoned Iila in a flash of green light. The winged snake hissed and lunged for the force, mouth open and fangs bared. The spellbook, now free of the confines of Aviva's satchel, withdrew from Iila's bite. Once it was out of reach, a loud snap echoed through the cave and Eira appeared, dangling the book in her hands. A proud smirk adorned her features, and her eyes gleamed as if she had already won.

Flaring his feathered wings, Iila rushed toward her for a second strike. Eira backed away. She summoned the flecks of gold-tinted magic and flicked her wrist. The air shimmered, creating a barrier between her and the snake's fangs. When she snapped her fingers, the barrier rebounded against Iila and knocked him to the ground. As the snake struggled to right himself, Eira lifted her foot and slammed her heel down on his head.

"Iila!" Aviva cried, taking a step forward. Uriah threw his arm out to stop her.

As soon as Eira withdrew her foot, Iila disappeared. Cold dread lined the pit of Tobias's stomach.

Eira sighed, inspecting the bottom of her shoe. "Such a shame. I only meant to frighten him off. It's amazing what this magic can do." She snapped the spellbook shut and raised her face, smiling cruelly.

Tobias stepped back as she advanced toward them. His wound ached with the memory of her blade in his flesh, and his breath caught in his throat. He gripped his sword tighter for stability.

"Eira," Kase ground out, lifting his sword and pointing it at her. He stepped between her and Aviva, who was still staring at the place where Iila had been. "Return the spellbook. Don't make us go through this again."

"It is rather funny, isn't it?" Eira chuckled dryly. "Doesn't it give you a sense of déjà vu? A cave, the book in my hands, you telling me to hand it over." Eira's hand slid to a knife at her waist. "But trust me, things are going to be different this time."

Icy cold gripped the air, twisting it into a piercing *wrongness.* The pressure heightened, pressing firmly against Tobias's shoulders and sending a shiver down his spine. Magic crackled at Eira's fingertips; even Kase took a tentative step back from her.

"I've learned a few new tricks since our last run-in." Eira lifted her free hand, drawing a symbol through the air with the glittering magic at her fingertips. A crown-like mark appeared on her forehead, black like ink and glistening in the moonlight. "Wouldn't you like to see what I learned?"

Tobias stood rigid, his heart threatening to burst from his chest. His hands trembled, but he didn't move. He couldn't tell if it was fear that kept him there or morbid curiosity. From the chill that laced through his blood, he guessed the fear outweighed the curiosity. *Move,* he begged his body, his urgency thrumming unanswered through his veins. *Do something!*

Eira had barely completed drawing her magic rune when Aviva's hand shot out and grabbed Kase by his cloak, yanking him back. With a brief flash and an ear-popping drop in pressure, Aviva vanished. Tobias, bewildered, turned to stare wide-eyed at where she had been, finding that Uriah and Kase had both disappeared as well.

A thorny root of despair choked the air from Tobias's lungs.

"Oh," Eira sighed. "Guess she didn't want to see."

Tobias spun to face her, pointing his sword at her the way Kase had. He begged his hands to stop shaking, but they didn't. She scrutinized him with her sapphire gaze which only made the trembling worse.

"What did you do?" he asked. His voice quivered, much like his hands. He cursed himself. "What kind of magic was that?"

"That wasn't me," Eira said, splaying her hands innocently. He kept his gaze locked on her right hand, where she still held on to the hilt of her dagger. "It was Aviva. It's something she does when she panics."

Tobias studied her, but it didn't appear she was lying. If anything, she looked… *relieved.* There was the slightest loosening in her stance, a droop in her shoulders, like she was more comfortable. Even her grip on her dagger had lessened.

"You can put the sword down. I just want to talk to you."

"I'd rather talk with my sword in hand, if it's all the same to you," he said, holding tighter to his weapon. Though his knuckles ached, it brought him some semblance of safety.

She sighed. "Why do you insist on being so untrusting? We have a similar goal—we both want to understand this." She lifted the spellbook and waved it, her expression softening into a more open, friendly smile. "You said before that you had an interest in my companion as well."

"I'm not doing this," he snapped, forcing his voice to remain firm. "I'm not like you. I won't turn against my friends for something as fleeting as power or secrets, and you're not someone I can trust. In case you forgot, you *tried to kill me* last time we met."

He clung desperately to that image of the fragile, helpless Eira he had seen at times beneath the gold of her borrowed magic. If he could get that Eira to resurface, he had a chance to make it out alive. Perhaps he could reason with her.

Eira's eyes flashed; sparks of magic gathered at her fingertips, making Tobias flinch back. "The power he grants me isn't fleeting! As long as I obey, it will last."

"How is that trade worthwhile?" Tobias bit back. "This person, whoever he may be, is using you. Can't you see that? You're being manipulated. You're being forced to do horrible things, and for what? A little bit of magic to throw around as you please? How is that trade worth anything to you?"

Eira flinched. Slowly, her hand reached to grip a pendant

that hung around her neck: a small, lime-green rock, dangling from a thin chain. Tobias frowned. Had she always worn that?

For just a moment, her gaze drifted away. The fragile Eira returned, releasing her hold on the magic she had summoned. Her lips pursed and she wrapped her arms around herself.

When she didn't respond, he took a deep breath and softened his tone. "Listen, Eira, I can't condone any of your actions. I can't allow you to continue to act this way. I can't excuse what you've done. But I do believe that something isn't right here, and I'm going to get to the bottom of it. If you would just give me the book—"

The softened look in her face vanished, replaced with a hardened stare. She recoiled, holding the book close to her chest and the pendant she wore. "If you won't be swayed, then I have no reason to discuss any more with you. Goodbye, Tobias."

"Hold on—"

All too late, he reached to catch her wrist and pry the book from her hands. His fingers fell just short. A swirling cloud of dust rose up from the stone and swallowed her form. When the cloud vanished, Eira had gone, taking the book with her. Only a few flecks of gold remained, drifting aimlessly through the air.

Tobias stood alone in the cave for several more seconds, his hand still outstretched as if he had a chance of catching her. But she was gone.

He curled his fingers into a fist, gritting his teeth.

There was something she was trying to tell him, something he still couldn't quite grasp. Like Smoke, she favored cryptic words. She had been dragging him in circles since day one, and this was no different.

No matter what it takes, I'm going to figure you out, Eira. He cupped his hand around one of the sparks that remained, holding it close to his chest. It flickered in his palm for a mere moment before dying out.

I promise.

21

ONE STEP AHEAD

SMOKE CIRCLED IN THE SKY another time before flying to the cave mouth, peering inside with one amber eye. A low hum rumbled from the back of his throat, but he didn't seem particularly unnerved.

Tobias sheathed his sword, releasing a deep sigh. The buzz of adrenaline finally faded, leaving him exhausted and empty. "She got away," he told the dragon, an edge to his voice that surprised him. "She used magic to escape, and she has the spellbook."

The old dragon pulled away with a grunt, exhaling a thin tendril of smoke through his nose. Unfurling his wings, he pushed himself away from the opening and took off into the sky again. Moonlight glinted off his red scales, though he was soon swallowed by the deep shadows of night.

Tobias guessed he was already relaying the information to Kase.

He gripped his arm, glaring down at his feet. It was so easy to promise something, but following through was proving to be a lot more difficult. Eira was always one step ahead of him, always inside his head. Ordinarily, he might have decided that was the signal that he should have listened to Kase and gone home. He might have allowed his resolve to crumble again, rendering him just as useless as a lost child.

But he had made up his mind, and something about Eira's behavior still didn't sit right with him. This time, he took a deep breath and steeled himself. This time, he lifted his head and pressed on.

Shoving his worries to the back of his mind, he turned on his heels and raced back to the blocked exit of the cave. It hadn't changed since he had left it, and the sight of it left a sour taste on his tongue. He pulled at any small, loose rocks, trying to shift the heavier ones and make them collapse. "Oliver? Are you there?" He hesitated a moment, then, "Arayna?"

"Tobias?"

The rocks shifted, opening up a tiny crack. Tobias knelt down to peer through it, meeting Arayna's gaze on the other side. "Finally," she said, grinning. "Someone else to help me move these rocks. You okay? What happened?"

"Where's Oliver?"

"Here."

Arayna stepped aside, allowing Oliver to come into view. One hand squeezed the other; blood coated his fingers. Even so, he smiled wearily. "I cut my hand on the rocks, so try to be careful."

Tobias nodded. Turning back to the rocks, he pried a few more loose and tossed them aside. It took several minutes, and his arms began to tremble with exhaustion. Larger rocks tumbled free as Arayna made progress on her side. The pile began to shift, and Tobias dodged out of the way as a couple chunks rolled over where he had been standing. Soon, the path opened up again and Tobias stepped through, breathing a sigh of relief as he let his arms fall loosely to his sides. Arayna stretched, her ears twitching as she flashed him a smile.

"Thanks," she said. Her smile faltered as her gaze slid past him. "Where are Aviva and the boys?"

Tobias jolted, reaching up to grip the hilt of his sword. "I was going to ask you that. She disappeared, taking Kase and Uriah with her. Then Eira managed to get away." He bit the inside of his mouth, waiting for Oliver to throw one of his sharp, disappointed glares his way, but he never did.

Oliver sighed instead, still pressing down on his bloody wound. "When Aviva panics, she tends to teleport away. It's how she's always been; it's why Kase believed she was alive for so long, and I guess he was right." He looked back toward the path they had taken to get there. "The spell doesn't have much range, so I doubt she even made it outside. They'll be back soon."

Tobias's fingers closed tighter around the sword's hilt. As much as he wanted to brush it off, Aviva had left him scrambling. Eira could have killed him—though, the fact that she didn't was confusing in and of itself. Bitterness welled up inside his chest.

"Sorry she left you," Arayna said, offering Tobias a consoling pat on the shoulder. She went to Oliver's side and grabbed his hands, yanking him forward so she could examine his wound. He yelped in protest, muttering a string of curses, but she ignored him.

Tobias reached into his satchel and pulled out a thick roll of cloth bandages. He was glad to have picked them up from Aviva's house before they left.

"Here." He pressed them into Arayna's hands, stepping back. She looked at them, scrunching her nose and furrowing her brow. He sighed and took them back, gently pushing her out of the way as he knelt down. Carefully, he wrapped the wound on Oliver's hand. Tobias had never been good at first aid. He really didn't know much of anything aside from *don't bleed everywhere*, but all he had to do was wait until Aviva came back. She would be able to heal it with her magic.

Magic... His thoughts leapt back to Eira, focusing in particular on the green pendant she wore. When he thought about it, the pendant did have a strange aura to it, and the look in her eyes had changed ever so slightly when she touched it. Shaking his head, he tied off the bandage, stepping back.

"She took the spellbook," Tobias repeated, raking his fingers through his hair. "She got away with it, *again.*"

Arayna looked toward Oliver, who kept his gaze focused on his hand as he flexed his fingers. He turned and picked up his bow, slinging his quiver over his shoulder.

"I can't really blame you." He shrugged and maneuvered past Tobias, stepping into the cave and looking around. "It's not like you have a lot of prior experience in battle—or even with thieves. Especially not thieves who somehow all of the sudden have magic that they didn't have for as long as you knew them." He growled, turning his back to the entryway again. "It's all so stupid!"

"I'm sorry," Tobias murmured, gripping his sleeves and looking down at his feet. His face warmed with embarrassment and shame, and he didn't dare lift his head to face Oliver and Arayna. "I caused this mess. I thought I could do better, but she's always ahead of me."

He wanted to punch himself, or at least knock some sense into his thoughts, but he knew he was right. It *was* his fault the book had been stolen in the first place. Aviva left it in his care, and Eira had so easily weaseled it out of his hands.

You told yourself you would move past this, he reminded himself. *Remember? Saving Eira and putting the pieces together and all that? That's what you're here for.*

Tobias straightened under the presence of that reminder. He was going to press on anyway, no matter what doubts tried to weigh him down. The fragile look in Eira's face was still present, and it still cried for help. Reclaiming the spellbook was one priority; getting to the bottom of things was another. It was a puzzle, and he was determined to solve it.

"We all make mistakes," Oliver finally said, his voice wavering. "I mean, look at Arayna. She's a walking mistake."

"Excuse me?" Arayna punched his arm, turning up her nose at him as he laughed. "You're an even bigger mistake—the worst friend ever!"

"Oh yeah?"

"Yeah, you… you…" She scrunched up her face in thought, folding her arms over her chest. "Give me a minute. I'll come up with something."

Tobias smiled, watching the two of them. Their bickering continued, and Arayna threw more punches at Oliver's arm, but he laughed them off. At the sight of that, Tobias's heart twisted. His grip loosened on his sword hilt, the weight of the key hanging around his neck suddenly growing more obvious. It pulled at his neck, a soft reminder of the home that waited for him when he chose to return. Though the house had most likely remained empty while he had been gone, the memory of it was sweet. Swallowing hard, he glanced down at his hands.

He could already imagine how tightly he would hug Talia and his father when he saw them again. His chest had never ached so much for their company. Now, it was like a thorny vine had wound around it and pulled until the sharp edges dug into his flesh.

When he returned home, he would be someone they could be proud of.

Arayna stopped her argument mid-sentence, her body stiffening as her ears pricked up. Her gaze snapped toward the passageway they had left behind. Following her lead, Tobias turned just as a light appeared on the path, breaking through the shadows that hung over the entrance. It wasn't long before Aviva, Kase, and Uriah emerged from the dark. Uriah spotted them first, and his face lit up.

"Finally!" He rushed forward and left the other two behind. Bursting through the entryway, he made his way toward the cave opening. He spread his arms wide with a sigh as he stared out at the sky. "Ah, fresh air," he murmured. After a moment, he turned back to face the others. "I guess Eira is gone? Well, at least you cleared the rocks away."

Aviva looked less relieved as she came to meet Tobias, her lips pressed into a thin line and her brows drawn together. Kase gently took her staff from her hands, and Tobias noted that he mirrored her tight expression.

"I'm glad you're alright," she said. She bent slightly at the waist, bowing respectfully to him. "It wasn't my intention at all to leave you behind back there. I didn't even realize you weren't with me until I had already left the room. I'm truly very sorry."

A little of his bitterness lifted. "Don't worry about me; I was fine. But she got away with the book. Shouldn't we regroup and go after her?"

Aviva straightened, her eyes gleaming as her frown lifted into a mischievous smile. "You mean this book?" She reached into her satchel and pulled out the white spellbook—the same one Tobias had seen Eira steal from her just moments ago.

Surprise dragged a gasp from his lips and his heart skipped a beat. "How—how did you do that?"

The book caught Uriah's attention, snapping his gaze toward them. He said nothing, but his lips thinned in a tight frown. As soon as Tobias glanced at him, he turned away to study the opening to the outside again.

Aviva slid the book back into her bag, covering it once again. "I knew she would be after it, so I created an illusion that she could steal. It feels real enough to convince her, but it won't last long. However, she surely went back to her companion, and she's going to lead us right to him. I want to know who it is that's so interested in my magic."

"What about Iila?" Tobias asked. The image of the snake's

head flattened beneath Eira's boot resurfaced, and he almost regretted asking.

She laced her fingers together, shifting her gaze to the ground. "He's… dead. I could summon another familiar, but it would take too much time."

"Oh," Tobias murmured, scrambling to find the right words. His heart sank. "I'm sorry."

Kase rested a hand on Aviva's shoulder. "For now, we're going to rest here. It's late, and we all need it. We can make a plan in the morning before we set off. Smoke will keep watch."

Weariness crashed down on Tobias, nearly toppling him over. He pushed it back and nodded in acknowledgement of Kase's plan for the night. Nothing sounded better than a moment to sleep and eat. On top of that, knowing Eira hadn't really thrown him all the way back to the beginning sent a flicker of relief throughout his body.

Arayna pulled Aviva away with an apologetic glance at Kase, explaining as the two walked that Oliver had a cut in need of healing. Oliver protested, but the Mage ignored him and tended to the wound. Tobias drowned the rest of the noise out as he collapsed in the nearest open spot in the cave, curling up and resting his head against his satchel. The cold of the stone seeped through his clothes, and the ground pressed uncomfortably against his back, but his eyes slid closed and sleep claimed him before he even had a chance to complain about it.

22

IMAGO

"YOU WANTED TO SPEAK WITH ME?" Kase sat at the edge of the open cave mouth. His feet dangled over the edge, far above the ground below. The sky still bore the deep violet of night, speckled with countless silver stars, a full moon in the center of it all. To his left, seated on a ledge against the mountain face, Smoke sat with his tail curled over his front feet. Kase guessed it was important—whatever the dragon had woken him for—and he rubbed the remains of sleep from his eyes.

When the dragon didn't respond, he ran his tongue over his lips and continued, "Everyone else is asleep," he said. "And it's still too early to wake them. You're not going to say we should move yet, are you?"

Smoke didn't turn to look at Kase, his gaze fixed on the distance. The very tip of his long tail twitched, and Kase couldn't help but notice the way his wings fidgeted.

Your little one is moving again, Smoke murmured softly as though the news might break Kase. *I believe he caught my voice when I opened myself up to your companions. In hindsight, my continued connection with Tobias did not help deter him. I apologize for that.*

Kase flinched back, curling his fingers tighter so that his nails dug into his palms. "What am I supposed to do about that? If he comes here, who knows what the others will do. And I'm still unnerved by this *person* Eira keeps mentioning. What if it really is the same dragonborn that was hunting Calix? What do I do then?" He raked his fingers through his hair, frustration rising. "I promised I would protect him, but what can I do against a dragonborn? And how can I protect him from the others if they were to meet? For crying out loud, Smoke, he's..."

He shot a look back, making sure everyone was still sound asleep. No one stirred, and the sounds of soft snores filled the silence. Still, Kase leaned forward and lowered his voice.

"He's a hybrid."

Smoke chuckled, his deep voice resonating down their bond. His presence glided easily along the thread, gently wrapping Kase in a comforting warmth. Kase sighed deeply, sinking in the security of Smoke's still calmness. It anchored him in a safe place where he could feel warm and secure until the storm passed.

Kase took a deep breath and loosened his fingers. A soft sting lingered in his palm, but he ignored it for the time being. He buried his face in his hands, resting his elbows against his knees. "Sorry," he said. "I'm leaping to all kinds of conclusions."

It is alright. Smoke turned his head toward Kase. *You are human, and I am learning that this is simply how your kind acts. Your lives are so short, yet you lack the focus to get things done. I do not think you should worry about things you cannot control. Time will present the problem to you when it is ready, and you cannot wrestle with it until then, so try to put your heart at ease.*

"I can't just stop thinking about him, Smoke," Kase snapped, his voice rising as bitterness and anger squeezed his chest. "I took him in and tried to raise him as my own brother, and then I *dumped* him without so much as a proper goodbye. How can I put that behind me? I promised to protect him, and I failed!"

You did protect him, Smoke reasoned. The calm in his voice made Kase's blood boil, his face warm as he glared at the dragon. *You simply did not like the method by which you did it.*

Kase spun toward the old dragon. "Because it was stupid! If it was up to me, I would have—"

I did not call you here to argue over Calix. Smoke curled his lip back, glaring at Kase with narrowed amber eyes. *I was simply informing you of something important. You would do well to control yourself before you wake someone else and attract unwanted attention.*

As quickly as it had come, Kase's anger ebbed away. Wearily, he nodded and eased himself back into his seat again. The cool night air helped to remove the stinging burn of anger, but it bitterly reminded him of the freezing night on which he had found Calix in the first place. How many years had passed since then? Five? He couldn't help but wonder how much Calix had grown since then.

Part of him ached to see the child again, but he couldn't promise that. His presence had drawn the dragonborn to them last time. Calix was better off on his own.

He swiped angrily at his tears as more and more memories flooded through his head. He didn't understand why his mind had to be such a curse. When one good thing was achieved, he couldn't enjoy it. The next bad thing was always thrown at him immediately. There was no time to rest or even to catch his breath.

He was always drowning in regrets.

Smoke sighed and nudged Kase's thigh until he laid a hand on the dragon's head. *I understand that you are upset, Kase. I am sorry that my advice back then hurt you so much.*

"It's okay." Kase stroked Smoke's scales, smiling a little as the dragon purred—much like a giant, scaly old cat. "What was it you wanted to talk about?"

Something even less cheerful, I'm afraid.

Laughing dryly, Kase tilted his head back to watch the sky

grow lighter. Dark, inky blues and violets were swiftly painted over by the pale azure of day, tinged with oranges and pinks beyond the mountains. He clenched his fists, knowing it wouldn't be long until they would depart again.

"Don't hold back then, I guess."

The old dragon exhaled, a thin tendril of smoke coiling up from his nose and drifting away with the breeze. *I managed to confirm my suspicions. The companion Eira boasts of is indeed the dragonborn Aurum. I can feel his magic, and I can see its tainted aura around the thief. I will do some more digging on the way if we intend to follow Eira, but I am sure it is him.*

Kase swallowed thickly, raking his hands through his hair with a growl. "What would you suggest I do about it?" Facing a dragonborn was the absolute worst thing he could think of doing. He had done it before and had barely escaped with his life both times. Considering the strengths of the others in the group, he couldn't see any of them making it out alive. The thought drove a thorn into his heart.

Kase, Smoke began in a solemn tone. *Lift your head and look at me.*

Without waiting for an explanation, he did. Smoke's amber eyes gazed back at him, twinged with grief and glittering with knowledge. Kase's throat constricted as the beginnings of tears welled up again. Smoke had told him, long ago, of a vision he had had. It was a gift of red dragons to catch mere glimpses of the future, and Smoke always caught lengthy and accurate ones. The specifics slipped through Kase's fingers like sand in an hourglass, but he could easily recall the overwhelming sadness that plunged both of them into the deep end when the vision first came.

He already knew his course of action. His lips quivered as he looked away. "I see."

I cannot stop what I foresee or else I would. Try as I might, the ends will meet regardless of my will. Time is mine to command, but it is not mine to change. A sort of whine escaped the dragon as he crawled closer to Kase, resting his chin in his lap. His ruby colored scales sent warmth through Kase's body, but it didn't ease the chill that crawled down his spine.

Have courage, dear friend, for I will always be with you. You know that. His eyes slid shut as Kase smoothed his hand across his scales. *But... how long do you intend to keep up this pleasant, heroic facade in front of your friends?*

Kase shrugged, feeling for the dragon keeper pin in his pocket and holding it tight. "Forever if I must."

Smoke chuckled, low and dry. He lifted his head and returned to his former position, his watchful gaze fixed on the sunrise. Sunlight flashed across his scales as his tail moved to curl around his talons. Perched upon the rocks, glowing in the early morning sunlight, he looked much more like the god—Imago—that he was.

Kase wanted him to remain as Smoke forever, but it was impossible. He had known since the day he agreed to their bond, and yet his chest ached with betrayal. The side to him that echoed of Imago had always been painfully distant and cold. He preferred the Smoke side, the one that exchanged wit with him and extended grace for his failures. As much as he wished, he could never have one without the other. They were one, and they were all Imago. Smoke was simply the affectionate side he had crafted through years of serving as the dragon's keeper.

With a bitter smile, he glanced down at his hands in his lap. *Empty promises. All we do is make empty promises,* he thought, keeping it locked deep inside his mind and warding off Smoke's intrusive searching.

Was his bond with Smoke an empty promise as well? Was that how Imago saw it?

Reeling Kase back into the present, Smoke sighed deeply. A flood of emotions raced down the bond, rushing past Kase too quickly for him to comprehend any of them. *You speak of forever without truly considering the word,* Smoke chided. *Forever is nothing to a dragon, or to a god. Humans know nothing or forever or eternity, and how could they? Everything you know has an end. Yet you throw the word around so casually.*

When he thought about it, he knew Smoke was right, just as he always was. Even so, Kase didn't cry. He couldn't. He had known his future for many years, ever since Smoke had spoken of his visions and attested to how unavoidable they were. No matter what he did, the truth of what lay in store always loomed over their heads. There was nowhere to go to escape its shadow, so Kase had stopped running.

"As long as you're with me," he whispered, "I know everything will be okay."

Then I will be with you.

Kase smiled, knowing that what Smoke said was true. He grabbed hold of their shared bond and held it tightly, curling up near the edge of the cave mouth so he could be close to his dragon. The stone pressed harshly against him, and the wind buffeted his face, but he savored the touch as long as it lasted.

Sleep greeted him the moment he closed his eyes, carrying him off to a world where his worries and fears didn't matter anymore. Somewhere he could smile easily and dream freely.

And that was how he knew the dream wouldn't last.

23

BETRAYAL

THE HAZY FOG of sleep faded before Tobias was willing to release it. A strangled shout dragged him back to the waking world, cutting away the remaining threads of tiredness. His eyes flew open, and he was met with the sight of a smooth stone wall across from him. A flickering, white light cast long shadows across the room, projecting the image of two figures locked in a fight. It was hazy and distant, yet familiar all the same.

"Uriah, please," Aviva begged, voice small and fragile. "Don't do this."

Uriah? Tobias shot upright, scrambling for his sword. His fingers closed around the hilt as he turned toward the source of the light. Aviva's staff lay broken on the ground, its light dimming slowly. Uriah had Aviva pinned to the ground, the spellbook trapped between his hands and Aviva's as they fought for possession of it. Threads of emerald magic bound the book to Aviva, but they trembled as Uriah pulled against them.

"Sorry, but there is something I must do," Uriah ground out. His voice shook with determination, his face pinched in concentration.

"Hey!" Tobias pushed to his feet and drew his sword. The

226

distance closed between them before he could fully process what he was doing, as though his legs had moved of their own accord. He swung the sword in a wide arc, grazing Uriah's cheek. Guilt choked him the moment blood stained his blade. *Is this really Uriah? What's going on?*

Uriah cursed as he leapt back, releasing his hold on the spellbook. His eyes flicked to Tobias and his familiar grin twitched the corners of his mouth upward. "What a surprise. I thought I sealed everyone out. Perhaps that magical blankness of yours kept you inside."

Tobias spared a quick glance around them, gripping his sword tighter. The cave was empty and dark; the air was thick with magic, and it pressed firmly against him, filling his mind with heavy fog. It was the same sensation he had encountered in the wyrm's cave.

Aviva scrambled upright, clutching the spellbook against her chest. The green threads multiplied and wound tightly around her to hold the book in place. "Think this through, Uriah. You're not yourself. There has to be another way."

"Oh, there you go again. Always thinking you know what's best for everyone." Uriah rolled his eyes as he wiped the blood from his cheek. "Seriously, Aviva, all you really want is whatever best suits *you*. Can't you see my side of things? Your time is running out. The Summoners will only ignore you as long as the corruption persists, and you can't live while it grows. You'll be snuffed out—all because you refuse to meet me halfway. I made a deal with the Shadowslayer: I *will* bring him the spellbook and your magic in exchange for the purification of this corrupted world." He laughed to himself. "Unlike Kase, I am a man of my word. I don't make empty promises."

The Shadowslayer? Tobias glanced at Aviva, searching her face for some sign that anything Uriah was saying was supposed to make sense. *That old Sheniirian legend?* It was the second time Uriah had mentioned it, and that made Tobias's skin crawl.

Aviva's expression gave nothing away; her emotions were sealed behind a thoughtful frown. "Do you know what kind of deal you're making with this man? Think of your family. Your brother, Uriah. What would he think?"

Uriah reached for his ax settled against his back. "Everything I do is for him. He'll understand when it all comes to an end."

Hesitation and fear rooted Tobias in place. Since when had Uriah made a deal to turn on them? He was Aviva's Guardian—more than that, he was her friend. Did he not hate Eira for doing the same thing he was choosing to do now? *Unless... he's also trapped the same way she is.*

Uriah rushed forward, raising his ax for a strike. Tobias ducked on instinct, swiping his sword out in an effort to stop him. The blade nicked Uriah's arm as he dodged, swerving around the path of Tobias's sword with ease. A swift kick knocked Tobias's legs out from under him. Cold stone met him as he collapsed, jarring him with the impact. Gritting his teeth, he pushed himself up again and spun to face Uriah. He was mere steps from Aviva, who stood frozen in place, glaring up at him.

"Why are you doing this?" Tobias called, begging him to stop if only for just a moment. "What changed, Uriah?"

His steps halted and the ax lowered. "Eira failed one too many times. I have to clean up her mistakes. It's nothing personal, really. You'll understand someday."

Tobias's mind whirled for an explanation. How long had Uriah been working with Eira? It stung to think about, yet he couldn't push it away. The more he tried to put the pieces together, the clearer the image became, pointing towards the shimmering gold of Uriah's eyes.

Perhaps he had always been against them.

An arrow pierced through the sealing enchantment, embedding itself in Uriah's shoulder. He stumbled back with a grunt and reached to grab the shaft, his face twisted in pain. Tobias seized the opportunity and ran to Aviva's side, shielding her from another attack. A hole opened in the enchantment, giving way to a clear view of the cave outside. Arayna leapt through the opening with a roar, throwing herself at Uriah and shoving him against the ground with ease. Oliver stood behind her, a second arrow nocked against his bow.

"There's two more," Uriah sneered. "The last one won't be far behind, huh?" He pried his arm free and slammed it against the side of Arayna's head, throwing her off. She collided against the stone with a resounding *crack*.

Aviva gasped and stepped out toward Arayna, magic dancing at the tips of her fingers. Tobias threw his arm in front of her and shook his head when she met his eye. Blood pooled on the stone—bright red against the slate gray. The sight of it made his chest constrict, but Uriah knelt too close to Arayna, ax in hand and a look of madness in his golden eyes. He was baiting Aviva for all Tobias knew.

Oliver drew the bowstring back to his jaw, his hand trembling. "Stay where you are," he snapped, cutting cleanly through the silence. "I won't miss a second time."

Uriah chuckled as he rose to his feet, pressing a hand to his wounded shoulder. "You never miss. What, don't have the heart to kill a friend? It would be so easy for you to do it from there."

Hesitation crossed Oliver's face and his grip faltered. The string loosened as he slowly lowered his bow. "I..." He trailed off, leaving his statement unfinished as he glanced at Arayna. She remained huddled on the floor, painfully still as her blood pooled at their feet.

Tobias gripped his sword tightly, desperately searching for a solution. The sight of blood made his stomach churn, and his throat clenched to think that Uriah was only going to get more violent if they stood in his way. There had to be a way to make it end as safely and quietly as possible. He scrutinized Uriah. There were no golden threads in sight and no desperation beneath his taunts. The only hint to the same magic as Eira was the shimmer of gold swirling in his eyes. What kind of promise did he make with the Shadowslayer to take things this far?

Uriah swung toward Tobias, his gaze sliding to Aviva beside him. Tobias stiffened, raising his sword. "Don't come closer," he said. The words came out in a rush, blurring together as his voice trembled. He swallowed hard. "If we… if we give you the spellbook, will that help you? Will that put an end to this?"

The words left a sour taste on his tongue. Every part of him screamed that it was a bad idea—he didn't know the consequences, he didn't know that Uriah would keep his word. And yet, it was the only thing that made Uriah stop. An inkling of a plan began to form in Tobias's mind, weaving together a fragile image of victory: the end of the back-and-forth game.

"I knew I liked you." Uriah returned his ax to the sheath against his back. "You're the most reasonable. It's not all about murder with you."

"Answer my question," Tobias snapped, narrowing his eyes. "If I let you walk away with the book, will that satisfy the Shadowslayer? Will he stop coming after Aviva, Kase, and the rest of us? Is the book all that he wants?"

"Tobias," Aviva hissed.

Uriah paused for a moment, pressing his fist to his lips as he frowned thoughtfully. The gold shine in his eyes dimmed slightly—a familiar sign that made Tobias's breath hitch. It was faint, but it was there. Perhaps Uriah *was* suffering the same kind of manipulation as Eira.

"I'm sure I can work out some kind of deal," Uriah said confidently. He held out his hand, a smile crawling across his lips. "The spellbook please, Aviva. The *real* one. I'll know if you try to pull something like you did earlier."

Aviva pressed the spellbook closer against her chest. Her gaze slid to Arayna and Tobias followed the look. Oliver had crouched beside her to examine her wound. His shoulders trembled, but he kept his head low to hide his face from view. Aviva drew in a deep breath, standing straighter as she faced Uriah again. The green threads fell away, but she still held tightly to the book.

"A Mage should never agree to part with her spellbook without first consulting both Guardians," she murmured as she lifted her hand, drawing a set of runes in the air. "Kase would be upset with me if I did that a second time."

"Kase," Uriah echoed, stepping back as though the name had burned him. He jerked toward the opening, reaching for his ax.

An empty cave lay beyond the jagged, shimmering edge of the opening in the enchantment. Faint, morning sunlight spilled inside, but it stopped at the barrier's edge, unable to cross through hole Oliver and Arayna had created. There was no sign of Kase beyond the spell's cage.

Aviva's runes took the shape of a thin spear. She shoved the spellbook at Tobias before dashing forward while Uriah's gaze was pinned on the opening. She thrust the spear out, piercing a slip of paper peeking out from his pocket. The paper came free as she lifted the spear. Uriah jolted and spun to face her. A growl tore from his throat as she took the paper in both hands, dismissing her spear into a shower of green sparks. Meeting his eye, she tore the charm in two.

The spell began to dissolve the moment the paper split. Sunlight penetrated the darkness, bathing them in its warmth. Fresh air flooded the cave and cleared the thick, suffocating pressure of Uriah's spell.

Kase stood behind Aviva. Cracked, red markings trailed up his arms, glowing in a fiery light. His eyes swept over the scene before landing on Uriah. Anger sharpened his gaze to a fierce glare, and the sparks that circled his fingers caught fire, licking at his arms. There was no surprise in his face, and that realization twisted Tobias's stomach.

Uriah shrank back from him. "Couldn't get through the spell

on your own, huh? You... always were weak when it came to magic."

"Smoke thought there was something off about you," Kase said as he reached for his sword, sliding it from its sheath with a sickening scrape. "I don't know why I ignored him for so long."

Tobias flinched away, though the malice in Kase's eyes was pinned on Uriah alone. If left to the mercy of Uriah's taunts, what would Kase do? In the past, he had never reacted well, and Tobias was sickened by thought of how he would act in such a state. There was no proof that Uriah was attacking of his own accord—not yet. If Kase acted out only to learn Uriah was being controlled just as much as Eira was...

This has to stop. Tobias gritted his teeth. He spared a quick glance at the spellbook in his hands, burying the urge that begged him to do nothing, and crossed to Uriah with clipped, determined steps. Tobias planted himself between Kase and Uriah, holding his chin high despite the prickle of Kase's glare on his back.

"Take it," he said, shoving the book at Uriah's chest. "Promise you'll leave and convince this... Shadowslayer to let us go. I'm tired of playing this game."

Uriah's face lit up and he took the spellbook with a grin. "If you insist."

"I do."

Uriah whirled toward the tunnel that led into the mountain and sped off before Tobias could have second thoughts. He was gone in a flash, his steps echoing as he raced into the dark, empty corridor. Just like that, the spellbook was gone once more. The aching emptiness in Tobias's chest returned, lacing his veins with ice and numbing the tips of his fingers.

Kase started to follow, his sword raised and his eyes murderous. Tobias jumped in his way, throwing his arms out to block his path to the tunnel.

"Do you have any idea what you've just done?" Kase

snapped. His hand landed firmly on Tobias's shoulders, fingers digging into his shirt. All it took was a sharp pull and Tobias was at the mercy of the dragon keeper's shimmering green blade.

Tobias swallowed hard. "We don't have time for you to fight each other. The longer it dragged on, the more Arayna would suffer." He gestured to her with the sweep of his arm. "If I didn't hand it over, he was going to fight Aviva for it—or worse."

"Who knows what he's going to do with it?" Kase hissed. "The things in that book… there are spells in there that should *never* be used."

"And you were going to kill him to keep it out of his hands, right? How is that better than whatever you're trying to protect in that book?"

The anger in Kase's eyes died down as he glanced at Arayna. Slowly, his grip loosened until his hand fell away.

Aviva had already knelt beside Arayna, pressing her hands against either side of Arayna's head. A soft glow enveloped her palms, and the air hummed with the presence of magic. Already, the bleeding had stopped, leaving behind a dark stain in Arayna's tangled brown hair. It didn't lessen the tension in Oliver's shoulders or remove the frown from Aviva's lips. A heavy weight pressed down on all of them.

Uriah, a man who had once been their friend, had turned on them as well. Tobias wasn't sure which one hurt more: the knowledge of Uriah's betrayal or the loss of the spellbook.

"I'm sorry," Oliver started, sinking back against his heels. "Arayna and I went to check the tunnel. When we came back…" He sighed, dragging a hand across his face. "I knew Uriah was rough around the edges, but this is hard to believe."

"There has to be a reason," Tobias added. "He mentioned his brother, do you think something happened to him? Or could he have been manipulated like Eira was?"

"It doesn't matter." Kase sheathed his sword and approached

Aviva. He raked his fingers through his hair, leaving it tangled and unruly. Dark circles lined his eyes and his shoulders sagged with exhaustion. "What's done is done. How do we intend to get the spellbook back?"

All eyes turned to Tobias, curious and distrustful. He pushed his shoulders back and curled his fingers into tight fists to keep them from trembling. He wet his lips, taking as long as he could to gather his words.

"We're going to let him take the book back to this Shadowslayer and we're going to follow him. We'll face Shadowslayer head on and reclaim the book. I want to deal with this problem at its roots," he said, lifting his chin. "I want to save Eira, but if we can cut off the source of everything—the gold magic user—that would be the best solution. We should... reach out to Uriah, too. I think he might be facing the same manipulation. I don't... I don't think I believe that this was his choice."

Silence fell over the group. Anxiety pricked Tobias's mind, sending a shiver down his spine. He kept his jaw clamped shut and his gaze locked on the floor. It was stifling; he couldn't help but beg that someone would say anything to put an end to the tense quiet.

"I agree with Tobias," Aviva spoke up. "Let Uriah take the book back. I want to know who is after my spells and settle this with them directly. I'm tired of watching everything fall apart around me."

Kase sighed as he looked away. The red runes finally began to dissipate, leaving him strangely shadowed. "Fine. Smoke will follow him from a distance and see where he goes. In the meantime, we should rest. Let Arayna heal and let Aviva recover her magic."

Aviva pursed her lips. The glow vanished from her hands as she pulled away, turning her gaze to her staff. It lay broken and discarded on the ground a few feet away. The light had gone completely dark. "There's only so much I can recover without Iila, the book, and my staff," she muttered.

Her words cracked Tobias's resolve. Pity flooded his mind and threatened to sweep him away into the depths of guilt, but there was no time for regret. He clung to the hilt of his sword at his side. "I'm sorry," he said. "I couldn't think of another way to stop things without hurting anyone else."

"It's alright." Aviva dragged her staff toward herself, scraping the shattered gem across the stone. She lifted the red and gold charms and snapped them free from the shaft. "I trust you. Though… my trust seems to end up misplaced these days."

Tobias opened and closed his mouth several times, desperate to respond. Nothing ever came out and the conversation died, giving way to the painful, tense silence once more.

A FEW HOURS passed before Smoke returned, settling himself outside the opening in the cave. Kase approached him slowly and they shared a moment of quiet as they exchanged information through their bond. Tobias itched to get going, but the seconds seemed to stretch on for an eternity. The longer he waited, the more anxiety pressed heavily on his shoulders. Doubt began to trickle in through the cracks in his mind. Had he done the right thing by giving the book away? Would they be able to get it back?

Kase turned to the group before Tobias could follow the doubting thoughts to their conclusion. The dragon keeper's face was grim, but he pushed away from Smoke before speaking. "Uriah went to the castle of Sheniir."

"That old place?" Arayna scratched her head, still seated against the far wall of the cave beside Aviva. "Isn't it at least a couple of days on foot?"

"He could have been warped there," Oliver said, examining

the tip of one of his arrows. "It would make sense. That must be how Eira has been keeping up with us despite that we have Smoke."

"If that's the case, this Shadowslayer person is no joke," Aviva murmured. "It takes a huge amount of energy to warp over long distances—even more so if you don't go yourself."

Tobias frowned, folding his arms over his chest. "If this person is so powerful, why would he need your spellbook?"

Aviva shifted and hugged her knees against her chest, resting her chin against them. "I don't know for sure, but... I used to study purification spells, which lead into the study of dark magic. That spellbook is filled to the brim with forbidden spells I would never use, but I wrote so that I could undo them." She sighed and buried her face. "It was stupid. I never thought someone would try to steal it."

A shiver raced down Tobias's spine. "He won't be able to read it, right?"

"I don't know," Aviva said. "I'm not feeling too confident that my spells can hold against him."

Arayna shot to her feet with a growl. She swayed but managed to catch herself on the wall. "He won't read anything if I claw his eyes out. That'll settle this. I'll kill him—him and Uriah!"

"No." Oliver shoved his arrow back into the quiver, shooting a glare at Arayna. It was enough to silence her, shoulders stiff as she sank back into her seat. She turned her face away, her ears flattening against her head.

Aviva dragged her fingers through her loose, tangled hair as she sighed. She spared a quick glance at Kase before pushing herself up. "Let's confirm before we decide what to do next. I'd feel better if I saw him there myself."

She didn't wait for permission or agreement before drawing a circle in the air. Magic rippled out from the middle of it like water in a pond. Tobias furrowed his brow and crept closer.

Recognition tugged at the back of his mind. As the magic circle solidified, creating a hazy, green mirror hanging in the air in front of them, his mind leapt back to the legends of Selini's Blue Head Dragonborn—he who could see the world through the surface of any body of water. Tobias felt a twinge of jealousy as he watched Aviva work. Magic was an incredible and boundless gift.

And yet, it seems to bring about an unfair amount of pain.

"He's there," Aviva cut in. All eyes turned to her as she snapped her fingers and focused the image onto the old, abandoned castle of Sheniir. She zoomed in until the image of Uriah appeared. The castle's walls fleshed out around him, bringing the picture to life.

He stood in a large room with a throne upon a dais at one end. Beyond the throne, a mass of black scales shifted, slivers of bright green flashing beneath their cracks. The image was fuzzy, and Uriah's face was difficult to make out through the shadows. But he was there.

The only other one in the room was Eira, who smiled as though pleased to see Uriah had come. There was no sign of the magic user—Shadowslayer, as Uriah called him—they both claimed to work with, but the dragon behind the throne was enough to make Tobias's blood run cold.

Uriah's head turned, his gaze landing directly on Aviva. Gold sparks flared to life in his gaze, and a grin broke through the hazy shadows that covered his face. With a gasp, Aviva recoiled, shattering the image into glass-like shards of magic which dissolved in the air. Thick silence blanketed the group, suffocating enough that Tobias's legs grew weak.

"Is… is that supposed to happen?" Tobias asked, his voice wavering.

"No." Aviva rubbed her temples and squeezed her eyes shut.

Arayna turned away, her lip curling to reveal her pointed canines. Her fingers curled into fists at her sides, and her body tensed. Oliver laid a comforting hand against her shoulder—perhaps the most tender thing Tobias had ever seen him do. A little farther off, Kase frowned, his gaze flickering darkly. No one said a word; the silence was stifling. Tobias's hands grew cold as he gripped his sword tighter.

"Ahtella sensed something was off about him, but I didn't want to believe her. I didn't want to believe what I saw here either," Arayna sniffled. With a growl, she swiped her nose with the back of her hand, shaking Oliver's hand away. "He's my friend too, you know? And now he's working with them? It's stupid."

"It's unpleasant, but it seems to be the truth," Aviva said. She cupped her chin in her hands, fixing her gaze on the ground. "But there was definitely something different about him in the vision, and I'm... I'm uneasy about the fact that he looked right at me. He shouldn't be able to see any kind of remnant of that spell—he's not powerful enough to sense scrying."

"Well, he senses scrying now. I think that tells us all we need to know." Kase turned sharply on his heel and made his way toward the open cave mouth. A frustrated groan tore from his lips and he raked his fingers through his hair, his head thrown back to glare at the sky.

"What do you mean?" Tobias asked, glancing between Kase and Aviva. "What does sensing your spell have to do with his... betrayal?"

"It means Uriah has magic now—his own magic. Not his brother's charms," Aviva said. Her hand dropped to her side. Her knuckles turned white as she clenched her fists. "The only one I know of at this time that's giving out magic to others is Eira's companion, who must be this Shadowslayer man. He made a deal with him—what I don't know is whether or not Uriah is there by choice."

"It seems pretty clear to me," Oliver snapped. "He left us for power. Don't you remember the way he spoke about it before?

How could you even think of considering this as anything other than a choice *he* made?"

"Why are you so eager to toss him aside?" Arayna growled. "He *told us* that day that Shadowslayer was behind all of this and you brushed him aside. Maybe he was trying to warn us."

"He could have killed you just now, Arayna. In fact, he seemed to be trying to!"

Arayna recoiled, pressing a hand to her head. Her lips quivered and she looked away.

Aviva hung her head. Waves of tangled, pale blonde hair cascaded over her shoulders. The pink and white flowers had wilted, leaving only a few dried-up buds clinging to the strands of her hair. "I want to think better of him," she murmured. "This can't be all there is to it."

After a beat had passed, Tobias lifted his chin and faced the group. "Then it's time to go. We'll get the spellbook back."

"Don't tell me you really intend to go there," Oliver said, withdrawing from Arayna and slinging his quiver over his arm. "Eira, Uriah, and the magic-user aside, did you not see the dragon in Aviva's vision? That thing is huge. It has to be the Venen that Eira got her poison from. Do you want us to fight that thing?"

"I have a plan," Tobias answered. Confidence surged through him and he gripped the key dangling around his neck. "All I ask is that you trust me."

Oliver studied him but said nothing, a thoughtful frown etched into his face. Arayna hung back from the group, her gaze still locked on where Aviva's spying mirror had been moments before. The silence stretched on, pricking Tobias's skin with nervous energy.

"I trust you," Aviva finally said, brushing a hand across his arm. She smiled when he caught her eye. "Tell us what you plan to do."

24

TRUST

THE SUN HAD SET by the time they arrived at the castle. A gentle pitter-patter of rain greeted them—enough to soak through Tobias's clothes, but not harsh enough to leave him shivering from the cold. Smoke touched down on the ground only a few feet from the castle doors, folding in his wings gracefully. He released a puff of smoke through his nostrils and bent down in the muddy ground.

Kase leapt down first. Mud caked the bottom of his white cloak. He turned around to help Aviva down, who shivered and wrapped her cloak around herself. Both clothed in white, they shone in the moonlight. Shadows stretched high across the mud, reaching out toward them with long claws. Neither seemed to notice, however, while they spoke to each in hushed voices.

Arayna and Oliver found their own ways down. He tried to help her, but she shoved him away. The red blotches had disappeared from her eyes during the flight, and the stains left behind by her tears had almost faded. She'd tried to hide it, but she had spent most of the flight crying silently.

Tobias's heart twisted with sympathy. Some part of him

wondered if Uriah knew the kind of impact he had had on Arayna. And if he knew, would he have thought twice about his choice?

Did Eira have those same second thoughts? Was that why she seemed so desperate for help?

Once everyone was on the ground, Smoke stood up straight. At Kase's signal, he took to the air once more, vanishing under the cover of the dark clouds.

Aviva smoothed her wet hair back from her face and turned to face the group. She cast a glance at the castle a few feet away, its broken spires towering over them. The fog of rain obscured most of its structure, leaving it as barely anything more than a shadowed silhouette.

Aviva gathered magic to the tips of her fingers. She formed a rough model of the castle's structure, much the same as the eerie illustrations Tobias had seen in the ghost stories Talia liked to read. Its massive entryway doors hung open and broken, lying crooked on its hinges on the left side. Many of its walls had collapsed, leaving only half of the castle as a notable structure. Two small, green sparks flared to life in the largest room left standing: the throne room.

She glanced at Tobias expectantly. "Once more."

He nodded. He had laid out a rough sketch of his plan before they left, but now that he was standing at the entrance to the castle, drenched in rain and cloaked in darkness, the reality of it all made him shiver. *But Eira is there,* he reminded himself. *You made a promise to her if nothing else.*

"Oliver, Kase, the two of you head up and search for the other companion," he began, tracing one finger along a staircase that headed upward toward the jagged, half-broken roof that spanned over the throne room. "I imagine he's going to want to be somewhere that he can keep watch over everything. Similarly, I want Oliver to be able to provide support from above. As long as the rain doesn't hinder your abilities?"

Oliver lifted his bow. "I'll be fine."

Tobias turned back to the model. "Eira and Uriah are probably going to be in the same place—these two dots here in the throne room, right? This is also where the Venen dragon is. Aviva will go around the back with Smoke and Arayna and try to draw it out. Once outside, Smoke can handle it." He glanced at Arayna. "You're sure your injury is fine now?"

"Of course." Arayna tapped the side of her head where she had been hit. "Chase Uriah outside for me. I'd like to slam his head into a stone somewhere too."

"Arayna," Oliver warned. "Don't. We don't know yet if he made this choice or if he was manipulated. Even if it was his choice…"

Arayna's eyes flashed but she didn't argue as she turned away.

As Aviva dismissed the glowing model, Tobias let his gaze drift to the real thing. The crumbling castle loomed over him, pelted by rain and surrounded by howling winds. It seemed fitting for someone claiming to be Shadowslayer to operate out of it considering the story of the original legend.

A man consumed by dark magic, left to haunt the ravaged kingdom of Sheniir. Desperate to escape the threat of war, pain, and suffering, he doomed his soul to the corruption of forbidden arts, he recalled. Talia had always loved the myth of Shadowslayer, but Tobias had never had a real opinion on it. Now, he stood before the source of it, and his blood ran cold. He was beginning to understand Kase's fear of the old castle.

Steeling himself, he faced the group. "I'm going to the throne room. To Eira."

Light touched Aviva's eyes as she met his gaze. "If you wish to free Eira from the control of the gold threads, you'll need this to cut them." She reached forward and took his hand. As soon as her fingers brushed against him, a spell rune appeared on his wrist, glowing silver before it faded into a barely noticeable mark. Aviva let go and stepped back.

Tobias furrowed his brow as he looked down at where the rune had been. "How do I use it?"

"It will activate on its own," Aviva said. "Because of your blank gift, you won't be able to wield it. It's the best I can do without going with you, but I don't think I should. I can't face Eira or Uriah again as they are." She paused, taking a deep breath. "Cut the threads and it should sever the connection."

"I understand." Tobias rubbed his wrist, itching to know what the rune would do if he couldn't wield it. He had no reason to distrust Aviva, but his curiosity still snagged easily on anything he didn't understand. His *gift* was a puzzle he would have to solve later.

When this is all over, I can ask Aviva more about it.

Kase fidgeted, wiping his palms against his pants. He cast an uneasy glance at the castle and at Aviva who was approaching it at a steady pace. "Okay," he began, keeping his voice low. "Remember what we're here for. We want this to end, but it's not worth risking any lives for. If things get too dangerous—"

"Pull away, we know." Arayna gave his shoulder a firm pat.

He answered with a shaky smile before pulling her and Oliver into a tight hug. Oliver stiffened, but Arayna melted easily into the embrace, burying her face in Kase's chest.

Oliver jerked free after a few seconds, glaring at Kase. He opened his mouth to argue, but no words ever came out. After a moment, he shut it and looked away with a huff.

"Sorry," Kase murmured as he pulled away from Arayna. "Be safe, okay? I don't know what lies ahead of us, and maybe I'm a little worried about that much uncertainty."

When no one else said anything, Tobias stepped forward, offering his hand to Kase. It took Kase a moment before he clasped it. Grinning confidently despite the nagging anxiety in his chest, Tobias shook Kase's hand firmly. The gesture was awkward, and regret squirmed in the back of his mind as soon as he initiated it, but it was the best thing he could come up with.

Clearing his throat, he pulled away. "We'll be okay," he said. "We've got you, Aviva, and Smoke here to back us up. This Shadowslayer guy can't be that scary, right?"

Kase chuckled, though the sound came across as hollow and humorless. "Right. No problem."

With a final look at the three of them, Kase left to catch up with Aviva. As he came and stood by her side, she glanced up at him, though her face was obscured by the rain. Similarly to what he had done moments before, he caught her in a tight embrace. Tobias looked at his wrist again, frowning thoughtfully.

What does Kase know that the rest of us don't?

Arayna's hand landed on Tobias's shoulder, jerking him out of the endless pit of his thoughts. He jumped and whirled to face her. She dipped her head to him—reserved compared to her usual actions.

"Since I know you're worried about facing Eira alone," she whispered. As she turned, she lifted her hand and traced a wide arc through the air in front of her. Ahtella's shimmering red form appeared in front of her, glowing with a warm, amber light in the darkness of the sun's absence. The wolf looked up at Tobias with a gleam in her dark eyes. Intelligence shimmered beneath the surface: a look he had seen in the eyes of dragons but never any other creatures.

He reached out tentatively, waiting until Ahtella dipped her head to him to brush his fingers across her soft, scarlet fur.

"Ahtella will protect you if things take a turn for the worse," Arayna said. "And if you can win Eira over, that would be a nice bonus. She seems to listen to you."

"I plan to. I don't believe she's acting of her own free will, and I can't leave her to suffer that way if it's true." Tobias paused, searching her face. "Take care, okay? I know we didn't give you long to rest."

Arayna squeezed his shoulder before taking off to rejoin Aviva. Together, the two of them split off toward the castle's left side—the side still enclosed by solid walls. Kase veered to the right, vanishing around the stone walls. Oliver lingered for a moment longer before he took off after Kase. It wasn't long before the sound of their footsteps sloshing through the mud disappeared, and Tobias was left alone in the rain.

This is what you wanted, he reminded himself. *This is your chance to make things right.* With that in mind, he gripped the hilt of his sword and walked forward.

The entrance to the castle loomed over the top of him. The left side door had all but fallen off its hinges, and a massive hole penetrated the door on the right side. The entrance was wide open, presenting him with the deserted halls within. Lanterns hung on the walls as he made his way inside, cracked and unlit. Blood stained the tile flooring, littered with dirt and bones that snapped under his boots. Ahtella's red fur glowed softly, guiding him deeper into the castle.

His skin prickled with unease, fear coiling tighter around him with each reverberating step he took. He clung to his sword and to the wolf's light. There was no reason to be afraid.

The old castle was cloaked in mystery and horror, having grown into something of a legend over time. It had fallen to the dragonborn in their war with the elves hundreds of years ago, yet the remnants of their fear remained hanging in the air. Talia had always found it fascinating, spending hours of her time as a kid entranced by the ghost stories that arose from the abandoned site. Tobias had never shared her fascination, especially not when the blood and bones left behind were evidence of the brutality of the Draconic people.

He shook himself. The stories were meant to frighten children. He was an adult by all rights; he had nothing to fear. The dragonborn who had come to Sheniir so long ago had all been banished or killed. They no longer wandered the halls, waiting for the next fool to wander in. No spirits of their victims haunted the castle grounds. Those were all just nonsensical legends.

And even if they were true, Tobias refused to fear them. There was no Shadowslayer waiting for them, nor any rogue dragonborn. Just a magic user and his twisted game of manipulation.

Eventually, he emerged into the throne room, an open space that stretched out large enough that Smoke could squeeze himself in if he wanted to. Stone walls rose up around him, meeting at the top to form a crumbling roof. Rubble cluttered the floor, left behind by the hole in the ceiling. Rain poured in from outside and pooled on the floor.

At the back end of the room, a raised dais housed a gray throne carved from smooth stone. There, he found himself face-to-face with the very person he had been chasing since the beginning.

Eira sat upon the steps of the dais, one leg crossed over the other as she leaned back, resting her elbows on the top step. She wore a twisted grin, magic circling around her fingertips. The blades of the knives at her waist gleamed in its golden light. She rose to her feet.

"Tobias," she greeted, her voice almost relieved. Almost.

Beside him, Ahtella growled, her hackles raised as she bared her teeth. Tobias swallowed his fear and peeled his fingers away from the hilt of his sword. He didn't have to fight Eira. He just had to free her.

His gaze flicked past Eira to the wall of scales behind the throne, the same as he had seen in Aviva's vision of the castle. The only difference was that there was no one else in the room.

A sense of wrongness slithered down his spine. Where was Uriah?

25

BEHIND THE THRONE

"I'M SURPRISED TO SEE YOU HERE," Eira said. She descended the steps slowly, her boots echoing loudly against the stone. Rain had plastered her brown hair to her face; from how soaked her clothes were, she had been sitting out in it for quite some time. The roof only provided cover in certain areas of the room, and she had chosen a spot directly beneath the rain.

Tobias stepped back, watching attentively in case she reached for her daggers.

"I didn't think you'd follow me. Did you take interest in my words after all?" She stopped, hands clasped behind her back. "The offer still stands. There's room for both you and Uriah to accept."

Tobias gritted his teeth, his gut sinking. *So Uriah did come of his own free will.* "I didn't come to accept," he said, forcing his voice to remain level. "I came to set you free."

Eira hesitated. She reached to grasp the bright green stone that hung around her neck, her lips pressing into a thin line. Gold gathered around her fingers; even standing several feet away, he could see it shining in her normally-blue eyes.

"To... set me free?" she whispered, voice breaking. Her hand

247

released the green gem and fell back to her side—awkwardly, as if something had forcibly pried her grip away.

Tobias kept his gaze locked on her. "Yes."

She chuckled. "You must misunderstand something. There's nothing to set free. I'm here because I want to be. I mean, look at all this power I have! Look at how much they respect me now!" She lifted her hands and called upon her magic again, tracing shiny gold lines through the air. She laughed as she twirled, her skirts flaring out around her.

Despite all this, Tobias could see she wasn't happy. There was no joy in her movements or even in her laugh. If he focused on her, he could see faint gold strings tied around her wrists and neck, pulled taut as though someone else was controlling her movements.

"That's not freedom, Eira," he said. "And what your friends feel toward you? It's not respect. They're afraid of you—they *hate* you."

Eira faltered, whipping around to face him. He didn't know if that was really what they felt, but there were times it seemed that way. They were certainly afraid of her. Or perhaps they weren't afraid of her, but of what she had let herself become. Of who she had tied herself to.

The moment was gone. Eira shook her head and stood up straighter, pushing her shoulders back. She grabbed a dagger from her belt, its blade glinting in the light. Ahtella growled, her red fur flickering with magic.

"It doesn't matter what they think of me, and it doesn't matter what you came to do," Eira spat. "I do as I'm told. Nothing else matters."

"Eira—"

Ignoring him, she rushed forward with her dagger raised to strike. Tobias fumbled to draw his sword as she drew closer, the pounding of her boots against stone matching his heartbeat.

Ahtella leapt, tackling her. The wolf sank her teeth into Eira's arm, and she yelped in pain.

While Eira wrestled with the wolf, Tobias drew his sword. The ground was slick with rain; Tobias cringed at the mirror-like appearance it granted the gray stone. Drenched, shivering from the cold, and wide-eyed, he certainly didn't look like anyone who deserved to be on this quest. The reflection painted the picture of a child, cornered and panicking.

The hilt of his sword bit into his palms. It didn't matter what sort of appearance the rain granted him. He made a promise to himself and to Eira.

Thunder rumbled overhead, and a flash of lightning lit up the dark room. Tobias caught a second glimpse of the massive wall of scales behind the throne. He couldn't find the head of the dragon in the dark, but he guessed it was just as large as Smoke—if not bigger.

Cold seeped into his bones at the thought of that dragon waking up. He prayed that it would sleep soundly, or at least ignore him when it woke.

Eira's knife sliced through his arm. A sharp gasp slipped from his lips as searing pain jolted him out of his thoughts. He lifted his sword automatically in an attempt to block her next strike, remembering only too late that her weapon was a dagger rather than a sword. She spun and sliced his shoulder, the path of her blade mere inches from his neck as he leapt back. He couldn't worry about the dragon. He couldn't worry about the others.

Right now, he had to focus on Eira.

At their feet, Ahtella reappeared in a flash of scarlet. Snarling, she clamped her jaws around the hem of Eira's skirt and pulled. Knocked off balance, Eira landed on her back with a shriek, dagger slipping from her fingers.

Her confident smirk morphed into a dark frown. She raised her hand, summoning the flecks of magic to her fingertips, and formed a thick thread of gold. She wound it tightly around her hand, holding for a second before flicking her wrist. A bolt of power shot out from the magic binding. Without thinking, Tobias raised his arms to protect himself, bracing for the magic to strike.

Warmth pulled from the silver rune on his wrist, reigniting its glow. It took the shape of a shield, expanding to cover him completely from harm. The bolt bounced off the shield and struck the ground at his feet, scorching the stone. Relief poured through Tobias, the moment allowing him to take a deep breath.

The shield dissipated as soon as Eira released her hold on the magic. She ground her teeth, glaring fiercely up at him.

"That Aviva," she hissed. "She really thinks of everything."

"I don't want to fight you, Eira. I didn't come here for that," he said. All he needed was the gold threads to reveal themselves, but it was too difficult to see while trying to avoid her attacks. *If Ahtella can hold her down, maybe I'd have a chance.*

Eira shot to her feet, taking hold of her dagger once again. She lunged, and he braced himself, raising his sword to shield himself. Her foot collided with the back of his knee. His legs buckled, sending him crashing into the hard stone. She planted her foot firmly on his chest, grinning down at him.

"Try as you will, you're still too soft for battle. No wonder you're always searching for ways to talk instead," she teased, leaning over him. The gem on her necklace dangled right in front of his nose. An eerie light emanated from its core, and it gave off a rancid smell.

Tobias gritted his teeth, holding his breath. The stench from the jewel overpowered his thoughts, blurring them into a meaningless lull. Its brilliant green color was familiar, but he couldn't place it—not with the constant white noise drowning out his thoughts.

Ahtella growled and threw herself at Eira, sinking her fangs into the thief's arm. Eira toppled, releasing Tobias. He scrambled to his feet and backed away, sweeping his gaze over the air around her. If he could pinpoint the location of the threads, he could cut them and release Eira from their control.

A string of curses flew from Eira's lips as she fought to pry her arm free from Ahtella's grip. Blood seeped through her sleeve and her face contorted in pain as the wolf pinned her. Summoning the threads of her magic, she conjured another bolt of flickering gold sparks. Her hand thrust out, flinging the bolt straight through Ahtella's chest. Immediately, the wolf spirit froze, body seizing up as black cracks spiderwebbed through her. She exploded into a shimmering cloud of dust without another sound.

"Ahtella!" Tobias cried. His throat tightened as he sucked in a deep breath. Had Arayna been hurt too if her Beast Spirit was killed? Would she die along with Ahtella? His gaze shot back to where the black dragon still lay, sleeping soundlessly against the far back wall. He wondered desperately where Aviva and Arayna were.

Eira rose shakily to her feet, her hand pressed against the wound in her arm. "Such a nuisance," she muttered. A warm glow encircled her fingers, weaving around the wound. The flow of blood slowed to a trickle before it stopped altogether. She scoffed as she pulled her hand back, shaking away droplets of crimson.

The sting in Tobias's own wounds crawled through his body; warm blood clung to his skin. As if it simply wanted to mock his inability to heal the way she could. *That magic doesn't belong to her,* he reminded himself. *I don't want it.* Even with those bold words echoing over the ocean of his mind, a sliver of envy still found its way to his heart. It made sense now that it was so easy for Uriah to turn to Eira's side.

He brushed his fingers across his wound, and blood clung to their tips as he pulled away. The sting had dulled to a slight throb—barely noticeable above the thrum of adrenaline racing through his veins. It would be fine for the time being as long as he didn't strain the arm. He could get through this without healing magic.

He took his sword back from his left hand where he had switched it to explore the wound. Once it was settled in his right, he faced Eira. "What did you do to Ahtella?"

"Hm? Oh, I just sent the Beast Spirit back to Arayna. She was getting annoying, and she tore up my skirt, see?" Though her words carried a playful, high-pitched tone, her gaze hardened. "But if Ahtella was here, then Arayna isn't too far away. So tell me, Tobias, where are the others?"

"There are no others," he ground out, teeth clenched. "I told you already, I came to talk with you, not to fight."

"A shame. Uriah said you would all be coming to meet our companion." She hummed to herself, tilting her head back. The gentle sprinkle of rain turned into a heavy downpour, drenching them both. Water plastered his clothes to his skin. Wet hair clung to his face, getting in his eyes, but he didn't dare take his hand away from his sword.

"It doesn't matter anyway," she went on, words almost inaudible beneath the rain pounding the castle walls. "I've stalled long enough. Now, how does Kase do it again…?" She pressed her fingers to her lips, whistling through them to produce a sharp sound, the same as Kase's call to Smoke.

Tobias's heart stopped. Time seemed to slow as the whistle sliced through the constant noise of the rain. Sheathing his sword, he rushed forward. He grabbed her by the wrists and peeled her hands away, cutting her whistle off. "Eira, don't!" he cried, pinning her hands to her sides. "Don't wake that dragon, it will—"

A low, rumbling growl cut him off. It reverberated through the air, shaking the ground beneath his feet. His breath snagged as he turned toward the throne and the wall of scales behind it. Silver light shifted across the surface of the black scales, the cracks between them laced with a vibrant green. The dragon's head raised up, its horns grazing the broken ceiling as it rose to its feet. It possessed a stout body and a square jaw lined with black spikes. Tusks protruded from its lower lip and its eyes were the same bright, acidic color as the liquid that oozed from its scales. Its gaze swept over them.

Tobias stiffened. As recognition flared in the back of his mind, dread dropped a heavy weight on his shoulders. All at once, everything clicked. The green gemstone, the rancid smell, the scales that covered its body.

A Venen dragon.

Tobias frantically shoved himself and Eira to the floor, hoping it would overlook them. He raced to remember the things Talia had told him of Venen dragons. They were part of the Celestial Class, much like Smoke. Thought to have been extinct, only a few of them remained in the world of Anticuus. They were high-class poison dragons.

Glancing to the side, Tobias's gaze landed on the green gem that hung from Eira's neck. There were rumors that one effect of the Venen's poison was a dulling of the mind, making one extremely open to suggestions. It clouded over organic thoughts, sapping away a person's will until they were nothing more than a puppet. Because of this, the Summoners had issued a hunt for the dragons.

If the gem was crystallized poison from the Venen dragon's scales, someone could use it to control Eira.

The Venen dragon spread its wings and took flight, slipping easily through the wide hole in the ceiling. It barely left the cover of the castle before Smoke collided with it. The two dragons crashed to the ground outside, the force sending a shudder rippling across the ground.

Eira shoved Tobias away and shot to her feet, craning her neck to peer through the gap in the roof. Lightning ribboned across the sky; a few beats passed before the crash of thunder followed. The ground shook again and Smoke's shriek tore through the air.

Eira cursed. "Of course Kase's stupid dragon was nearby!" Her gaze shifted to Tobias, and she shoved strands of wet hair out of her face. "Where is he? Where's Kase? And if Kase is here, then where's Aviva?"

"I'm not telling you." Tobias pushed himself upright, meeting her eye. There was still no sign of the threads, but the pendant on its own was enough to twist his gut. If he got rid of it first, would the threads appear?

Eira groaned, gripping the green gem that hung from her neck. "You don't understand anything! If you really wanted to help me, you'd tell me! If you really wanted to help, *you would have brought Aviva.*"

Tobias gritted his teeth, his gaze shifting down to her hand gripping her necklace. "If I really wanted to help, I'd do this." He snatched her pendant and yanked.

The chain snapped and fell away. Her grip on the gem loosened and he pried it free, tossing the necklace away. It clattered uselessly against the stone, and the glow that surrounded it fizzled out.

Eira's hand shot to her neck, feeling for the pendant. Her eyes widened. "What just—"

"I need you to tell me something," Tobias said. "Who is this Shadowslayer? What is he after, and why use you to get it?"

"Shadowslayer?" Eira furrowed her brow, shaking her head. "There... is no Shadowslayer."

"But Uriah—"

"There is no Shadowslayer!"

Confusion pulled Tobias's lips into a frown. "Then who's manipulating you?"

She screwed her eyes shut and turned away, hanging her head. "I can't," she said. "I can't tell you."

"You can," he promised. "He can't do anything to you. I'll

make sure of it. You can and you have to, because I can't help you if I don't understand the problem."

Thunder rumbled ahead, mingling with the roars of the two dragons. Rain poured down from above, and Tobias shivered. He ignored these things, shoving them aside to focus on Eira, eagerly awaiting her response.

Sniffling, she turned to him with watery eyes. Gold flashed in the depths of her gaze. The silver rune on Tobias's wrist lit up, and his gaze locked on Eira's chained neck. His arm sliced through the air, snapping the gold strands that bound her. With a flash, they fell away, dissolving like they had never been there at all.

Eira gasped, eyes wide. "Aurum," she whispered. Despite the softness of her tone, he heard it clearly above the noise around him. "He's Aurum, the Golden Head Dragonborn of the goddess Selini."

Tobias inhaled sharply. Vivid memories of tapestries and paintings depicting the face of the golden dragonborn flashed through his mind, coupled with the stories Talia would tell him. Aurum was the leader of Selini's five servants, each one of them bonded to one of her heads—blue, red, green, black, and gold. He was the servant to her golden head, the strongest of them. He was the reason the elves and druids had been wiped from the face of Anticuus.

Aurum was the reason the Summoners had banished the hybrids and dragonborns to their own corner of territory.

Tobias pushed those thoughts aside, forcing his hands to stop trembling. Smoke's cryptic words from the forest rang in his ears, melding with his frigid fear of the dragonborn. *Pray that, if it is a dragonborn, it is not a Head Dragonborn,* Smoke had warned. *For if it is, you will all perish.*

Bile rose in the back of Tobias's throat, and he swallowed hard against the bitter taste.

"Can you… can you really set me free?" Eira murmured, voice breaking.

Fear and uncertainty clouded the surface of his thoughts. Looking down at her, he couldn't see any hint that she was lying. In fact, it was the sad, frightened look he had seen on her face several times before, though it had been buried beneath the magic she had been given by Aurum.

He forced a slight smile. "You *are* free, Eira."

She brushed another lock of soaking wet hair out of her face. Laughter slipped from her lips, but this time it was light and genuine. A laugh that sounded clear and happy.

A scream pierced the moment. Tobias's head snapped up just as someone fell from the ceiling, slamming against the stone floor with a sickening *crack*.

Horror seized Tobias's heart. His feet slipped on the wet floor as he raced toward the body. A pool of blood spread around the figure, and their form lay mangled. Regret choked Tobias like smoke in his lungs. Sliding to his knees, his gaze slid over the figure as tears leapt to his eyes.

"It can't be," he whispered. "It can't be."

A round, silver pin slipped from the bloodied hand. Crimson splotches stained the imprint of the dragon on its surface.

26

OF GOLDEN EYES

Kase looked down at the runes traced across his hands and arms. They glistened with rain, infused with warmth which fought off the cold threatening to seep through his drenched clothes. He took a deep breath before pulling his gloves back on, sliding his sleeves down over them. In the few minutes since his and Aviva's paths through the ruins diverged, he still hadn't recognized the weight of their plan completely. It was better that way. They hadn't told Tobias or anyone else, and he wasn't sure he could bring himself to—especially not if he couldn't process it himself.

"It's the last resort spell," she had said before pulling away with a smile. *"If the future you saw comes to pass, I'll make sure the connecting half gets passed on. This way, your promises can be fulfilled—the way you and your dragon desire."*

"This will kill you. You know that, right?" he had asked, reaching out to grasp her hand. She stopped to look at him, and he pressed on. *"You're putting yourself into a spell. You won't survive that."*

"Neither of us will."

He clenched his jaw as he climbed the steps that led to the

roof—which was more like the remains of the upper floors than an actual roof. Dark, ominous clouds hung heavily overhead, snuffing out the last rays of daylight. Shadows seemed to sneer at him from every corner of the destroyed room. The ceiling was gone, left with only half of a waist-high wall on the left side to prove it had once been a room at all. Jagged stone edges jutted out on the far side of the floor, rain pooling in the places where it dipped slightly. He clung to the edges, placing each step carefully. He didn't trust the floor not to crumble beneath him if he walked across the center.

Overturned bookshelves, some splintered and broken, littered the floor. Years of weathering had worn the scattered books. It twisted his heart to think about what this castle may have once been. Now, it was a sad reminder of the history of Anticuus. He kept to the broken remains of the wall, running his gloved hand across the surface of the stone bricks.

"Where are you?" he murmured. "Where are you hiding?"

Tobias had tasked him with locating the companion Eira had bound herself to—though he still hadn't told him or any of the others about what Smoke had revealed in secret. The knowledge still sent a shiver crawling down his spine.

Oliver had split off, taking the opposite side of the castle, where many of the upper rooms were still intact. Looking up, Kase's gaze landed on a spire of the castle, still standing tall against the battering wind and rain. Oliver's navy coat moved slowly past one of the windows near the top of the tower. The sight of him brought a flicker of relief to the tangled mess of Kase's mind.

He had no faith in Tobias's plan. It was scattered, disorganized, and hastily thrown together. A gamble he had been forced to make in a desperate attempt to settle things as calmly as possible. Uriah's betrayal had shaken all of them. They had little hope of reclaiming the spellbook as they were, but he couldn't refuse the plan when it was laid out before him. If he could use it to meet with *Shadowslayer* face to face, then he would settle things once and for all.

Then, Calix would finally be free.

Unease tainted his resolve, cracking it down to the core. Kase curled his fingers into tight fists, pausing halfway to the jagged edge. He knew he should trust Aviva's spell, trust that Tobias could take care of himself, but something about it all made his gut twist. It wasn't right. Everything was so painfully *wrong.*

Trust that instinct, Kase, Smoke interjected, circling above. The rain stopped momentarily each time his massive form flew over Kase's head. *This place is steeped in dark magic. I suspect even Aviva is uncertain about how to deal with it. There is too much to wrestle with here.*

You think we shouldn't have come?

There was a pause as Smoke circled another time. *I think you should not have come,* he finally said. *But I could never have stopped you or anyone else. As much as you hate to admit it, Eira is still someone you care about, and it pains you to see her like this. You are driven by your heart, Kase, and your heart truly cares for others.*

How nice of you to put this blame on me and my 'heart.' Though he tried to play it off a joke, he knew there was an inkling of truth in Smoke's words. If he were to look back on everything he had done, it was always driven by the flame of emotion burning deep within him. It was why Smoke chose him as a partner. A bitter smile rose to his face. *I guess it is my fault.*

You need to press on for now, my friend. The faster you can find this companion, the faster things will end.

Kase nodded. Inhaling deeply, he forced himself to relax. His fingers uncurled, aching from being clenched so hard. When he managed to rein in his thoughts, he continued toward the edge. Rain cooled the warmth of his skin, sizzling as it touched his hands. He didn't have to look down to know Smoke's power had surged forward in response to his unease.

He stopped at the edge of the broken floor. Far below, Tobias stood in the throne room with Ahtella at his feet. He was talking stiffly with Eira, who sat on the steps of the dais. Their words were lost in the storm, but from Eira's flourishing movements, he guessed nothing was getting through to her.

Kase frowned, surveying the room once more. Where was Uriah?

Smoke? He reached out to the dragon again, feeling for their bond. *Let me see through your eyes for a moment. I can't see—*

Behind you! Smoke snarled. The bond snapped against Kase, spinning him around to face the open roof.

A figure appeared at the top of the stairs, his ax resting on his shoulder. Disheveled black hair plastered itself to his face, and his cloak draped awkwardly over his body. His golden eyes glowed in the dark as a wide grin found its way to his face.

Kase grabbed his sword and drew it from the sheath at his back. "Uriah," he sneered, though his voice shook. The blade of his sword began to glow green, and it hummed with power.

Uriah chuckled to himself. "I knew you'd come."

Kase could feel Smoke's growl building in the back of his throat. He shoved the dragon back, closing off their bond to ensure his thoughts were his own. "And? What are you waiting here for? Tell me why you betrayed Aviva."

He laughed, swinging his ax and resting its head against the ground. He leaned against it, his posture relaxed and his expression lazy.

It made Kase's blood boil—and this anger, he knew was his own.

"Betray her?" Uriah asked. "What makes you think I betrayed her?"

"You attacked her and joined up with the thief that tried to kill her! Not to mention the dragonborn that's here somewhere, feeding off this mess!"

Ribbons of lightning raced through the storm clouds above,

followed by a deep rumble of thunder. The wind raked its freezing talons through him, battering rain against his body. Thanks to Smoke's bond, Kase had no trouble seeing despite the heavy rainfall and the darkness of night. Uriah's eyes shone like a beacon among the shadows. It was eerie and unfamiliar.

Uriah leaned his chin against his hand. "Dragonborn? What dragonborn? I only know of Shadowslayer."

"Don't play dumb with me!" Kase lifted his sword and pointed it at Uriah. "This mess has a dragonborn's fingerprints all over it. Nothing else has such a foul stench, reeking of death wherever it goes. No mortal would conceive of such a plot as this. I *know* what's really going on here, and I won't be fooled by you."

"You say that," Uriah drawled, "but you are as foolish as ever, Kase."

With a roar, Kase charged. He lifted his sword, willing Smoke's magic into his arm, and swung. The blade clashed with the handle of Uriah's ax, ringing in the still air. Kase gritted his teeth and tugged on his bond with Smoke, drawing on more of the dragon's power. Warmth raced through his body, sizzling against the rain.

With each swing that missed or that collided with Uriah's ax, Kase's anger grew. Heat seared every inch of his body, building painfully in his core and begging to be released. His vision tinted red at the edges. Sparks danced at his fingertips, signaling the beginning of magic leaking through his guard. But he didn't care anymore. If Smoke's magic consumed him and he was burned alive, he would at least take Uriah with him.

The blade of his sword sliced Uriah's shoulder, spilling blood onto the crumbling floor. Uriah hardly seemed to notice. He swung his ax with the same arm, pulling the same amount of force. Kase jumped out of the way. His foot caught on an overturned bookcase, sending him tumbling onto his back. The impact knocked the wind from his lungs and his vision flickered. As he fought to catch his breath, Uriah's foot slammed down on his hand. A shout tore from him as he pried his hand free, releasing his sword. Uriah kicked the sword away, sending it skidding right off the floor's broken edge.

His heart leapt to his throat as the magic coursing through him spiked, burning holes through the fingers of his gloves. His head snapped up, meeting Uriah's golden gaze as he grinned down at him. Kase rolled out of the way and shot to his feet, narrowly missing the blade of Uriah's ax as it crashed into the stone. A crack zig-zagged across the floor.

"Powerless without your sword, Kase?" Uriah swung for his head, and Kase ducked. "Nothing to do but run away now, hm?"

Kase lunged forward, grabbing Uriah's wrists and squeezing. White hot magic raced from his chest down to the tips of his fingers, burning away Uriah's sleeves. Uriah yelped and pulled back, his ax dropping heavily to the ground. While he surveyed his burns, his face contorting in pain, Kase doubled back and dragged up mental walls between himself and Smoke again. The magic had already turned the skin on his hands a bright red, blistering with the beginning of a burn. He heaved a deep breath, sweat dripping down the sides of his face.

This is why I warned you against using my power, Smoke chided. Concern laced his voice, weaving together a sliver of regret.

Kase ignored him.

Uriah gasped in pain, the glow in his eyes flickering. As he lifted his head, his pained groans turned to laughter. Thunder rumbled overhead; the rain steadily grew heavier, blown at an angle by the wind. Lightning flashed across the dark sky, granting Kase a glimpse of something in the shadows on Uriah's face. It clung to the sides of his face, following the angle of his cheekbones in a cluster of round, inky, plates.

Black scales.

It was just a few seconds, and then it faded again. But it was enough to make Kase's breath catch in his throat. He stepped backward, hands closing into fists. Never before had he wished so badly for the comfort of his sword.

"What a clever trick," Uriah sneered, advancing forward and grasping his ax. He hauled it up to rest it against his shoulder. It was a motion Kase had seen him do countless times before, but now it set him on edge. "Channeling a dragon's power through your body takes a lot of skill: I applaud you for your efforts. But it looks like you're quite worn out now."

Kase knew he was right. Weariness tugged at his body, weighing him down. It sank its claws into his chest, cutting off his supply of air. His body swayed when he tried to step forward, sending him a step backward instead—nearing the cracked edge which would lead to a harsh drop to the floor below. His vision flickered, black and red, making it nearly impossible to see through the rain. Distantly, he could feel Smoke supporting him. Though the dragon had flown down to the ground outside, he could still feel his presence through their bond.

But he knew using the magic any more would be fruitless. The burns it left behind pricked his skin, cooled slightly by the constant stream of rain against them.

His trembling hand slid into the pocket of his tunic. "I still have a few tricks up my sleeve, don't worry."

A rush of air from behind knocked both of them off their feet. Stumbling forward, Kase gritted his teeth and shot a glance back just as the black-and-green dragon from Aviva's vision took off into the sky. Smoke immediately shot up from the ground, colliding with the dragon and carrying it off into the dark of the storm. The bond snapped as Smoke closed it off. Deafening silence rolled over the connection, and Kase stiffened.

The blunt side of Uriah's ax smashed into the side of his head. Dazed, Kase fell backward. The cold press of the stone slammed into his shoulder, his hand dangling off the edge. A crack spiderwebbed beneath him. Panic clawed its way up his throat. Painfully long seconds ticked by while his vision tried to clear. Uriah's fist curled around the front of Kase's tunic, hauling him up. Kase gripped Uriah's wrist tightly, but his legs were lead beneath him. He planted his feet on the edge, attempting to ground himself as Uriah shoved against him. His grip tightened until his fingers ached. His heart dropped to his stomach at the emptiness behind him. One foot slipped off the edge.

More black scales crawled across Uriah's face, lightning catching on them as it flashed through the dark clouds. His grin spread wider, revealing a set of fangs and making his golden eyes spark with magic. His grip on Kase began to loosen, pushing against his chest until Kase's whole body seized in an effort to cling to the ledge.

"Look how far you've fallen, oh mighty dragon keeper," Uriah said in a low voice, a glint in his eyes. "And you're about to crash."

Kase swallowed. His head throbbed. Time seemed to slow. Every sensation was painfully real: the stone crumbling beneath him, the pressure of Uriah's hand against his chest, pushing him back. His legs trembled as he slipped closer to the edge. Desperately, he reached for Smoke through their bond, but it was still closed off on the dragon's end.

He had known this would happen, and yet tears still sprang to his eyes. The runes itched against his skin as Aviva's spell latched onto him. Regret choked him, but it was too late to turn back.

"Why are you doing this?" He gripped Uriah's fist, though his arms shook and his hands were slick from the rain.

"Why?" Uriah chuckled. "Because the goddess commanded that it be done, and you stuck your nose in the way of fate."

Calix. Kase realized with a jolt he must have been talking about Calix. Horror seized him, squeezing his chest until it began to burn. He was vaguely aware of Uriah's grip loosening even more, of the truth staring at him right in the face. There was no one to blame but himself—him and his heart. If he had kept to himself, if he had stayed away from the tangled threads of fate, none of this ever would have happened.

It was his fault.

Uriah let go, and Kase's tunic fell through his fingers. With nothing left to support him, the pull of gravity yanked him away from the edge. The wind rushed past him, and a startling moment of emptiness surrounded him. There was nothing he could do. His gaze locked on Uriah's glowing golden eyes above him, and he could have sworn Uriah's grin faltered for just a moment.

"Goodbye, Kase."

A distant scream cut off Uriah's goodbye, a broken, tortured sound from somewhere far above him. Briefly, Kase heard a second voice call his name. A painfully familiar voice, cracked with grief.

Despite the tears being torn from his eyes by the wind, despite the helplessness of falling, Kase smiled. Bitterly, pitifully, painfully, he smiled.

Sorry, Calix. It seems I couldn't keep my promise to you either.

His back crashed into the ground below with a sudden snap. Pain like claws ripped through him, followed by a numbness that rushed forward to wash it all away. Darkness swallowed his vision, and the cold touch of rain faded to nothing.

27

FALLEN

"KASE!" Tobias cried, his voice tight, on the cusp of breaking. His vision blurred with tears, and he desperately scrounged his thoughts for something—anything—he could do.

Kase's eyes fluttered open, dull and half lidded. He groaned in pain, his fingers feebly searching. Hurriedly, Tobias scooped the pin up and pressed it into his palm, closing his hand around the cold, metal trinket. Breathing a deep sigh, a smile spread across Kase's face—bittersweet, tinged with pain.

"S-sorry," Kase choked out, his voice breaking as he tried to take in a deep breath. "Sorry, I... Uriah was... Uriah was..."

Eira sat at Kase's other side. He flinched as his gaze drifted to her, his grip tightening on the pin. When she remained still, he slowly began to relax. "I don't... have a lot of time," he murmured.

"Don't say that," Tobias snapped. He cringed at the force behind his words, but it was all he could do to keep his voice from trembling. Hot tears blurred his vision. In some ways, it could be regarded as a good thing: it made it difficult to discern the growing pool of blood beneath Kase's head from the shadows. "Don't say that, please. We can fix it. We can heal you we—

266

we just have to find Aviva! Eira, stay with Kase. I'm going to find her!"

Before Tobias could even stand, Kase shook his head. The movement was stiff, barely even movement at all, but it was enough to convey a message.

For once, Tobias understood. Biting down on his tongue, he sank back to his knees. Seeing Kase like this made his chest tight, squeezing his heart. Kase was supposed to be a dragon keeper, a powerful knight with a magical sword who could withstand any blow. He was supposed to protect Tobias and help him catch his thief.

Tears slid down his cheeks, coupled with a choked sob. Kase was his friend. His first one aside from Talia.

And he had gotten him killed. All because he was too selfish, too cowardly. All because he wanted to do something right, to step out from Talia's shadow so that she could recognize his potential. So that he could prove he wasn't just her useless little brother.

"This is all my fault," he whispered, scrubbing at his tears. "It's all my fault."

"Listen to me," Kase said. He lifted his hand, holding the silver pin out for Tobias. His voice was surprisingly clear, despite the pain that twisted his face. His chest heaved as he tried to take in another breath, and his hand trembled in the air. "I want you to take this for me... Give it to him. Give it to Calix. And tell him... tell him I won't be able to keep my promises. I have to... break another one."

Tobias stared at the pin. Blood had been smeared across the silver, matching the red jewel in the center. He shook his head and closed Kase's fingers around the pin again. Keeping his head low, he refused to meet Kase's unfocused gaze. "I can't. I can't. I won't know where to find him, I won't know... I..."

Kase turned his hand over and dropped the pin into Tobias's

lap. "He will come to you. I need you to give this to him. Can you… can you do that for me?"

Tobias hesitated. The sound of the rain battering against stone filled the silence. For once, the castle was still, waiting for him to speak.

Looking at Kase, he knew it would be cruel to refuse. He only had a matter of minutes left, and he was asking Tobias to do something simple—something that was important to him. Swallowing his own emotions, Tobias nodded and took the bloodied pin in his hands. He cradled it gently, reverently in the palms of his hands. "I will. I can do it."

Eira fiddled with the hem of her skirt, hanging her head. "Kase… what did you find up there?" she whispered, so faintly that her words were almost snatched away by the wind.

Kase chuckled, though it faded into a rasping cough. His chest heaved as he fought for another breath. Wincing, he let his eyes slide shut. "I should have known I ticked him off that day… and that it would come back to bite me." He paused for a moment. "Uriah," he finally murmured. "Uriah was there… and he's not who you think he is."

Tobias leaned forward. "What about him? What about Uriah? What did you find up there?"

Kase only smiled his bittersweet smile, his face relaxed despite the blood that pooled around him. "So many questions… right until the bitter end, huh?"

"Kase?" Tobias straightened, reaching forward to shake his shoulder. Kase's eyes had gone dull: empty and unfocused. "No, no, no! Kase, please, don't go. Look at me. I'll go find Aviva and I'll be right back, I'll be quick! You'll be fine, everything will be fine. Please just *look at me*."

"Tobias…" Eira murmured.

Tobias shot her a look, a sharp retort on the tip of his tongue. If it weren't for the tears in her eyes, he would have snapped at her. If it weren't for how drained he felt, he would have snapped at her.

If it weren't for the fact that Kase fell still beneath his hand, he would have snapped at her.

Kase was dead. Tobias jolted back as the realization swept over him, dragging him down into the cold depths of a reality he fought to brush aside. He yanked his hand back as if he had been stung and cradled it close to his chest. If he didn't know better, he might have assumed time had stopped, freezing Kase in an eternal, peaceful sleep. But he knew the truth. Time wasn't kind enough to freeze. It had simply cut Kase off.

Trembling, he wrapped his arms around himself. He barely even registered Eira's hand on his shoulder—he hadn't noticed her coming and kneeling beside him.

It wasn't fair.

"I… I didn't even say goodbye."

"I know." Eira tugged on his arm, guiding him to his feet. "We need to make sure everyone else is okay, and we need to find Uriah. I don't have a very good feeling about what Kase said."

Tobias forced himself to look away from Kase's body. The beginnings of a headache throbbed in his temples, and his eyes burned from crying. Swallowing hard, he slid the pin into his pocket. He nodded to Eira, wiping away the last of his tears. Together, the two of them left the throne room behind.

His feet froze in the doorway. Though every inch of him begged to keep going, he couldn't help but glance back. Kase was still lying there, drenched in rain and soaked with blood. Broken and alone.

Tobias tore his gaze away and pressed on.

As Smoke howled outside, Tobias knew the dragon had discovered the bond had been severed. Talia had described the feeling to him, having experienced it twice herself.

"A pain like no other, like a very piece of your soul is torn from

your body," Talia had said after the loss of her first dragon. Her tearstained face appeared in his memories, and her voice shook with grief. *"You should count yourself lucky. You're unable to form a Rider bond—you will never know this kind of agony."*

There was nothing lucky about it. Tobias didn't need a bond to hurt.

By the time he and Eira made it outside, the torrential downpour had come to a stop. Thunder still rumbled overhead, threatening with the return of the rain. For the time being, however, Tobias was thankful for the break in the storm. His clothes had been soaked through, and his hair was plastered to his face. He shivered in the cool night air, wrapping his arms around himself.

Mud clung to his boots as he stepped out from the cover of the castle—or what little its remains could provide. Eira followed, her hand gripping her knife as she pressed against his side.

He steeled himself, remembering his promise to her. No matter what came, he said he would protect her. The tremors had stopped, signaling that Smoke must have conquered the Venen. Kase had only briefly mentioned Uriah, and Eira had shifted to their side. But what of the dragonborn? Was he still hiding somewhere?

He's Aurum, Eira had said. *The Golden Head Dragonborn of Selini.*

A shiver trailed down his spine at the reminder. Perhaps it was better if he remained in hiding.

"We should look for the others," he said, mostly to himself, but Eira nodded anyway.

"Do you know where they went?" Eira made her way out a bit farther, glancing around the deserted entryway to the castle. Nothing remained of the court but mud and an overgrown path. Darkness hung thickly over them, the moon blotted out by the ominous clouds.

It would be hard to find anyone. Tobias frowned and cupped his chin. Blood clung to his fingers, and he inhaled sharply, quickly withdrawing his hand. "I do but… I'm not sure where to begin. I don't know if everyone will still be in the same spot."

Eira studied him, her lips pressed together in a thin line. She opened her mouth to speak but closed it again before any sound came out. Her gaze flicked away.

"Let's look for Aviva first. Arayna should be with her, and she should know how to find Oliver." He looked down at his wrist for the silver rune, but it had vanished. He couldn't feel the warmth of her magic either. There was only the cold, pressing against him and seeping into his bones.

"Why are you trusting me?" Eira asked as she wrapped her arms around herself. "How do you know I'm actually free?"

Tobias glanced back at her. The gold threads that bound her before were gone, as was the ominous, sickening aura that had surrounded her. There was sincerity in her eyes when she looked at him, and the stillness in her person spoke volumes about her state of mind. Either way, she was still the woman that had sold herself to the dragonborn and betrayed her family.

"I don't," he finally said. "But I'm giving you a chance to set things right."

A laugh slipped from her lips, but it wasn't the high-pitched mocking titter. "Your heart is too soft for this tangled web, but… thank you."

With a hiss, an arrow flew from the dark and scraped past Eira's cheek. She yelped and leapt to the side as another struck the ground where she had been. Ice burst from the tip of the arrow, crawling across the muddy ground. Eira and Tobias both scrambled back from it.

Oliver emerged from the shadows, bow in hand. He rushed to Tobias's side and yanked him away from Eira. Reaching back to his quiver, he nocked another arrow on his bow and pulled back the string in one smooth motion.

"There you are, thief," Oliver growled. "What did you do? I heard Smoke, I heard the screams, so don't try to lie to me. Where's Kase?"

"Hold on!" Tobias shoved Oliver's bow down, aiming the arrow at the ground. Before Oliver could react, he threw himself between the two, hands outstretched to block Eira from view. "She's with me now, I swear."

Oliver scoffed and lifted his bow again. "Yeah, right. That's just what she wants you to think!"

Eira stiffened. "I…"

"Oliver!" Arayna's voice cut through the silence, sharp and ringing with worry. She came running toward them, mud splashing against the soles of her boots. She grabbed Oliver's arm and pulled in the direction she had come from. "Come quickly! Aviva—she's…"

For once, Tobias didn't need to ask any questions. He took off in the direction Arayna had come from, the others trailing behind him. Lightning raced across the dark sky, lighting his path for a brief handful of seconds. It was enough to allow him to see Aviva crouched behind a chunk of rubble from the wall that once surrounded the castle. Her green and white robes were caked with mud. Her blonde hair had tumbled down from its tight ponytail, splayed across her back in tangled clumps. There were no flowers to break up the sandy blonde this time, only spots of dirt and mud. Her hands were outstretched, both palms alight with white magic. The area around her brightened as she squeezed her eyes shut, muttering a spell under her breath. Silver runes traced across her skin in a script he couldn't read, but it bore a resemblance to the writing within the pages of the spellbook.

"What are you doing?" Tobias called, creeping closer. "Your magic isn't fully recovered, is it? This much could kill you, Aviva!"

Aviva refused to meet his eye, bowing her head as she gritted her teeth. "Kase and I had an agreement. If things went wrong—if they went the way Kase knew they would—then I would seal my spellbook and use his remaining lifeforce to purify my forest and this castle. Corrupted energy has flooded this place for some unknown reason, and I'm going to get rid of it all. I'm creating a last resort spell."

Tobias's breath hitched. "The way Kase…? I—I don't understand. Where is the spellbook? I'll go find it. Uriah and the… the *companion* are still out there. We can still fix this!"

A pen formed in her hand, coupled with a thin sheet of paper much like the charms Uriah used to cast his brother's spells. She scribbled furiously on the scrap of paper, her letters glowing deep crimson as she wrote. Tears streaked down her cheeks and her lips quivered, but she didn't stop.

"Aviva." Tobias knelt down beside her. The air around her crackled with magic, warm and calm despite the steely glint in her eyes.

"My master was right," she whispered. "I should have destroyed that book in the beginning. It has brought me nothing but pain."

Though there was truth behind her words, the thought of destroying the book drove a thorn deep into Tobias's heart. All that effort to protect it, all those years he spent watching over it, would go to waste if she got rid of it. Yet, as far as he could tell, the spellbook was already in the hands of the dragonborn. He stood no chance of getting it back from Aurum.

No, he reminded himself, his gaze sliding to Eira. She stood frozen in place, eyes wide and lips parted. No gold threads circled her, binding her to an unseen master. *It's not all going to waste.*

But it hurt to let go. He could only imagine how Aviva felt.

White light rippled through the air in a wave that expanded out from where they stood, sweeping over the castle. A screech echoed in the distance as the light faded. The shadows shrank back, no longer reaching out toward them with long claws that seemed desperate to snag their flesh. The air felt lighter and clearer—purified.

Aviva's cold fingers closed around Tobias's hand, pulling him closer. She pressed the paper into his palm, closing his fist around it. Unlike Kase, she didn't even ask.

"Take this," she whispered. She gripped his hand so tightly that it began to ache. "This is the last resort spell. The book is gone, but I sense the magic user—Shadowslayer or not—has fled. It's only a matter of time before he returns. When he does, use this spell against him. It can only be used once, so make it count."

He swallowed hard. "What am I supposed to do?"

A soft glow enveloped the Mage; at the same time, the paper in his hands lit up with the silver sheen of her power. Aviva looked down at her fingers as they began to dissolve. Flecks of magic drifted toward the paper, melding with its surface to form a shimmering set of unfamiliar characters—the same ones that filled her spellbook. As her body began to fade, the paper grew warm beneath his fingers. Despite that she was vanishing, she smiled pleasantly and her expression carried no hint of fear. Her eyes were dark with sadness, though.

"Aviva?" The call was feeble and small as it left his tongue, barely enough to express the whirl of his thoughts. He glanced between her and the paper, her fading body and the growing set of words he couldn't read.

She was writing herself into the spell.

"Whatever you believe is right," she said. "There's nothing else I can do for you. I'm leaving this spell with you, and I ask that you use it to uncover the plot of that magic-user—Eira's companion. His corrupted aura is corroding the natural flow of magic, and if this continues, it spells terrible things for Anticuus."

"But I don't even know where to begin!" he cried. Frustration sharpened his tongue, and anger lit a fire in his chest. "He's not just some companion, Aviva. He's a *dragonborn.* If I keep fighting a monster like that, I'll—"

"Listen," Aviva hissed, her gaze boring into him. The set of words on the paper was nearly complete, and only the faint outline of her body—etched in silver and green—remained. "Find my apprentice, Nari. Tell her what has happened. She will know what to do."

He didn't have time to protest. The moment he opened his mouth again, she was gone. All that remained as proof she had been there at all was the faint imprint of where she had sat in the mud. The paper glowed brighter, humming with the same aura of magic as she had possessed. With the set of letters complete, the light flickered out, snatched away with the warmth that had infused it. Again, he was alone.

He sank back against his heels, overcome by an aching numbness. Writing one's self into a spell was something he had only ever heard rumors of. He never expected to witness it. The paper crinkled as he tightened his grip. A curse rose to the tip of his tongue, but he swallowed it. There was no point in spiting someone who didn't exist anymore.

Even if he used the spell, Aviva would never come back. Just like Kase, she was...

Oliver crouched at his side, sighing as he examined the place where Aviva had been. "A last resort to stand against a drag-onborn," he muttered. "She mentioned this kind of spell before, but I had no idea she could—or would—do it."

"Kase is dead," Tobias choked out. The words weighed heavily on his tongue, and the sound of them grated against his ears. "Maybe that gave her some sort of push."

"Dead, huh?" Oliver pushed himself to his feet. "Dead." His voice wavered, but he gave no other hint to the way the words cut him. For all Tobias knew, they didn't at all.

Sliding the paper into his pocket with the pin, Tobias rose to his feet as well. As he turned to leave, he didn't even spare a second glance to the empty place where Aviva once was.

As she had said, there was no sign of the dragonborn. They searched the entire castle, but he was nowhere to be found. All that remained to hint to his presence was the spellbook, discarded in one of the outer rooms. Its pages were scorched, empty of the writing and sketches they once held. Several were missing. Tobias curled his fingers against his palms, hoping it was just another sign of the destruction.

Deeper in the collapsed section of the castle, they stumbled across Uriah. A black arrow stuck out from his chest, the tip piercing straight through his heart. His eyes stared blankly at the sky above; his mouth hung open as if he had died mid-cry. Tobias shuddered and stepped back while Oliver moved forward to pull the arrow from the wound.

"Is it one of yours?" Eira asked.

Oliver frowned, looking at the bloodied tip of the arrow. His face was blotchy and red from crying. "No. It's not mine," he snapped, his voice twinged with exhaustion. "There was no one else here, right?"

Eira shook her head. "As far as I know, it was just me, Uriah, and… and the dragonborn."

Oliver gritted his teeth and tossed the arrow aside. "How convenient that our only lead is dead and you can't give us an idea of where the dragonborn went."

"It's not my fault," Eira bit back. "I was under a spell. Everything is hazy and I can't pick out anything I was told. What am I supposed to do, remember anyway?"

"That would be nice, yes."

"That's not how it works!"

Oliver's fingers balled into fists at his sides, but he kept his mouth clamped shut. Arayna glanced over at the two, but she stayed far away at the other end of the hallway. Even as she looked back at Oliver and Eira, she refused to turn her gaze down to meet the sight of Uriah.

Tobias fingered the key that hung around his neck, drawing comfort from its familiarity. It did seem odd to find Uriah dead rather than to learn he had fled with the dragonborn. Still, if Eira was right, and the dragonborn truly was Aurum, then he was crafty and would not be afraid to get his hands dirty. If he believed Uriah knew something and couldn't risk having the secret spilled, he would have killed him. What made his skin prickle with unease was the memory of what Kase said.

"Uriah was there, and he's not who you think he is."

Tobias bit the inside of his mouth. Who did he think Uriah was? *More than that, why would he mention the Shadowslayer legend when Eira knew the magic user was Aurum?*

With a sigh, Oliver turned away from the body. He rubbed his shoulder, folding his arms around himself. "We should probably bury the body. Kase deserves that."

"Uriah too?" Arayna asked tentatively. She crept a bit closer, her hands folded together in front of her and her ears flattened down. "That's fair, right?"

"For Kase, I'll dig a grave with my bare hands. For Uriah, this castle is his grave. He chose it himself, so let him rot here." Oliver left for the throne room.

Arayna flinched. She hesitated a moment, her gaze drifting between Eira, Uriah, and Tobias. She stiffened as Eira looked back at her. Curling her lip, she finally turned and followed Oliver.

Hurt flashed across Eira's expression, but she made no move to follow. Tobias could only assume she knew as well as he did that it would take time before anyone else believed her, even though Oliver had already questioned her until she could do nothing but repeat that she had no memories of what the dragonborn had disclosed.

Tobias bent down, carefully picking up the black arrow between his thumb and index finger. The puzzle pieces didn't fit together in his mind. Kase's death, the appearance of Head Dragonborn, Aviva's last resort spell, and even Uriah's death. None of it made sense. No matter how he tried to weave things together, it always seemed as though a piece was missing.

How was he supposed to be a key if he couldn't even craft the lock?

He took a deep breath and dropped the arrow, stepping away from the scene. One step at a time. He could tackle this puzzle if he just took one step at a time.

Reaching into his pocket, he fiddled with the bloodstained gift from Kase. The next step he had to take would be to fulfill his promise.

28

IMPERFECT HYBRID

Wind whipped through Calix's hair, stinging his eyes and nearly throwing him from Stiria's back. He gritted his teeth and curled his fingers tighter around the dragon's fluffy mane. Screwing his eyes shut, he pressed himself closer.

Late. He was late again. His skin crawled with danger, and his scales burned with fear. He didn't need to be told; he could *feel* it.

He was late, and Kase was in trouble.

Are you sure you're not overreacting? Stiria asked, folding in his wings and dipping lower to avoid the worst of the growing storm. Rain battered his side, soaking both of them to the bone. *Kase and Imago told you to stay away, remember?*

"I know they did," Calix snapped. His hold on the bond was too shaky to communicate through, and he could only hope Stiria would hear him over the storm. "But I think something's gone wrong. I—I can feel Aurum nearby, and Imago, but… when I reach for Kase, it's like… like he's not there."

I'm sure everything is fine. Try not to worry yourself. Stiria swerved around, swooping down until his talons scraped across stone tiles. He touched down on the roof of one of the spires of the old castle of Sheniir, shaking rain from his mane. Twisting his head around, he met Calix's gaze with his gentle blue eyes and held it.

Calix inhaled sharply and slid down from the dragon's back, grabbing his bow and quiver. The old castle of Sheniir reeked of dragonborn, and the air was thick with magic. Though the storm raged overhead, that wasn't what made Calix shiver.

Tile shingles slipped under his boots as he ran to the edge of the roof, peering down at the open second floor of the castle. Voices drifted up toward him, faint beneath the constant roar of the rain.

One tone dragged Calix's fears to the surface, hauntingly familiar. A voice that spoke in his nightmares, always paired with golden eyes or a taunting laugh.

Aurum's voice.

The second one, pleading and desperate, caused an ache in Calix's chest. Aurum held Kase over the edge of the floor, his feet dangling over open air. Gold threads encircled Aurum's wrists. They had fallen slack as if cut on one end. Kase's usual red aura, his connection with his dragon, flickered. Up close, he could sense it, but just barely.

Late. Calix was too late.

He lurched forward, nocking an arrow on the shaft of his bow. Before he could pull back the string, Kase slipped from Aurum's grasp.

Ice gathered on Calix's fingers, cold despite the numbness that gripped him. His breath hitched; tears leapt to his eyes, and his scales burned against his arm.

It started with a whimper that slipped through his guard, then turned to a scream.

"*Kase!*" he cried, rushing toward the edge and peering down. "Kase!"

By then, Kase had already hit the ground below. The crack echoed in Calix's ears, ringing over and over in his mind.

Dead.

Tears spilled down his cheeks. He gripped his bow, pressing his quivering lips into a thin line. It couldn't be. Not Kase. It couldn't be Kase.

"Would you look at that," the dragonborn said, his voice lifting into a mocking laugh. "All I had to do was kill the man to draw out the imperfect hybrid."

With a gasp, Calix spun around, pulling back the string of his bow. Mere seconds ago, the dragonborn had been on the floor below him. Now, he stood between Calix and Stiria, his hands folded behind his back. Stiria growled, his hackles raising. Fear spilled down their bond, forming a headache at the back of Calix's skull.

Looking down at him was the face of a man, though his eyes shone with the same gold as Aurum's. No scales covered his face, and there were no horns jutting out from among his tangled mess of onyx-black hair.

Red hot rage swept over Calix's fear. His gut twisted with the realization that it wasn't Aurum; or at least, it didn't look like him.

But it didn't matter. It didn't matter who he was or what he was.

Calix let the arrow fly before the man had another chance to speak. It pierced straight through his heart, drawing forth deep red blood. The man didn't even have a chance to look down and survey the wound before he collapsed, the gold fading from his eyes.

It didn't matter who he was.

Tears blurred Calix's vision, and the bow fell from his trembling hands. With a sob, he collapsed on his hands and knees, his palms sticky as they touched the blood that pooled from the golden-eyed man's wound. Gasping, he pulled back.

Blood. There was blood on his hands.

"Stiria," he whimpered, trying to wipe the blood clean in the rain. All it did was smear it all over: his hands, his clothes, the roof. The metallic stench was overwhelming. Bile rose in his throat. "Stiria!"

I'm here. I'm right here.

Stiria's tail curled around his waist, his scales ice cold against Calix's wet clothes. He turned and buried his face in Stiria's mane, smearing blood across the dragon's brilliant blue sides. His whole body trembled, his sobs muffled by Stiria's mane. Images flashed through his mind—memories of Kase from long ago, his nightmares about the dragonborn Aurum, his arrow piercing the heart of the golden-eyed man.

And of Kase's body, broken on the floor far below.

There was blood on his hands. Blood under his nails. Heat rose in Calix's scales, searing the skin around them. With a whimper, he clawed at his arm, tearing through his skin.

Calix, please don't hurt yourself, Stiria whispered. Using his talon, he pried Calix's fingers away from the deep scratches he had cut into his arm. *Please. It won't make it better. It won't undo what is already done.*

Calix heaved in a deep breath, but it caught in his throat. "Stiria." He coughed into his hand, pulling away from the dragon. "Stiria, take the body away. I'll be alright here until you get back."

Stiria scrutinized him, his azure eyes narrowed. Frost fogged his breath when he exhaled, and a chill hung from his end of the bond. He flicked the tip of his tail, shaking droplets of rain from the fluffy end of it. *Are you sure? You will be okay?*

Calix nodded, wiping his tears away. He cringed as he smeared the blood across his face and tried to force a smile to hide the fact that he wanted to throw up. "Yes. I'll be fine."

Stiria hesitated a moment longer. When Calix said nothing more, the dragon turned and bent down to scoop up the body of the man in his jaws. The man's torso was all that fit in Stiria's mouth. The arrow wound stuck out awkwardly on one side, and the man hung limply from the dragon's jaws. There was truly no life left in him. Calix tore his gaze away as Stiria leapt down to another level of the castle.

I don't want to risk being spotted if I take flight, Stiria said, his gentle voice floating through the bond. *I'll leave him here in the castle.*

Calix said nothing, and Stiria didn't push. Alone, the numbness began to fade. Pain bit through the skin on his arm, spiking each time the rain hit the deep gashes he had left with his nails. Cold seeped through his clothes, plastered against his body like his tangled mess of dark brown hair. Stained with blood, his iridescent blue scales visible, he surely looked like a monster.

His gut twisted. If she saw him like this, Kiara would hate him.

His eyes stung with the beginnings of tears again. His heart ached as though he was the one who had been shot. Breathing in too quickly, he backed away from the edge and the puddle of blood. He sank to the ground, raking his fingers through his hair as he buried his face in his knees.

It should have been him. It should have been him who died. Not Kase; it should never have been Kase.

Shakily, he clawed at his scales again. His nails dug into his skin, and he winced, biting down on his tongue to suppress his cry. *It should have been me.*

And what good would that do? Imago's deep voice rumbled through his mind, wiping away his storm of emotions and replacing them with a warm feeling of comfort.

Calix winced, his shoulders tensing as he lifted his head. The old red dragon circled above before gently landing on the side of the tower. He spread his wing over Calix's head, shielding him from the last of the rain as it began to thin out.

"Imago," he murmured, suddenly feeling small and childlike beside the ancient Celestial dragon. "You... You're still here."

You must calm yourself, little one. There are humans below, and you cannot risk being seen by them yet. He nudged Calix with his snout, breathing a plume of smoke from his nose. *I know of what has happened. Where is Stiria?*

Here. Stiria nudged his way underneath Imago's wing and came to stand beside his Rider. *The body is gone. I hid it in the castle, but I'm sure someone will discover it soon.*

Calix shuddered, pressing closer against Stiria. He never thought he would hear those words from his dragon.

You must leave this place for now, little one, and wash this blood from your hands. But lift your head high, for you are Caeruleus. Imago peered down at Calix with a gleam in his amber eyes. *But more importantly, you are Calix, and Kase would not wish for you to curl up here and throw away all you have accomplished.*

It was easy to nod and agree while he was in the presence of the dragon, but Calix knew his grief would crash down on him the moment Imago left. Swallowing thickly, he forced a nod.

Take Stiria and fly away from here. Wait until I call for you. With that, Imago pushed off the ground and took off into the sky again.

Calix watched until the dragon's crimson scales were no longer in view. *Goodbye, Ima—no, Smoke.*

Come, my friend. Stiria tugged at Calix's tunic with his teeth, pulling him to his feet. *Let's go.*

Calix heaved himself into the saddle on his dragon's back. As Stiria flew away, he shot one last glance back at Kase. He was far away now, but Calix felt a tug in his chest all the same. He knew what Imago was saying was right and wise beyond Calix's own ideas, but that didn't mean it didn't hurt.

He forced himself to face forward again. The wind battered against him; the rain pelted him until he shivered from the cold. He gritted his teeth and buried his face in Stiria's matted fur.

He didn't have time to grieve. He had a goddess to kill.

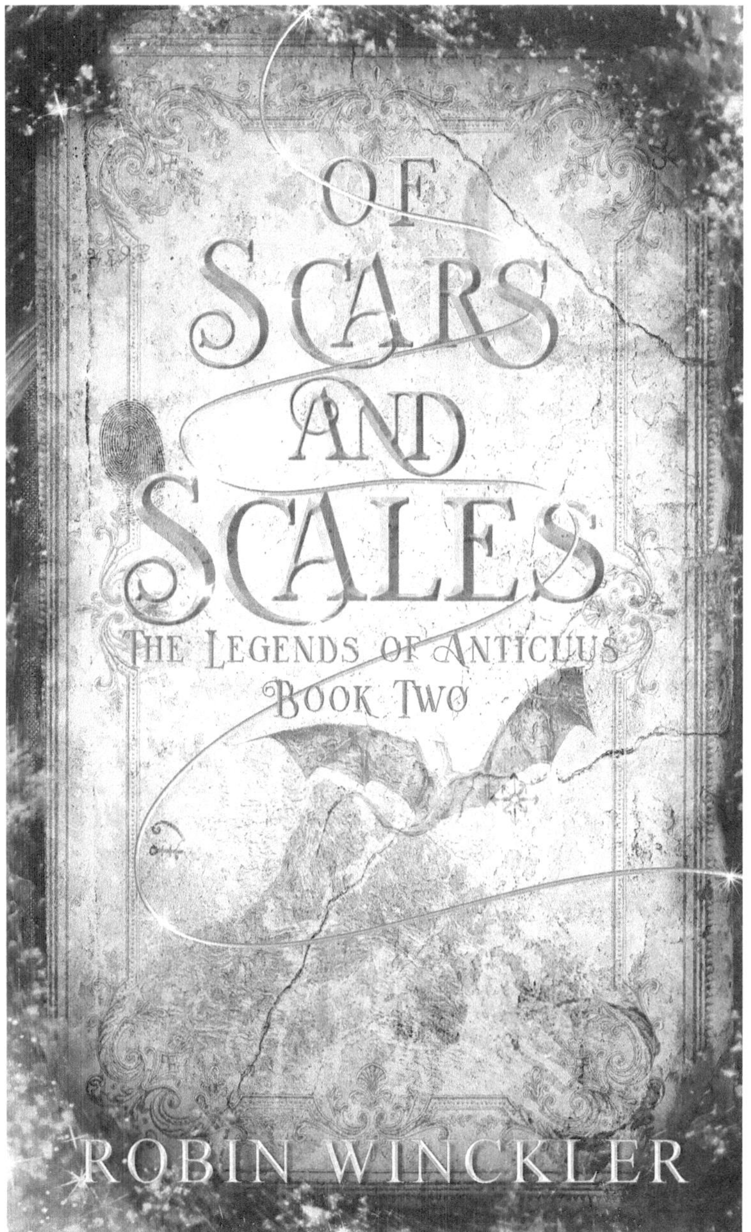
OF
SCARS
AND
SCALES
THE LEGENDS OF ANTICLUS
BOOK TWO
ROBIN WINCKLER

ACKNOWLEDGMENTS

I feel it's not that surprising of me to say there's a lot of people I want to thank. This is true for most authors in my opinion. Despite my introverted dreams, writing isn't really a solo career. There's a lot of other people involved in the successful production of a book. So, I'd like to take a moment to thank some of those amazing individuals.

First off, I want to thank my family. More specifically, my mom, who taught me to write and who first introduced me to the idea of including conflict in my stories. Although I refused to let her read this story until I was certain it was polished enough that I wouldn't be embarrassed by the idea of that, she is most certainly my biggest supporter. Without her, I would probably still be writing about princesses having happy play-dates with unicorns. Thank you, Mama. You gave me the ability to break so many hearts.

I'd also like to thank my sister, who suffered through many of my ramblings about this story. Thank you for listening to me —or at least pretending to.

And to the rest of my family, thank you as well. I didn't say much about OSaT to many of you, but I appreciate your encouragement in my hobbies as well as my studies. Someday, I'll learn to let you all read things before they're "perfect." Maybe.

Secondly, I'd like to thank Grace and Larissa, who experienced the very first draft of this story way back in 2017. I know that first draft wasn't the prettiest, but you both encouraged me to keep working on it over the years. You supported my ideas and guided them into proper plot points and characters. I'm proud of where the story is now, and I wouldn't have gotten here without the two of you.

Where would writers be without editors? Thank you to Laine and Aria Nichols for doing a fantastic job of polishing my story. I wouldn't be here without the two of you, and I am grateful to have had the opportunity to work with you!

Following that, I would like to thank my cover designer, Sarah Penney. It was a pleasure to work with you and thank you for bringing my story to life with such a beautiful cover!

Of course, I would like to thank my beta readers, my workshop partners, book club readers, and all the other people who read and supported the story in its early days. I would like to specifically thank Sabrina, Emma, and Nicole, who have quickly become some of my closest friends and critique partners. Thank you for supporting me on my bad days and my good days. I have loved bouncing ideas off of you, sharing drafts and brain dumps, and talking about the story with you when I should be writing it. You are my favorite readers—but don't tell the other ones.

Lastly, I would like to thank everyone who supported my story even if they aren't mentioned here. Thank you for your enthusiastic questions, for listening to me as I struggle to explain the plot without spoiling it, for encouraging me, and of course, for reading! I'm so very thankful for each and every one of you!

I hope that you have all enjoyed reading as much as I enjoyed writing, and I'll see you all in book two!

About the Author

Robin Winckler is a YA fantasy author with a love for magic, dragons, adventure, and all things high fantasy. She is currently pursuing a degree in English, which she hopes to use to grow her writing skills. When she is not writing, she can be found drawing, reading, or playing with her beloved dog, Pippin.

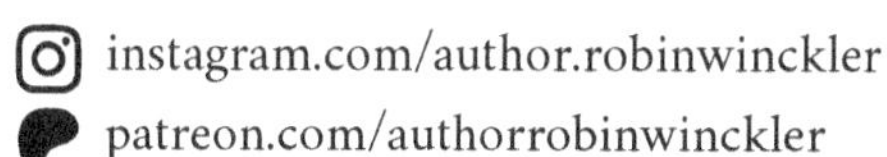

instagram.com/author.robinwinckler
patreon.com/authorrobinwinckler